Sold for a Status

Janet Collis

Published by New Generation Publishing in 2021

Copyright © Janet Collis 2021

First Edition

ISBN

      Paperback   978-1-80031-092-6
      Hardback   978-1-80031-091-9

www.newgeneration-publishing.com

 New Generation Publishing

I would like to dedicate this book to my husband Peter.
He encouraged me to write and gave me a lot of help, so I
could just sit and write.
Also to thank Robbie and Vera for all their help through
my early years.

Chapter One

July 1836.

The man's sudden appearance from the bushes caused the horse to rear, but his quick reaction to grab the reins, soon had the animal calm.

Isobel fearful of the situation, raised her crop high above her head, but as he turned to face her, the intended weapon fell to the ground.

Shocked, she stared down in disbelief. 'Dune.' She whispered.

He smiled as he carefully reached for her. Legs like jelly, she slid down into his arms and melted against him, the kiss, when his lips descended was magnificent.

A loud noise broke the spell, and he gently released her from his embrace.

Isobel suddenly aware of how near to the stables they were, pleaded. 'Dune. Please, please you must go. It is not safe for you here. If you are seen…'

'Hush.' He smiled, as he pulled her even closer, he kissed the tip of her nose, brushed her lips, with his own, then whispered. 'Meet me later. The usual place. Yes.'

Isobel nodded, as he turned to disappear back into the thick shrubbery.

She continued to stare at the greenery, frighten to move, in case he returned.

Unable to re-mount, she eventually turned towards the

stables, but luckily a lad caught sight of her and rushed to retrieve the animal. She smiled and thanked him, then turned and quickly made her way back to the house.

Draped in happiness from head to toe, Isobel rushed up the stairs and into her rooms.

Elated, she could not wait to tell Alice, tell her Dune was back. Yes, tell her that the boy they had not seen for the last two summers, had at last returned. But not as a lad, no, he was now a fully-grown handsome man.

Who had almost stopped her heart from beating?

Isobel danced about as she told Alice of her meeting with her beautiful Dune. The girl was so happy for her mistress as she helped her out of her riding habit, and into the warm bath water.

Eventually, dressed in a blue day dress, Isobel took Alice's hand and whispered, 'I think I am going to try and meet him now, because it will be so hot out there later. Alice, will you come with me?'

'Yes. Yes of course I will.'

The girls made their way quietly out of the house. They quickly hurried to the usual place, which was at the top of an extremely high hill, which stood a good way back from the house.

Isobel's joy was for all to see because Dune was already there. They walked towards him and without a word, he reached for Alice, and kissed the top of her head.

'How be thee my sweet Alice.'

She smiled and returned the kiss to his cheek. 'Good, thank you Dune.' She looked at her mistress. 'I'm away to pick some fresh flowers, see you both later.' And she was gone before either could speak.

Isobel saw the blanket already splayed onto the grass, and they both sat down on it. They chatted and laughed, then, Dune told Isobel about his father's terrible accident with the horse he was training.

'Oh Dune, how is he now.'

'He's good, almost well again, but his fall was the reason I have not been back for so long.'

'Oh, I see. It has been two years since we last saw each other.'

'Yes, yes I know. But at least now, we are both all grown up.'

'Well, yes, yes, we are.' She whispered. 'I am now seventeen, and you are twenty-two.' She smiled. 'See, I know a lot about you.'

'Well, so you should, we did grow up together, even though our lives were so different. Me the son of a gypsy, and you, the Master of the Manor's daughter.

They laughed, he kissed her, then they laughed and chattered until Alice appeared again.

'Mistress.' She nodded and curtsied. 'I be sorry, but your lunch is ready.'

'Thank you, Alice.'

Dune took her hand and help up from the cover. He then took her face and kissed her mouth; he took his time. He reluctantly let her go with the promise to meet up again later.

'Yes, later when it is cooler.' Isobel stated, as she and Alice finally walked away.

'*Isobel is to be married.*' Arthur Fordham's blood shot eyes bored deeply into Mary's shocked ones. '*And the service will take place at the end of this month. Surely woman, I cannot say it any clearer, or louder.*'

She stifled a sob as she reeled from the vicious, verbal attack. So, this devastated news, was his reason for the quick return. Usually, his trips to the card tables of London, lasted a good many months. But, back after just eight weeks, she knew his cup was full to overflow to deliver this news to her personally. He knew, these words would break her, finish her in fact.

Slouched in the chair opposite hers, the sight of her husband's smug- pleasure at her terrified, reaction, Mary begged, 'but Arthur, Isobel is just a child. Surely, Agnes, our eldest daughter should wed first.'

'Woman, for goodness, sake, how long do you think she would hold the attention of a man? Especially the suitor I have chosen for your precious Isobel.'

Unable to contain herself, she continued. 'But who…who is this…this person, you would have her marry?'

His anger was visible, as he lifted the tankard to his lips, and Mary was horrified as she witnessed the liquid cascade down the front of his tunic. A deep silence hung across the room. The wine finished; Mary, jumped when he banged the empty vessel onto the table, his mouth wiped with his sleeve, he lent forward. 'Now let me see. The man I want her to marry is a noble man my dear. Lord William Belington, to be precise. Whom I believe to be a few years older than myself.'

'What. …older than you? How old is this person?' Mary could not contain herself, and again, she witnessed the glow of sheer satisfaction ooze from him at her anguish.

But Fordham just ignored her outburst and continued, 'I'm told that his ancestral country estate, which boasts many thousands of acres, is somewhere in Sussex.'

He reached for the decanter and replenished the goblet.

Slouched back in his seat, Fordham sipped the wine. To have plunged a knife into your chest, dear wife, would have caused you less pain, than this announcement, you now must digest. He silently told himself.

The quietness of the room was vibrant, but Mary eventually stammered.

'Older…did…you say, the man is older than your fifty years.'

'Mm, give or take a year or two, although, it could be as much as ten, so I've been told.'

'Sixty. But why? How can you do this. Isobel is just seventeen.' Mary struggled to breathe, 'And Sussex. Where is this place, you'll have her go?'

'I know not where this place is, and she is the same age

5

you were when I swept you off your feet. Remember.'

The sight of her silent tears as they fell onto her clenched fists, enhanced his pleasure dramatically.

'I had no sisters.' She whispered. 'The oldest of the daughters are always wed first.'

'Well, that's not going to happen in our family. I want this arrangement with Belington to last until either his or my demise.' He smiled. 'Isobel's, youth and virginal beauty will secure that for me.' The vessel placed back on the table, he edged forward and rubbed his hands. 'No, from this union my dear wife, my new son-in-law will give me a status so strong, I possibly will be welcomed into Royal circles.'

He retrieved his wine and sneered.

Mary knew to continually badger him would bring his wrath down more strongly, but without a care, she blurted. 'But why. Why does the wedding have to take place so soon?' She cleared her throat. 'The end of this month, I mean. Isobel, and… I have not met the…him yet. This man, who will take her so far away from me.'

Mary's throat hurt and she started to cough, it was a severe bout, and racked her thin body. Woozy and lightheaded, she retrieved the muslin from her pocket and held it to her mouth. The attack started to ease, but it was the sight of the fresh, deep, red blotches on the cloth, that caused her to shake inwardly.

Fordham slammed the goblet down, 'Enough, no more talk. This marriage will take place. Our daughter will become, Lady Belington, and leave here for good.' He reached for the decanter. 'Now get out woman and let me drink in peace. No wait.' He slurred.

'Pull that cord before you go, my supply is low. I need more wine.'

Fordham sneered as he shrugged her look of pure, hatred away. 'Now, woman, I want it now.'

Mary dragged her weary body from the chair and did as he requested. Numb from head to foot, she closed the library's ornate doors behind her, then slowly walked the corridor that led out into the garden.

Seated beneath the shade of the old oak tree, despite the intense heat, Mary shivered uncontrollably. Completely stunned, unable to digest his words, she stared at the scorched grass. Her husband gained great satisfaction when he could inflict pain on people, and the deeper they felt it the happier he became. The evil, darkness inside him had broken many a man. Now, he was about to do the very same to her, because with her beautiful child gone, her reason to live would diminish, and he would be free of her at last.

How she had grown to despise this man, who had been her husband for the last twenty- three years. Despise him with a vengeance, and still to this very day, Mary could not remember, what the attraction towards him had ever been.

She and her mama had visited friends, on the Cornish coast where they lived. Fordham had been there as a guest, and somehow, he had seduced her, a carefree girl of seventeen into a false sense of desire for him. And, despite her mother's heartfelt plea against it, when he was ready to leave, six weeks later, she had been a young bride swept away to a new life in Durham.

The marriage was horrendous from the start. Her young body constantly subjected to his drunken, sexual, brutality, twelve months later Agnes was born. Traumatized and mentally incapable to tend the baby, Mary was overwhelmed by her mama's sudden appearance. But it was the lady she had brought forth with her, she was even more grateful for. Always attired in black, the efficient woman simply known as Nanny, moved straight into the nursery to care for the little one. Fordham made no qualms about her position there because, his mother-in-law was to pay her yearly wages. Agnes grew into a peculiar child, who never wanted to mix or play. Once she could read, she never took herself away from the big room full of books. Through the years as Agnes matured, Mary learnt to honor the solitude this daughter always desired. Now aged twenty- two, she imaged her father. Extremely tall, her brown, lanky hair she pulled off her plain face into a tight bun. But mostly like him, she was completely cocooned in her own selfishness. Mentally and physically scarred through his continual sexual activities, five years, and many miscarriages later, Mary had eventually carried full term. From the instant the beautiful baby girl was delivered and put into her arms, her reason to carry on living returned. The pink bundle, she named Isobel, after her mama. The woman, whose care and love from afar, had truly sustained her sanity. Fordham wanted sons, and again showed no interest in the new-born. And, ironically after the birth, he no longer demanded his evil way with her. Also, he was rarely at home, but when he was, he kept to his own rooms, and left Mary in total peace.

It was a complete turnaround from his previous ways regarding her and the sex he always demanded. But, mostly, Mary's life now, was more peaceful, and happy.

Distant thunder interrupted the intimate silence of the early afternoon. She began to cough; she removed the cloth from her pocket, and her body shook. A sob escaped her as she noticed more fresh blood spots. She looked upwards and every trace of blue had disappeared, and angry, grey clouds now moved across the sky.

'Oh no, dear Lord, no,' she cried into the emptiness. 'Please help me. What can I do to save my dearest, beautiful, child? What can I do to keep her safe and close to me?' She shuddered. 'Safe. Safe from her evil father, and this terrible man he intends to give her to.'

The first drops of the desperately needed rain started to fall. Pale and drawn Mary eased herself from the seat, her grey, day dress dragged the damp flag stones, as she slowly walked back into the house.

Chapter Two

Isobel looked up and smiled as her mother entered the room. Mary's throat constricted; the lump threated to choke. So, fair, so beautiful, at seventeen, this daughter was a mirrored reflection of her own lost youth. Tall like herself, Isobel wore her flaxen hair up during the day, then she would clip it to the nape of her long, neck for the evening. Deep emerald eyes enhanced her flawless oval face. Her beauty and gentle ways came from deep within, and the feisty spirit she had shown signs of late, Isobel had certainly inherited from her namesake, her grandma Isobel. Fatigued, and completely drained emotionally, Mary bent to kiss the top of her daughter's head. Concerned over her mother's health, Isobel asked. 'You are very pale, Mama. How do you feel today?'

'Yes. Yes, my darling, I am quite good. It is the heat. It's terribly warm out in the garden, but the rain has just started.' Isobel knew the statement was just for her, but said, 'that's good, we need some rain desperately.'

'Indeed, we do my lovely one.'

'Mama, are you sure you are feeling, okay? Would you like a cold drink?'

'No, my dear, nothing to drink, and yes I am fine. Did you enjoy your ride this morning? You went early.'

'Oh yes, very much thank you Mama. It was one of the happiest I have ever been on.'

Mary smiled. 'Good. But I sense something different about you child. You seem to have a glow.' Isobel wrapped her arms about her body. 'It must be the sun from the ride. I feel so exhilarated,' her eyes searched her mother's sad face. And I saw my beautiful Dune. He has returned, and we kissed. She added silently. Mary looked across at Agnes curled up asleep in the chair. She took a deep breath then muttered. 'It's much too hot to do anything now. But once I have had a little nap like your sister, there, I'll be fine.' The cough took hold once more, and her body convulsed. Isobel stood and quickly walked towards her, she noticed how hard she clung to the high back chair for support. The muslin was quickly hidden as she helped to manoeuvre her mama into the seat. Then, she walked towards where the carafe of cold water stood, poured some into a glass and took it over to her. Mary smiled at her daughter, 'thank you my dear.' She drank thirstily, 'that's much better.' Then settled back more in the chair, she closed her eyes and, thankfully sleep soon took her.

The month of April was when the dry cough had started. Lack of appetite, constant tiredness, and terrible night sweats had followed. The doctor eventually summoned had diagnosed a severe chill. A sweet brown liquid had been left for her mama to take. Now it was the first day of July, and since his last visit, Isobel knew her mother, now took more and more to her bed. The summer heat was unbearable, the embroidery splayed across her lap, she turned to view the garden. The small amount of rain had ceased, but damp scented aromas crept into the quiet room. Heavy eyed, she welcomed the breeze as it tantalized the long white nets attached to the back of the French doors. In sleep, Isobel journeyed back to her earlier encounter with Dune, Dune O' Mallery, whose sudden appearance still had her head in a spin. Two long summers had passed since he had last worked her father's fruit fields. Consequently, to see him stood there, had completely overwhelmed her, and left her breathless. Deep, almost black eyes had smouldered as his smile revealed perfect white teeth. And to have been held, held so close, had been sheer heaven. Dune's warm breath had caressed her face as they stared at each other. Then his strong hand had carefully tilted her chin upwards towards his beautifully shaped lips, and the kiss, the kiss, she had wanted to last for ever. But end it did.

'Isobel, so beautiful,' he had whispered. Before his hasty retreat. She could see his tight fitted black, leather trousers tucked into knee length boots. The gold round ring that hung from his left ear, had mesmerized her. Coal black curly hair cascaded onto the white, ruffled collar of the open shirt tucked into his waist. Dune's magnificent physique would not leave her.

The Romany gypsies had worked her father's fruit fields, long before either she or he had been born. She was six, he was eleven, when they had literally bumped into each other at the back of the house. Isobel had fallen and hurt her knee, he had helped her up from the ground, and his hand had continually stroked her white hair. Young as they were, an instant chemistry flared between them. Consequently, from that summer, and all the summers after, she and Dune would secretly seek each other out. Sadly, through those years, they both learnt that such a friendship between them was absolutely forbidden. Isobel had last seen him in June two years ago, it had been her fifteenth birthday. Hand in hand they had run to their usual place hidden from the house. Exhausted they had laughed and fallen onto the grass. It was there, Dune had tenderly taken her face into his hands to gently kiss her lips. Next day, Mama had whisked her, Agnes, and Alice away to visit Grandma Claremont in Cornwall. Sadly, the trip lasted for almost three months and on her return, every trace of Dune and the gypsies had gone. But now he had returned, and she knew despite the extreme happiness she felt, they could never resume their friendship. Because the consequences, and reprisals, each would face if her father, the Master, ever had any inclination of what they had shared for so long, would be indescribable.

Fordham staggered into the room, a goblet and decanter clutched in each hand, he booted the door shut. Isobel instantly awake saw wine spill as he fell into the chair opposite hers. He refilled the vessel and lifted it to his mouth. Shivers ran through her body, as his blood shot eyes bore into her from over the rim. She lowered her head and stared at her needlework, but it was the red stain that snaked across the flagged stone floor, that really held her gaze. This man had always frightened her, but recently a strong anger towards him had started to rise within her, especially, when she witnessed his despicable behaviour towards her mama. His cruelty at times was so intense his face would distort, plus he never cared who was in the room, when these outbursts occurred. Isobel seethed when she heard him boldly brag of his sexual escapades down the back streets of the bordellos. His long trips to London to visit these clubs, where crucial card games were played. Sometimes, if he had won a great deal of cash, he could be gone for months and months. Although, the loss of money, was of no consequence, because he was one of the richest coal merchants in 'Coallstone,' near Durham.

'It's simply a game of enjoyment my dears.' He would often say to them. 'And how I love to see those who can ill afford to lose, squirm and sweat.' He would stop and laugh, before he continued. 'Especially, when they realize all their assets brought to the tables now belonged to me.' Isobel knew him to be an evil, spiteful man, and his early return from this latest trip concerned her a little. She knew, he would not have returned for any old thing, so, she was eager to know, what had brought him back so soon.

The tall Grandfather clock in the hallway struck four, and Alice's knock broke the tension that had developed. A white cap perched on top of her black piled hair; the cream apron tied round the slim waist of the long black dress; she pushed the laden trolley into the room. The sight of the Master sprawled before her, she stopped and curtsied, then quiet as a mouse she steered the wheels towards where the Mistress was asleep. The task finished, she smiled at Isobel as she turned to walk towards the door, but the master's voice halted her.

'Wait girl. Wait.' His hand in the air he beckoned her towards him. He gulped the remains of his wine, then nodded to his grey knee length boots. 'Come here and get these bloody things off. There in need of a good clean. And I mean spotless.' Instantly by his side, she reached for the offered foot. The sole grasped tight, she tried to remove it, but it would not budge.

'Put your back into it, girl.' He yelled. 'You, stupid idiot, tug it. Pull the bloody thing off.' Alice tried, but it would not move. Fordham angrily raised his other booted foot to the middle of her back, and pushed against her with such force, she flew across the room and hit her head on the corner of a wooden table. Anger consumed Isobel, she could see Allice was dazed as she staggered up and dabbed the blood, that oozed from the cut above her eye, with her apron. Appalled by her father's behaviour, she wanted to go and help, but to do so would have made him angrier. Isobel knew cook would tend the wound once Alice returned to the kitchen, and she prayed the other boot would remove more easily. Fordham sneered lecherously as the girl lent forward to try and free the other one, but luckily it was off with the first tug. She quickly moved from the man, collected the other boot, curtsied, and left the room. Isobel fumed at the sight of the inflicted wound, and has soon as she could, would seek her friend out. Outside in the hall the girl's tears fell freely, what a disgusting man he was, with the boots held tight in her hands, she rushed back to the kitchen.

Alice had been born here in the Manor house eighteen years ago. Her mother Nellie had been a young parlour maid, and had been employed for almost nine months, when one night the cook had found her huddled in a cupboard. She was in a terrible state because she was with child. The woman, a kind Motherly figure had been the one to inform the Mistress of the poor girl's dilemma. Nellie had been completely alone in the world, and was a good hard worker, who rarely left the premises, even when time off was due to her. In the past, Mary had found it necessary to dismiss young, members of her staff for their own safety. It was well known that most of society closed it eyes to the Masters indiscretions, with the girls and boys housed in their homes. But sadly, she had not been able to help young Nellie. But the Mistress, had not sent the girl away, she kept her in the house, and Nellie had been put downstairs to work in the kitchen areas. The whole household had been kindness itself with the care they had all shown towards the girl, while she awaited the birth of the baby. Alice arrived six months later, and beneath stairs, she became their pride and joy. Every person Nellie worked alongside, contributed towards the little ones needs. The Mistress brought clothes, and necessities, and spent a great deal of time below stairs with Mother and child, because with them, she watched and learnt. A year after Alice's birth, Mary once more heavily pregnant had her prayers answered, and that's when Isobel, her second daughter was born safely. This time the pink bundle brought love and joy from the minute she was placed into her arms. Desperate to hold her little one close to her breast to enable her to feed, as she had witnessed Nellie do so often with sweet Alice, she bonded immediately with her beautiful, new daughter.

Chapter Three

Agnes aged five was so peculiar, she did not even, want to play with her new sister. She just continually stayed in the big room full of books. So, when a tutor arrived to teach them both, as soon as lessons were finished, she simply returned to the books. Isobel's third birthday was when the four-year old Alice was taken along to the nursery to play with her. The room full of toys, dolls, and picture books, the two little ones loved to be together in. Consequently, over the following years a great, strong, friendship, developed between the girls. But eventually, Alice had to do some light duties in the kitchen. She was ten when her mother suddenly died. Everyone in the house, plus Mary who had come to love the child made sure she was well looked after. One of the larger rooms in the female's quarters was turned into a new bedroom, so she could sleep in there protected by the old cook, who also loved her like her own. But, by the time her small bed, basket full of toys and books, plus the set of three drawers filled with clothes was placed inside, there was not much space for the dear, elderly lady's small possessions to be put into. Mary loved to spoil young Alice, after all it was her birth right to be treated in such a manner, not that anyone away from her home would ever learn of it. The girl was often puzzled and shocked by the items her mistress insisted she had. Even, now as a young adult she was still laden with gifts and clothes. And her great, friendship and closeness with Miss Isobel was known by every servant and maid, and, if, Miss, Agnes, knew of it, she obviously did not care, because Fordham was completely, ignorant of the fact. Mary had stipulated to each member of staff, that Alice was never to be left on her own when gentlemen guests were in the house. She also stated that, when the Master was at home, the child was to be given work below stairs, for her own safety. But with his unexpected early return today, plus his devasting news, this rule had gone by the wayside.

Fordham looked across at his wife. '*Wake up woman.*' He shouted. 'How could you sleep through all the commotion. The tea needs to be poured if you please. Now woman.' Isobel's needlework fell to the floor as she stood. 'No please, Papa. Let me do it, Mama is very tired.'

'No, no forget it,' he blurted, the goblet held high in his hand. 'Wine. I want more wine. Get it now will you.'

His attitude and tone when he often spoke to anyone, Isobel hated, and she was extremely angry with him now. Disgusted again by his verbal behaviour, she took the vessel from him and walked towards the sideboard, where to her horror, she saw the large silver tray had not yet been replenished. But, then thankfully, tucked slightly from view, she found a half -filled decanter.

'Do not bother to fill it girl, bring the whole thing over to me.' She did as he asked, and, in his eagerness to grab them, she noticed how badly his hands shook. Isobel collected the material up from the floor, then seated again she looked over to her sister Agnes, who was woken when poor Alice hit the floor, and rare smiles were exchanged. Mary roused from her heavy slumber, looked round and frowned. Isobel knew since she had started to take the syrup for her cough, she always woke heavy eyed, and woozy headed.

'Oh.' She uttered. 'I did not hear the tea trolley arrive my dears.' She sat upright and smiled at her two daughters. Isobel, desperate to change her father's foul mood, wanted to enquire about this last trip, and was quite eager to know, what the reason was for his early return. 'Papa, how was your trip to London this time? Although, it was not for very-long, was it?' She smiled as she looked at him.

'Not now dearest.' Mary almost shouted, as she handed her a cup of tea and passed one to Agnes. 'Your Father will be tired from his journey.' Fordham looked at his wife, then started to clap his hands. 'Woman, you are such an idiot, do you know what, I have never known any- one as stupid as you are.' He looked at Isobel then continued. 'You know this daughter needs to hear the news that has brought me back so soon.' He smiled. 'After all it does concern her, does it not.' Isobel confused by his words, took the offered plate from her mama, and automatically picked up a small square of the cucumber sandwich to nibble on. Fordham, the goblet raised to his mouth, shouted. 'But first, I want more wine. Pull the cord, woman, would you. Now, not in half an hour, now woman.' Isobel noticed her mother's stern icy glare, she knew her father would not be pleased to witness the look, but her mother did as the man demanded, and silence prevailed while they waited. Isobel was relieved when the butler knocked and entered, she hoped dear Alice was resting after her run in with her father. Fordham waved the empty decanter up in the air. Then hissed. 'Wine man. Another full one. I want it full.' The man bowed and left, but was soon back with the silver tray, that contained a full decanter of red wine. The tray placed onto the table next to her father, the man bowed and quietly walked from the room. Fordham looked at the three women before him, his smug pleasure for all to see. The silence in the room deafened him. His goblet replenished he sat back, drank, then cuffed his mouth.

'Well, now let me see. My trip, Isobel, you want to hear about it. Although this one was short, it turned out to be an extremely, eventful, one for me.' Isobel with no real interest in what her father had to say, picked up her needlework and stared at the material. Fordham looked at his youngest daughter, really looked at her hard.

'You know my dear wife.' His eyes focused on Mary. 'We certainly produced a beautiful woman in Isobel.' He sat back and slowly sipped more wine. 'Why,' He continued, 'Her beauty is even more breath-taking than yours had been at this age, his Lordship, should be eternally grateful to me for the gift he is about to receive. He finished the liquid, refilled the goblet, and smiled. 'Isobel, you want to hear about my trip. Yes.'

'Oh yes Papa. Yes.'

'Good. Because you are my reason for my quick return.'

'I…I am the reason, I do not understand, father.' She never did fully understand the man when he spoke, because most of the time his words were slurred. Sometimes you could not understand one word he said, possibly like now, she could not make any sense from the man. But he continued. 'I play cards with many important men, but this man, Lord, William, Belington, owes me a great amount of money, but, he does not have any to give me. Plus, he is in debt to many more gentry, and again does not have the funds to pay them.' Isobel shivered, what was he talking about, none of this had anything to do with her. She silently thought, as she watched him gulp down more liquid. Fordham wiped his mouth with the back of his hand, then continued. 'So, Isobel, this is going to happen.'

'What will father.'

'Why, the wedding. Your wedding girl. You are to marry Lord William Belington.'

Isobel looked towards her mother, she tried to speak but no words would come.

'Yes, I am back now to make the arrangements.' He looked at his wife and smiled. 'At the end of this month, Belington will arrive here, and you will become his bride. And when you are wed, you will travel to his family, estate, somewhere in Sussex.' Silence in the room was intense. The women were not interested in the food or tea. He smiled as he reached into the square silver box on the table, he withdrew a long cigar, he studied it for a few seconds, then the brown flakes bitten from the bottom end of it he spat onto the floor. The candle protector removed, he drew deeply from the glow, then fully lit, he sat back, and smoke trailed from his mouth. He looked across at his wife's ashen, frightened face, and declared 'Now, where was I. Oh yes the agreed transaction. This man, Isobel, is to bestow a great honour upon me, once you and he are married.' Mary's body shook as her throaty cough broke into his words. The deep silence returned once the cough stopped, and the man waited for his wife to drink the liquid, Isobel had quickly leapt up to get for her.

'Thank you dear.' She smiled. 'That's better.' The glass clutched tight in her hand, Mary looked towards her husband, who when Isobel was seated, continued.

'You see I'm to become an honorary member of his Lordship's elite club, which will grant me entrance through many doors. I am to be introduced into the man's noble circle.' He stated. 'I will be introduced into London's top society, why I might even rub shoulders with Royalty.' He puffed hard on the cigar. 'You see, Belington needs heirs for his ancestral estate, which as I have said is somewhere in Sussex. So, the man needs to marry.' Mary breath shallow, sweated profusely, as she silently, whispered to him to shut up talking.

'I intend to pay a large settlement to him when you and he are married, and as soon as I hold the wedding certificate, I have vowed to pay all his debts. Consequently, he will start his married life with a great deal of money, and not owe anyone a single penny.' The room was vibrant. Smoke curled upwards. Total shock grabbed all the three women, but Mary wanted to kill her husband, there was no other way, he had to die.

He refilled the goblet, and has he lifted it to his mouth, his eyes never left his beautiful daughter's face. The wine finished he pushed the rest of the cigar into the vessel and threw it across the table.

'Isobel, you will become Lady Belington at the end of the month.' Stunned, her material held so tight the needle entered the skin of her hand, she did not cry out, has she looked at her mother's pale frightened face. Her gaze caught Agnes's look of sheer relief. Eventually she muttered. 'But father, I thought Agnes would marry first, for she is the oldest. Is this not the way it is done?'

'No. No. You never presume.' Her father shouted. 'No. No. You do what is demanded of you.'

Isobel knew, he was angry, so she stayed quiet.

'Your bridegroom, will arrive two days before the service.' He stopped the silence of the room was powerful. 'After-which,' he continued. 'You will travel to Sussex with him to begin your new life.' He lifted the decanter to his mouth and downed the last few drops, then slumped back in his chair. He declared, 'the amount of cash this is going to cost me will be extremely high, but the status I will gain from this marriage will be reward enough.' Satisfied with all he had accomplished, he uncurled his tall, thin frame from the seat, and moved unsteadily towards the door. His hand on the handle he shouted over his shoulder.

'Oh, wife I will be away later. Not sure when I'll be back, but, be assured I will return before the groom appears for the ceremony.' Then he was gone. Fordham climbed the stairs slowly, but half-way up, he stopped to grab the handrail. Sweat fell from him, and a strange, numbness consumed him. 'Guilt.' He spoke aloud.

'Rubbish never suffered from it.' He continued up to his room, and once inside, the slammed door echoed throughout the silent house.

Chapter Four

Isobel instantly by her mother's side was gathered into her open arms. Despite the intense heat, cold fear pulsated through her, and Mary shivered uncontrollably.

'Oh Mama, Mama, what shall I do? I... I... am to marry a stranger.'

'Hush little one, hush, all is not lost... I will speak with your father and beg him not to let this happen.'

Desperate to comfort Isobel, Mary held her close, and rained kisses onto her hair as her own silent tears, streamed down her face.

Agnes stood and moved towards them. 'Oh Mother, for goodness's sake, you know, Father, will never change his mind. And you of all people, should know that.' She declared.

'Quiet. You know it is you who should wed this man, as the first born it is your duty to your father.'

'Well, as you heard, Papa requires Isobel to be this man's wife, and we all know he is to be obeyed.' Agnes did not flinch as the moist eyes scolded and condemned. Neither did she waver at the disgust she saw in them. Instead, her brown skirt skimmed the floor as she carried on past them and silently left the room.

Isobel back in her own quarters cuddled Alice tightly, 'I am so sorry about what happened to you dear friend.' Isobel kissed her forehead, 'the eye is very swollen, and black, bruising, is coming out beneath it.'

'Yes, cook bathed it and put this creasy stuff on it.'

'It looks sore, is it? You hit that table with some force, the way you went across the room.'

'It is but cook said, if I put some more of her cream on tonight, it should be a lot better by tomorrow.'

'Oh, well that's good Alice, lets, hope she is right.'

The girl went off and made some more tea, when she returned, she could not believe what Isobel told her, 'Miss, you mean your father is going to make you marry, a stranger, who is an old man, then send you away to a place called Sussex.'

'Yes, Alice, that is what he intends to do.'

In the small hours, Mary sat and wrote a heartfelt letter to the one person who could possibly help her and her precious daughter, her Mother, Isobel Claremont.

This horrific, evil deed, Fordham was about to bring down upon them had to be stopped, and her beloved Mother, was possibly the only one who could make that happen.

Isobel Claremont suffered no fools. A strong business-woman with an excellent brain, she possessed only two weaknesses, her only daughter Mary, and her second grandchild Isobel. Thrilled that the baby had been given her name, family and close friends now called her Bella. Medium height, deep autumn-streaked hair, at sixty- two, signs of her youthful beauty still glowed.

The heat through June into July had been unbearable. Relaxed and seated in her majestic garden, she inhaled deeply. Grateful the late afternoon rain had cleared the hot stifled air she welcomed the slight coolness that caressed her face.

Scented aromas entwined with the gentle breeze, tantalized the heavy leafed trees, and a little color had returned to the scorched grass. Flowers, shrubs and rose bushes swayed for their audience of one. Bella watched the bird's splash in and out of the deep concrete font that centered her view, while their songs to greet the encroaching night filled her ears.

The sudden sound of horse's hooves as they pounded the bridle path towards the house, shattered the intimate silence of dusk's slow descent. Concerned over the lateness of the hour, Bella stood and walked towards the open arch. Her breathe faltered, and fear took hold as she recognized her daughter's young rider. She immediately knew something was terribly wrong. Only a few weeks had passed since he had left Cornwall to return home to Mary, there was no way he would be back so soon, unless there was something very wrong.

Panic stricken, she gathered up her green muslin skirt, and hurried across the lawn to the open French doors.

This young lad would bring Mary's news and gossip every four to six months, and then after he had rested, he would return to Durham with all Bella's news and correspondence. Whatever could have brought him back so soon? She stopped and watched the boy dismount, and hand the reins to the stable man who had walked out to greet him. A few words were exchanged, before the youngster hurried off towards the back entrance of the house. The lad must be absolutely, exhausted, she thought. But, from her staff she had learnt just how much he loved to saddle the animal and ride the rugged countryside, till he had reached the Cornish coast.

The journey in accordance with the weather, could take roughly, three to four weeks each way. However, fortunately for him on these trips, he had stopped and encountered several kind Blacksmiths. Luckily, all had offered water, a little food, and rest by the warmth of their forges.

Bella agitated, wondered where her butler was. Relieved to finally hear his knock, she called, 'Enter.' the sight of the battered, brown, leathery bag, he held instead of the usual silver tray, disturbed Bella even more.

The man cleared his throat. 'Madam. Miss Mary requested by note that she wished you to receive this, he held the tight buckled pouch out, 'un-opened on this trip.'

She took it from his hand. 'Oh…I see,' she murmured more to herself. Fearful now, of the whole situation, she placed it onto her desk. 'The boy must be exhausted? I know you will see he is well looked after and rested before his return.'

'Indeed, Madam.'

Bella smiled at the short bald man who like all her staff, had been in her employment for many years, 'thank you, William. Oh, and I think I'll have a brandy for a nightcap please.' She had a fear, she might need one.

'Very well, Madam. I'll fetch it straight away.'

Reluctant to open the bag, she sat and stared at it for some time while she sipped the rather large, smooth liquid. Eventually with hands that shook, she undid the buckle and retrieved the eight- paged, letter inside. Unable to believe the written words before her, she read it over and over. Shocked by their contents, the papers fell from her hands and landed at her feet.

For the first time in many years, Bella felt vulnerable, and very, very much alone.

What on earth could she do to help her two girls out of the agonized, dilemma that hateful Fordham, had dared to bring down upon them.

'What dear Lord, can I possibly do?' She whispered. It was late and she was tired, perhaps she would think clearer in the daylight. She stood and walked towards the bedroom door, perhaps after a night's sleep, she might have some answers.

After an extremely restless night, dawn's arrival clearly, indicated another hot day. Strong anger replaced her previous fear, and seated at her desk, Bella read the letter again.

Mary and Isobel were the two people she loved with all her heart. Also like her daughter, she wished she could include Agnes in her heart, but it was impossible. Oh, she had tried many times to love the child and show affection, but, sadly without success. It was a simple case of like father, like daughter, both were completely impossible, selfish, and extremely dislikeable. And of course, there was also young Alice, and the mystery that shrouded her.

Bella knew her beloved Mary cared for the girl very much, and the child was extremely lovable. Plus, the fact that Fordham, had fathered the girl was of no consequence to Mary, because she loved the child like her own.

Bella thought her daughter a wonderful person for the way she had accepted Alice and taken her to her heart.

The Claremont wealth came from her husband James's trade ships, which still sailed the seas this day. She was nineteen when the tall handsome Irish sailor, twelve years her senior had anchored off the Cornish coast, where her village was situated, due to the persistent storms.

Bella had literally bumped into him in the local town while he collected supplies. It had been, love at first sight, and against her family's wishes, they married six months later.

Never once had she regretted their hasty union. Their love, happiness, ships, and wealth increased with every second spent together.

They were absolute soul mates.

Three years after the marriage, their greatest gift of all arrived, with the birth of their daughter Mary. But James had perished at sea in a terrible storm when his precious baby girl was four. Alone with a child and a business it was only with the help of her husband's dear friend and solicitor, Benjamin Bronte, that Bella had been able to continue to build his empire.

Mary's marriage to Fordham had been a great disappointment. But her love for her daughter was unconditional, and she had been fully supportive. However, still to this day, she could never understand what had drawn her beautiful daughter to him in the first place. She knew Mary had never been happy with Fordham, and now the nasty, despicable, man wanted to sell her precious granddaughter to this, this, old man, Lord, or no Lord.

She remembered her daughter's long visits when the girls had been so small. They would come and stay for months at a time, and she had cherished every moment they had spent with her. She remembered how very reluctant her girls were, when eventually they had to return to Durham, even Agnes at times seemed content to be there with her, and her many books.

Many balls of paper later, desperate to undo the hurt and harm Fordham wanted to inflict upon her girls, pen in her hand, the words began to flow.

Bella prayed with everything she held sacred, that her generous offer would prove conclusive. Also, if she did succeed, she would bring Mary, Isobel and possibly Alice back to Cornwall to live with her for good, which she now realized, should have happed years ago.

Chapter Five

Desperate to see Dune, Isobel rode as if the devil himself was after her. Anxious to tell him the terrible news her father had returned with, she reached their favourite spot, and almost fell into his arms. And, as he pulled her tight to his chest, floods of tears fell. He had no idea of what troubled her, so he just held her tight to his body and let her cry.

She suddenly, stopped, because his extreme closeness made her feel really- strange.

Nether-the-less, from his strong embrace she drew comfort, and wished with all her heart they could stay locked together, like this forever. Isobel, eventually still and quiet, Dune led her to the blanket he had previously laid on the grass. He walked to the crystal, clear water that cascaded over the rocks, and filled the tin cup he always had attached to his saddle. The water soothed her throat, and as she turned to look at his face. She murmured.

'Dune, I am sorry, but it is far too hot here.' She gave him her hand, and he helped her back up onto her feet. She walked towards the old oak where the horses were sheltered.

'Dune, I am sorry.'

'No, it is very, warm.' He said as he collected the blanket and placed it back onto the ground, in the shade of the tree. 'There, is that better, my darling?'

Isobel sank down, 'Yes thank you. Oh, Dune, I am to be

married. Married at the end of this month.'

'What. What… did you say. Married.?'

She nodded, and tears fell again as she told him what her father had arranged for her, and that it was all to happen in three weeks-time.

'No. No this is impossible. You cannot do this I have only just returned, no, no. No. No.'

Isobel a little calmer, murmured, 'Sadly, there is not a thing I can do, and I will have to marry this stranger, who also happens to be older than my father.' She looked at him hard. 'I will have to do this Dune it is expected of me. Agnes should wed this man, but my father has said no.' Her lips trembled, and he pulled her tight to his body. 'I, do not know why he has passed my sister over, but, he has, and I am to be sacrificed to this old man.'

'But we must be able to do something to stop this evil deed. Anyway, you cannot marry him because I love you, dear sweet Isobel, and I have for years.'

Tears fell once more, and cuddled close together, neither spoke, and silence hung in the air for some time. Content to be in Dune's arms, and because she had not slept much of late, Isobel closed her eyes.

Several hours passed, and when she woke, she was lying flat against him on the rug.

'Oh, Dune.' she uttered. Wide awake now, she slowly moved away from him, and he helped her to her feet. She yawned and stretched her arms above her head. 'Sorry, Dune I am tired, I have not slept well lately.' Isobel smiled as he again handed her the cup to drink from.

'That was nice, it was lovely and cold, thank you.'   He pulled her tight to him and kissed her hard on the mouth.

'Oh, Dune, Dune, what you do to me when you kiss me like this is…wonderful.'

'My darling, I will not let you marry this man, because you are mine.'

'No… no. I have told you many times, we can never be together. You know this to be true.' She took his hand and kissed it. 'Dune please do not talk like this, because the thought of my father finding out about us, well it terrifies me.' She pulled him close to her. 'You must promise me, that you will not do a thing to endanger yourself. Please, Dune, I mean it. You must, never, never try to help me.'

He nodded, then moved towards the blanket and picked it up.

'Dune I must go; Mama will be worried about me. But I will meet you as much as I can before, my terrible marriage takes place.' She looked at his face.

He smiled, bent to kiss her, then he walked towards the horses. 'Come, we will ride together some of the way.'

'No, no, we cannot, because I have been longer than normal, Mama will have fretted, she may have sent some staff out to look for me. Please you go and I will meet up with you tomorrow.'

He reached for her again, and the kiss was magnificent.

'I must go now.' She whispered, as he helped her up into the saddle. She turned back to look at him, he blew a kiss, then, stood, and watched her ride away.

Isobel gently urged Tranquil to trot on and in no time, they had gathered up speed and were back at the stables. Her horse settled, Isobel went straight into the house, and made for her Mother's room.

'Oh, my dearest I was so worried. What happened to you?'

'I am so sorry; I never meant to alarm you Mama.' They embraced and Isobel said, 'Silly me, I fell asleep. Since father told me what he wants me to do, I have not slept very well.' Mary kissed her beautiful daughter's chcck. 'Yes, my darling, that I can fully understand. But never mind your home safely, and that's all that matters.'

'Yes, I shall have a nice bath, then after my super I will be back to see you Mama.'

Her mother smiled and pulled her close once more. 'You go my darling and come back when you're ready.'

'Yes, I will Mama, thank you.'

She opened the door and quietly walked back to her own room.

Alice's relief at seeing her, she took her hand. 'Mistress, I was so worried. What happened?'

Isobel still very tired smiled, 'Dear Alice, I met Dune, at our special place, out near the great mountain, it is such a beautiful spot there. I have not slept, well lately, so I fell asleep. I am sorry, I did not mean to worry anyone.'

'Never mind, let's get this riding habit off you, so you can have a nice warm bath.'

Isobel ate a light supper, then went across to her mamas to read some more of 'Pickwick Papers,' the serialized story, written by a young man called Charles, Dickens.

Mary relieved by the sight of the dishevelled lad before her placed two pennies into his grubby hand and muttered. 'Thank you dear -boy. I know by the time factor that you must have ridden long and hard.'

The battered, bag clutched tight to her chest, she smiled again as he turned to follow the young maid from the room.

Out in the passage, the dumbstruck boy quickly tucked the coins down into the safety of his mud splattered boots.

Mary seated at her desk, through a haze of tears read her mother's words, and they gave her such hope. Oh, how she loved this strong woman, who had always been her rock. Fordham had returned two nights ago; many days had passed since the man had delivered his devastating news.

Elated paper in her hand, she found her husband in the library. 'Oh, Arthur, Arthur, listen.' She held it up for him to see. 'Please, I have letter from, Mama. Would you like to read it? She writes that she will help us, so, Isobel, does not have to marry that old stranger.'

He completely ignored her and waved his hand dismissively.

Still not to be deterred she offered it and continued, 'Mother, can solve the matter. She wants to give you a substantial amount of cash, and with it you can clear all this...man's debts. Mother also wants to replace every penny that you are owed, and...' She stopped and looked at the despicable man sprawled before her. 'And' she insisted, 'If you accept her offers, she will give you an extra-large amount on top for yourself. Oh, Arthur, if you do as she suggests all that you have lost through your card escapades with this person, will be restored, with much more besides.'

'Blabber, blabber. What the hell, woman, are you on about?'

Out of his seat he staggered towards her. The stench from his breath so close to her face caused her to fall back, luckily, into the seat of a chair, near her. His hands splayed across the arms, he leant forward and blasted. 'Mother, this and, Mama, that, I don't care what the old hag has to say.' He straightened. 'This marriage will take place, and your precious, Isobel, will be leaving here to live far away in her new home, with her husband.'

Consumed by a strong anger, Mary screamed. 'No. No, she will not!' She coughed, but thankfully it was not a severe attack. She wiped her mouth and continued. 'The money you have been offered can free Isobel from the deal you made with that...old man. Mother wants to give you so much more money, than you are owed.' Mary looked at the man, you disgust me, Fordham. Absolutely, disgust me. She spoke silently, but she pushed those thoughts aside and whispered. 'Please Arthur, please do not let my beautiful Isobel be sent away from here. I beg you.' She stopped and heaved as she inhaled the stale odour that oozed from his sweaty body.

So very weak and tired, she uttered. 'Arthur, please, please, do not send my, child, away...I...' She coughed, and it was a severe bout. Her body shook, coloured lights dashed in-between her closed eye lids, pain tightened in her chest, and her head throbbed.

Fordham moved, and his drunken body almost fell onto her. 'My dear, wife,' he slurred.

'As... as I have told you many times before, you are the most stupid, female I've ever had the misfortune to know.'

Mary knew the despicable man was extremely rattled.

'Woman, it's the status, pure and simple. It is the status this marriage will bring. *That's* what I *want, the status.'*

His sneer inches from her tear- stained face, Mary was relieved, when he finally resumed to his full height, and staggered back to his seat.

Silence prevailed for some time, but disgusted to sit and witness, the liquid from the raised vessel run freely down his clothes. Mary whispered. 'I know your reason for this deed is to punish me, Arthur, is that not so? Agnes, is the oldest, she....'

The tankard slammed onto the table, vibrated the room. '*Yes, y*es, the man is so desperate he would have taken our eldest.' He wiped his mouth and stared at his wife.

She had just turned forty and signs of her beauty had faded vastly, not that it bothered him.

'But.' He continued. 'Again, as I have stated, with, Agnes, as his bride, just how long do you think his Lordship's interest in me would last? This union will take place, and your precious, Isobel's pureness will seal it for me. So, woman, bloody well get out of here and keep away. I want to drink in peace.'

Drained and mentally exhausted, she whispered. 'What, kind of man are you? She's only a child, seventeen, and this, this man you said is older than you?' How badly she wanted to slap the hateful face. If she had had a gun in her hand right now or a sword, she would not have hesitated to kill him.

Numb, she stood, and defeatedly left the room. In her despair, she walked the long corridor, and there she cursed the demonic man for all eternity. Little did she realise it would occur, sooner than later.

Chapter Six

Fordham's extreme wealth came from his ownership of many of the richest coal collieries near Durham. Ruthless in business and family, he too suffered no fools. His estate situated on the outskirts of the city, consisted of thousands of acres. The tenants of his hamlets paid dearly for the privilege to plough and work his fields. Their rents were high, and most of what they grew, ended up in Fordham barns, which never left much for the people to sell.

His Manor house was in desperate need of repair.

Dull and very dark throughout, it was only through Mary's insistence of the utmost cleanliness through the daily chores that hid and covered the neglect.

Household money for Mary had always been extremely sparse. Neither was she allowed to replace or repair one item without his authority. Her husband even expected her to go to him when she wanted to buy material for clothes and bed sheets.

It was her mother who had come to her rescue yet again. Bella aware of her daughter's situation had set up a monthly allowance for her with a solicitor in Durham Town.

Mary extremely grateful for her generosity, only drew on the money when she had an urgent need of it. Consequently, a substantial nest egg had grown.

She only went into the big city, when Fordham was absent on his trips to London town. On her last excursion, she had purchased several bales of materials. Day gowns, household uniforms, and some frayed linen needed to be replaced. Four old chairs re-covered in a new fabric the man had not even noticed.

On her return, Mary had been overly, excited about the deep, green, velvet cloth, she had purchased. The local seamstress had been immediately sent for and put to work. Uncontrollable tears had fallen, when her youngest daughter, had stood before her in her first off the shoulder, evening gown. The material almost the color of Isobel's eyes, her blonde hair piled high had left Mary speechless. Agnes's refusal to have the same dress made for her, from the rest of the bale, had brought forth, a new riding, habit for Isobel to wear on her daily rides. Nurtured flower beds, well-kept lawns, and trees surrounded the house, again because of the Mistress's persistence. Although, Fordham did agree the outside should look respectable. He had even given instructions, for several of the farm hands to help his wife with the large grounds. The atmosphere on the whole estate, was always lighter, and happier when Fordham was far away from it.

The butler opened the door and bowed. 'Lord, William Belington. Sir.' The men walked in, the man left, and quietly closed the library doors, behind him.

Fordham slumped in his chair did not stand. His temper was explosive. His Lordship was a day late, and the sight of the two unsavoury characters, he had, had the audacity to bring into his home, fueled him even more.

Belington sneered. You, Fordham, are one of the most arrogant, bastards, I have had the misfortune to ever meet, he silently told himself. You are obviously under the illusion you hold all the aces. Although, for now, I really need you to believe you do. But after tomorrow's union, the only thing you will gain is a great downfall. And, of that, you can be damned sure. He continued to stare at the man, who was too re-in-state him with much of the wealth he had lost many decades ago. Oh yes, he silently continued. I am the one who has the best hand, and I will always have it.

The silence in the room was intense. Belington inhaled deeply, as he whispered, my only pleasure at this precise moment in time, would be to inflict the greatest pain upon you, Arthur Fordham, that I was capable of. But instead, I must hold out my hand, fixate a smile, and walk towards you to declare. 'Arthur, dear friend, please forgive the lateness, but you know how it is when one is caught up in a game?' He turned to beckon the two unwanted guests. 'I believe you know my cousins, Lord… and Lord…?'

But Fordham was not interested in names, only the titles.

'Oh shit,' he whispered, as he stood and staggered towards them. 'Welcome, welcome, your Lordships to my humble home.'

Belington sniggered as he watched the man grovel. Oh yes. He continued silently. I knew that introduction would change your attitude towards me and my kin. The man's smile broadened, especially as I only met them two days ago, in the long game of cards, which made me late.

43

Eventually, wine and beer flowed, and a game began, and as usual the despicable man Fordham mostly won.

It was Friday, and tomorrow her precious child was to be married to the old man who had just entered the house. With a few meals already arranged with cook, Mary and Isobel waited apprehensively in their rooms, for the dreaded sound of the gong to echo the hall.

Isobel stared into the full- length mirror at the long, green day dress she had chosen to wear. Alice on her knees pulled at the hem till it touched the tips of her cream pumps. The girl stood, and at the sight of her mistress's tears, she whispered. 'Oh Miss, how I wish I had a magic wand to make all this go away for you.'

'Oh, Alice, I prayed when the man failed to arrive yesterday, that he might have decided not to come here after all. I had hoped, he had changed his mind.'

'I think the whole household wished for that, Mistress.'

Isobel smiled. 'You always make me feel better dear girl.'

The gong sounded and it was time for her to go down and meet her suitor. Alice opened the door to the dreaded knock, and Isobel walked straight out into her mama's embrace. Agnes already down in the large hall, looked up as her mother and sister began their slow decent. Isobel shuddered as each step took her closer to the unwanted stranger, who tomorrow would become her husband.

The four men managed to stand respectfully, when their

hostess and her two daughters entered the room. The girls stayed well back as their mother moved towards the table. Fordham slurred. 'You're Lordship, my wife, Mary.'

The repugnance of the man caused her to sway, and Isobel immediately by her mother's side supported her.

'Are you un-well, Madame?' Belington enquired.

'No sir, I...I... Please. It's just the heat.' She gripped her daughter's supportive hand while led to the chair next the open French doors. Seated, she whispered, 'Thank you dear child. I came over all hot.' Mary shuddered, she was not going to tell Isobel, it was the man's terrible smell, that had turned her stomach.

Fordham's anger over his wife's behavior was obvious as he beckoned Agnes, forward.

'Your Lordship...this is ...my...'

'William. Please, my dear friend Arthur.' He sneered, and silently added. For now, at least. But it was the beauty who stood next to her mother across the room, his bloodshot eyes were transfixed upon.

'Oh, yes...William.' Fordham slurped. 'Mm, this is my eldest daughter, Agnes.'

He took the offered hand and slobbered over the white glove. She curtsied, then moved from his side, and quickly made her way towards her mother and sister.

She sat straight on the second chair, and never said one word, about the repulsive, smelly man a great deal older than their father.   Isobel was more concerned over their Mother's health at this moment in time, because she had been utterly shocked to see just how loosely, the long deep burgundy gown, hung on her thin body.

Deep in thought, she had not heard her father's approach, but having sensed his presence she turned, and her mouth gasped at the sight of the ugly stranger, whose red perspiring face, also had an extremely long scar attached to it.

'Your Lordship…, I mean William, my daughter Isobel, your bride to be.'

The man bowed, took her hand, and feasted his eyes on his virginal prize. 'My dear,' he whispered, 'you are more beautiful, than I was led to believe.'

Mortified by the sight of the man she had been sold to, the lump in her throat threatened to choke.

The sixty -year- old man before her was short and extremely plumb. Long, greasy, dark hair fell onto his thick shoulders. Two red slits for eyes, above a large nose in the round face, repulsed her. The stale odour that oozed from his body was fouler than his breathe.

His once white shirt, now grey, he wore beneath a badly stained brown velvet tailcoat. The paisley cravat tied about his thick neck, with mud splattered cream trousers tucked into long brown knee length boots, his full attire, was a complete disgrace. But it was the deep scar, that started from behind his left ear, down his cheek, and finished beneath his bottom lip, Isobel visibly cringed at.

The man put his hand to his face and smiled. 'Ah do not be alarmed my dear, it does not hurt. It's a keepsake from a duel many years back.' He released her hand, and as she turned back towards her mother, Belington smiled. 'Oh yes, Arthur, you certainly have done me proud, for she surely is a great beauty.'

Fordham grunted, 'tell me, I've often wondered, about that.' He touched his own face.

'Ah this was from one of my mistress's husband. Oh, what a woman she was.

Such passion, so much fiery lust. But not worth to die for. After the man inflicted this upon me, I gained great satisfaction to return the deed, as I thrust my blade straight through the man's heart. The woman became a merry, easy widow.'

Isobel like her Mother found the dinner extremely, stressful. She too realized the grandness of the table was completely lost on the guests. The French, designed blue and white dinner service, trimmed in gold a gift from her grandmother, looked grand on the pale cream Damask cloth. Stemmed glasses stood by the knife tips. The silver, candelabrum with the five candles aglow, centered the table. A round glass bowl filled with fresh cut flowers stood each side of it. Flagons of wine and beer stood on several trays for the men, and a jug of freshly made lemonade was for her and Agnes. The usual Sherry decanter was near her Mama, who sometimes enjoyed a small glass.

The warm potato soup, followed by roast goose and fresh vegetables, the white cream cheese with fruit, was all cooked to perfection, but Isobel, like her mother ate very-little. Even Agnes's hearty appetite, seemed to have disappeared.

Belington peered over the top of the goblet towards Agnes. Mm, for the promised money and dowry, I would have taken you. He silently told her, then his gaze sought the pale beauty. But my what a prize you are. All the pleasures I will endure with you my sweet, excites me already. His wine finished he placed the goblet back onto the table.

Finally, the men lit their cigars.

Mary stood, followed closely by her daughters, they excused their-selves, and walked from the room, out in the hallway, their Mother whispered. 'I am nervous about those men in the house. I want you girls to sleep in my bedchamber tonight.'

'Not me Mother.' Agnes declined, 'I will go to my room and lock the door.' But before she did, she took Isobel's hand. 'Sister I am truly- sorry about that awful person, that terrible man you must marry tomorrow. I truly am.' Then she hastily disappeared, and as promised, the door was bolted and secure behind her.

Isobel sauntered into the far end of the garden and thought of her beautiful Dune. It was only the fact, she had been able to ride out, and secretly meet him so many times since his return, that had kept her sane over the last few weeks.

Lavender entwined with honey suckles clung to the night air. Fragrances drifted into her hair, she sneezed as they tantalized her small nose. Orange, yellows, fiery, scarlet, streaks sailed across the darkening sky, it was beautiful to see. She listened as the choral of birds filled the air, and uncontrollable tears fell. She had been so strong for the sake of her mama, but now alone, she trembled with fear as she thought of the old man, who tomorrow would become her husband.

A sudden sound caused Isobel to jump, she quickly reached for the bottom of her dress, grasped tight in her hand, she hurried back into the hall and quickly climbed the stairs to seek the sanctuary of her mother's room.

Chapter Seven

Mary on her return to her rooms, was physically sick and, had succumbed to several bouts of her terrible cough. Exhausted, bodily, and mentally, she was fast asleep when Isobel entered the safety of her chambers.

Much later, awake in the darkness the sudden arrival of horses to the front of the house, accompanied by a great deal of noise, caused Isobel to slip from beneath the covers. With her wrap about her body and guided by the moonlight, that crept into the room, she walked to the window.

It was her father, followed closely by those terrible men she had seen earlier that night. They were all extremely rowdy as they stepped up into the carriage, and as she watched it drive off, she wished, with all her heart, they would never, ever return. But it was a stupid wish, she knew, because her father, and the man Belington, would, be back there for tomorrow, for certain.

She stared out across the black fields. And her second wish was for her beloved Dune to gallop to the front of the house, call her name, then when she appeared, he would reach for her, and held tight against his body, he would ride off into the sunset with her never to return there again. She sighed loudly, no she could never do that, she could not leave her beloved mama behind here on her own.

Isobel sighed, what was she too do, the man was absolutely, repulsive, and so old.

There would be no Mama, no Alice, and worst of all no Dune. 'I would be better off dead.' She muttered quietly.

She moved away from the window, and slowly walked towards the make do bed. Thoroughly despondent, Isobel decided to go back to her own rooms. The men had gone and would not come back until morning, so with no worry, she quietly gathered her things together.

She tip-toed over to her mother's bed, and in the silence of the room, she heard the same throaty noise, that had come from her yesterday. Tears fell as she leaned down to kiss her sweaty forehead, then she quietly walked to the door, which she closed carefully behind her.

The door handle turned but it would not open. Isobel tried several times more, then gently tapped and called. 'Alice, are you in there?' She heard noisy movement before it opened, and the girl a blanket about her shoulders, declared, 'Oh, Miss, I'm so sorry.'

'Did you put that by the door?' Isobel pointed to the large wooden trunk half filled with her clothes.

'Aye, I did. Because I knew if anyone tried to enter it would wake me.'

'Well, my father, and the men have left, thankfully, and hopefully will never come back.' Isobel looked towards the wooden chair. 'Alice, surely you have not tried to rest in that rocker?'

'Yes Mistress. I thought you might be back to your bed.'

Isobel held her hands towards the fire embers and shivered.

'Oh, my you are so cold. Come, get under the covers and I'll make the fire up nice and warm.' The girl urged.

Grateful for the help, Isobel climbed in and snuggled beneath the blankets. 'I should have taken a thicker wrap with me. It is strange how these rooms, and hallways are always so chilled and damp from dusk onwards. Yet on the long hot summer days, we welcome the coolness of them.'

'Yes, Miss, they are all very cold by night. Would you like me to go and make you some warm, sweet tea?'

'Please Alice, do you mind?'

'Not at all. I won't be long.'

Isobel smiled when the girl left the room, and more tears fell. The thought of her and Alice being parted, was horrendous. On her own somewhere strange, no, the very thought of it was unbearable, and without her, she would be completely lost.

The girl returned with their hot drinks, and a few biscuits, then after a lot of chatter between them, the heavy trunk was eased back into its previous position.

Isobel knew her friend did not care where she slept this night, because she just wanted to be with her Miss Isobel, who was also her friend.

'That's it we'll be fine now.' She uttered.

'But those men have left, Alice, and I am certain, they will not return until tomorrow.'

'Well just in case my lovely.' She looked at her mistress and continued silently, because you my dear one, never saw the lecherous looks, they all gave you, so I will just stay put.

52

The deed finished, the fire banked up, Alice snuggled back onto the hard seat.

'Oh Mistress, I almost forgot,' the girl whispered, and checked the door again.

'Dune, was here.'

'Here. Alice, when, and where was he?'

'I saw him out the back. I had to tell him to go away, he was to near the house.' The girl's pretty face was serious. 'But he declared his worry for you. And his need to see you in your usual place, if you possibly could, before you... leave...'Alice fought to keep her own tears in check.

'Oh no, there's no way I will be able to go. I must marry that vile man tomorrow, then we will travel to his ancestral estate. 'I do not think I will ever see my beloved Dune again.' Floods of tears fell, and Alice rushed to comfort her.

Much later, still wide awake, Isobel dismissed all thoughts of the new dawn.

Instead, mesmerized by the high flames that licked the chimney breast, she let her mind run rampant. But she was also extremely, concerned over the noise that had started to come from her mother's throat. She would send for the doctor first thing tomorrow, her mama needed to see him urgently.

Her eyes were extremely heavy, and Dune her beautiful gypsy love, came to her, tears fell, then sleep eventually claimed her.

Sluggish, her slim legs over the side of the bed, Isobel stood. It was the day of her marriage. She sauntered to the window and opened the curtains. The dark, grey sky sent shivers through her. 'Alice, even the birds have not bothered to sing their dawn chorus, this day.'

'No, dear one, I think, like us, they must also be sad.'

'And the desperately needed rain, has decided to fall.'

'Yes, let's hope your clothes don't get wet.'

'Mm, yes.'

'Come please sit. You must try to eat a little breakfast. Cook says these eggs still be warm, when put into the basket.'

'Alice.' Isobel, stopped, tears welled. 'The thought of food makes me feel physically sick.'

'I know Miss, but you must try to eat a little, it will then hopefully make you feel a little better.' Alice pulled out the chair and reluctantly, Isobel sat and tried to eat some food. Under normal circumstances, regardless of the Master, the marriage of his youngest daughter would have heralded great happiness and joy, throughout the house. Instead, an eerie atmosphere like moth eaten net descended throughout. Now with just a few hours to go before the ceremony, an agonized silence filled all the rooms and hallways. It was as if Fordham's evil deed had ripped the heart from within the walls, and all who dwelt inside.

'It hangs so loosely on you Miss. Let me remove it and stitch the sides in for you? Although it does not surprise me you have eaten so little these past few weeks.'

'No, please leave it.' Isobel cried. 'I do not care how it looks.'

The girl took her mistress's cold hands and rubbed them

vigorously. The lump in her throat made it impossible for her to speak, and as Isobel's tears fell freely, they wrapped their arms about each other.

'I'm sorry dear, Alice. I know you want to make it all better for me and take all of my unhappiness away.'

'Oh, dear sweet Miss, I want too so very much.' They pulled apart and wiped their eyes. The girl collected the blue bonnet that matched the simple, blue dress, then asked 'Are you ready for this now Miss Isobel?'

She nodded, and the two long ribbons tied once about her neck were left to hang loosely. Lastly, long white gloves were drawn up over her hands to her elbows, and the bride who ignored the full- length mirror was ready.

Alice looked at her pale Mistress, and asked, 'would you like me to come down with you?'

Isobel whispered. 'Yes. Yes, please, dear friend.'

Deafened from the intense silence within the house, side by side they slowly descended the stairs. Isobel stumbled and might have fallen, but for the girl's steady hold.

The last step reached, together on the flagstone floor, Alice's uncontrollable tears finally fell. Consequently, this time, it was her mistress who conjured up the strength to turn and comfort her. 'Hush dear, Alice, please, no more tears.'

'After tomorrow, what will I do without you here for me to serve? The thought of not seeing you each day, and not being able to talk to…oh dear sweet …?'

Isobel retrieved the white handkerchief tucked into the

top of her right glove and passed it to her. 'Come on wipe those lovely brown eyes and get yourself to the church. Otherwise, this pretty lemon dress you've chosen to wear will go to waste.' Isobel shook inwardly and wondered at her own, composure. Locked in an embrace, they held each other tight. Then, without another word, Isobel pulled away, turned, and walked across the square hall, and in the blink of an eye, she was gone.

The coachman smiled and helped her up into the seat opposite the Master. Numbed from head to foot, she welcomed her father's silence.

The two black Mares coaxed to trot on halted at the church gates. Fordham uncurled his tall frame, stumbled past Isobel, and almost fell out of the door. He turned and sneered as he witnessed the tenderness the servant showed towards his daughter, whilst he helped her to alight onto the gravel.

'Thank you, Joe.' She smiled at the elderly man who had worked in her father's stables for most of his life.

The man removed his hat and bent as far as his arthritic bones, would allow. Then he stood and watched the dear girl, who had first come into his stables, a baby in her mother's arms, follow her father slowly along the path, that led to the chapel's entrance.

Every seat in the small church was filled with her mother's loyal staff, and all had donned their Sunday best.

Mary, seated next to Agnes, looked on in horror as the

vile man soon to become her son-in-law, scurried past their pew without time to spare. Disgusted to see he was still attired in the previous night's clothes, she whispered to Agnes, 'Thank God. It doesn't look like those other awful men have returned with him.'

Her eldest daughter shuddered and answered. 'Yes, Mama, I think you are right.'

The sight of the empty space beside her, Mary stifled a sob. It was where Bella, would have sat, and the letter from Cornwall, had been a terrible shock. It had been delivered by someone Mary had never set eyes on before, and the note had informed her that, Bella was ill with a severe chill, and unable to travel. Mary's heart had been very, heavy when she had told Isobel, this news. (But the truth was, Bella had suffered a stroke, and it had been quite a severe one. Consequently, at this moment in time, she was unable to walk or speak clearly.)

Isobel stepped inside the porch and lent against the thick, black door. She wanted to turn and run. Sickness hit the pit of her stomach, her body shook, and her head ached.

The sight of dear old Joe had awakened so many, happy memories. She remembered him from when she was small. She had loved all the creatures, but it was the horses she had truly longed to be with. Through those joyful years Joe had taught her how to nurture her passion for all God's animals. So, like her mama, she too had developed into a great horsewoman.

Chapter Eight

Fordham's patience thin, he grasped his daughter's arm. 'Come on, girl, move yourself, if you go any slower, you'll stop.'

The walk down the aisle past the congregation was slow. Isobel's distress was such, that she was completely oblivious of the effort her father had made with his outfit. His light brown frock coat, high necked white shirt, chocolate, colored cravat, top-hat and long, brown leather boots, were all, unusually clean and smart.

Due to many sleepless nights, and little food Isobel swayed, and might have fallen, but for her father's tight grip. His hold slackened when they reached the altar, where the smelly bridegroom waited with the priest.

She was aware someone had removed the white gloves from her hands, and her father had distanced himself from her. And that, the man in his black frock, and white hassock stood ready to conduct the service.

The sight of the stranger, the Master had betrothed this beautiful daughter to wed, made the priest cringe.

The man of the cloth was a truly kind person, who always tried to help those who lived on and around the estate, especially those in genuine need of him. The Master however, he hated with a vengeance. And this terrible deed, the man was allowing to happen this day, he classified as an unforgivable sin. No one should sell a child, not for any reason, especially to gain a status.

The pale faced beauty before him, had attended his sermons every Sunday, since a wee one on her mother's lap. He had watched her grow into an extremely beautiful, kind, thoughtful young woman, always eager to help those much less fortunate than herself.

Finally, with a great reluctance, the man cleared his throat to begin.

'We are here today to join... And this will be, one of the saddest ceremony's I will ever perform,' He silently told himself, as his sad words echoed out, into the thick, haunted silence of the Church.

Belington still intoxicated from his night of debauchery, frowned at the man stood before him. You have a voice, that goes straight through me. He silently screamed. It penetrates, through my dulled head, this day. And you my bride, you stand beside me like a stone stature. I am completely ignored. He used his sleeve to wipe the spittle from his mouth, and he continued to frown at the small fat man.

Isobel nauseated from the staleness that seeped from the man's overweight body, heaved, and feared she might be violently sick.

'Mm, Miss... Miss...mm... Mistress Isobel. I do, dear child. I need you to say, I do.'

The man smiled at her kindly.

Snapped back into a dazed reality, she whispered, 'Oh yes...sorry.' She inhaled deeply.

'I…I...do.' She placed the small bunch of fresh cut flowers into her other hand, to allow the man to take the hand he needed, but it was the sound of the priest's intake of breath that caused Isobel to follow his gaze. Blood oozed from the deep cut, the clutched stems had made, she felt woozy, he stopped the service. He moved towards the alter and collected a small cloth, he dabbed the wound dry, then rolled the material into a ball, and carefully closed her hand over to compress the area. Muzzy headed, she found it hard to breath when the thin gold band brought by her father, was eventually placed onto her finger.

It was then, with a great reluctance, the man of God pronounced them man and wife.

After the necessary documentation, had been signed, Fordham pounced on the witnessed marriage certificate. 'I'll keep it safe for now William, as we agreed.' He muttered as he tucked it securely into a leather wallet, and then back inside his jacket.

He needed to keep the document extremely close to him. His knew this man was capable of anything. Fordham, turned to look at his wife, and the sight of Mary's distress and fear, thrilled him beyond words.

Isobel Fordham had ceased to be, she was now Lady Belington. Therefore, as she turned to walk with the repulsive man, it was Lord and Lady Belington, who side by side now walked down the aisle to leave the church.

Cold, frightened, and absolutely shrouded in numbness, she silently prayed. 'Dear Lord, what can I do? I cannot stand the very sight of this vile man, who I must now call husband.'

Relieved to be out in the daylight, Isobel looked to the sky, and let the steady rain caress her face. Then to her sheer relief the man beside her stated.

'My dear. I never allow anyone to ride my horse, so I will see you back at the house. Do you mind if I ride him back?'

'No, sir. Not at all.' The dampness of the day caused her to shiver.

His hat back on his head, she watched him waddle off to find his animal.

Isobel deeply distressed to see the support her mother needed, from Anna, her personal maid and Alice, her emotions in check, moved towards them. She had heard her Mama cough several times during the service, and now, she looked physically, and mentally exhausted.

'Please, get the Mistress into the carriage.' Isobel turned to beckon Joe, who immediately came to help. While the trio carefully settled Mary into the coach, Isobel wandered over to one of the un-kept graves and, laid the tiny bunch of flowers across it.

The horse returned at a much slower pace, and from her seat, Isobel watched the women and men scurry across the fields that led back to the house. The animals halted in the courtyard, stayed still and quiet, while her mother was carefully helped from the seat and taken into the house and up to her room. Isobel, who followed close behind, was surprised to see just how many of the staff were already back in uniform. As she watched from the back of the room, tears welled as she witnessed, the love and care Anna, and the staff showed, while they tended their beloved Mistress's needs.

Much later, washed and changed into a clean nightgown, propped up against the pillows, Mary smiled at her daughter, and tapped the cover beside her, but Isobel waited until she had leant forward to receive her spoonful of syrup. She moved towards the bed and sat down, how she loved this woman. She held back her tears, as she managed to murmur through the large lump in her throat. 'Mama, how do you feel now?'

'Better my dear, but I am very tired. I think I'll try to sleep.' She took her daughter's soft hand and held it to her lips. 'Little one, we both need to keep strong.'

Isobel nodded, then whispered. 'Rest now, and I'll come back later and sit with you.'

'Yes dear, I would like that.'

'Would you like me to bring the next instalment from that new writer, Charles Dickens, so I can read for you?'

'Oh. Pickwick Papers that will be nice. I didn't know you had managed to get the new one.'

'Yes, Alice, and I brought the next part of it when we went into Durham last week. Now, you snuggle down and try to sleep.' Isobel smiled and stroked her mother's long hair until her eyes closed. Once more in the silence of the room, she heard the rattle noise in her mother's throat, but now it seemed, a little louder.

With no word from the man or her father, Isobel anxious to be rid of the clothes she wore, returned to her own quarters. The blue dress almost ripped from her body, was thrown to the floor onto her hat and wet pumps. 'Alice, I don't remember what happened to the white gloves, do you?'

The girl busy with the last of her garments to be packed, quickly picked up a robe and helped her into it. 'No, Miss, I never saw. I was more concerned over your poor hand.'

'Never mind, I'm not worried about them. If you find out who picked them up, tell them they may keep them.'

'Very well, Mistress. I'll be sure to do that for you.' Alice smiled, 'your bath is ready for you, Miss.'

'Oh, lovely, thank you.'

'Keep your poor hand in the water, and I'll see to it when you have had your soak.'

Isobel smiled as she entered the small room with the bath. With the silk wrap removed from her body, Isobel stepped into the warm soapy water.

She sighed and closed her eyes, and Dune's magnificent image was before her. If only she could see him, just one more time, before she left tomorrow. Perhaps an early ride, but no that would be no good, how could she let him know.

'Oh Dune, darling Dune, where are you now?' She whispered.

The water was chilled, when Alice helped her out, and once dried and re-robed, utterly refreshed, she sat on the stool in front of the mirror, while the girl crooned and brushed her beautiful, long blonde hair.

'You know this always calms me Alice, thank you... I'm... going... to... shall miss... you so very much...I.'

'Oh Mistress, dear one...' But tears fell freely, completely heartbroken over the terrible banishment, both comforted each other.

Alice knelt to pick up the heaped clothes. 'I'll take these down to the wash- room, Miss.'

Isobel turned she pulled the wrap tight about her. 'No, no. Burn them, give it all away, or you keep them but, I never want to see any of them again.'

Alice looked at her Mistress. 'I'll see to it. Cook may want them for her niece.' She stared at her mistress and said, 'Your, Ladyship, you've had no food since early this morning, please would you eat a little now?'

The very thought of it nauseated her, but, yes, perhaps she should try. 'I will, just as long as you bring back something light please. And, Alice, never again address me by that title, when, we are on our own.'

The girl nodded, smiled, and with her arms full, took her leave.

Still, with no sign of the man, she now called husband, Isobel in a clean gown, and, after a small, meal of fish with rice, went to sit with her mama.

Mary, eager to hear the next episode, smiled and beckoned her daughter to sit by her on the bed. Isobel's serene voice filled the room, and for a short while, the pain receded from her, face, and Mary looked content.

Isobel's voice turned into a whisper, as she noticed her mother's struggle to keep awake, so thc last few lines she never uttered. She stood as Anna walked towards the chair. This dear lady, had been her and Agnes Nanny for many years. Then, when she was no longer needed for the children, the lady, had been honored to become Mary's personal maid and companion.

She smiled at Isobel, 'I'll sit and watch over, the Mistress, Miss, please do not worry about her.'

'I know you will dear Anna. Thank you. Also, has the doctor been this afternoon, to see her?'

'No, Miss he is coming in the morning.'

'Ah, good. Thank you, Anna.'

The woman curtsied and smiled again.

Back in her own room, her relief as a new bride, was obvious when she found only Alice there. It was late, and mentally exhausted, and very tired she was ready to retire.

With all thoughts of the man dismissed from her mind, Isobel bolted, and secured the door herself from intruders. And, once more her dear friend insisted, she wanted to stay with her.

The fire banked up high and a cover around her, Alice again settled down to sleep in the wooden rocker.

Chapter Nine

Fordham, and his new-son-in-law, had made their way straight to the library, and while the promised dowry was made ready for his Lordship's eager hands, the wine flowed freely. Belington drew his breath in deeply as he sighted the bank draft placed onto the table.

'That's not for me I hope, because that will be no bloody good at the card tables. No, no I want cash. You promised me cash Fordham. No this is not what we agreed upon, I want money. I need money.'   He banged his fist hard onto the table. 'You said, I would have the whole amount, after the marriage took place, so where is it?'

'Well yes, I did. But I'm sorry about that.' Fordham sneered. 'But this is the only way you're going to get it. After all, five thousand pounds, is an extremely, large amount for one to carry around in London, do you not agree.' He coughed, then, continued. 'The rest you can claim from my London Bank. I will give you a note to hand to them.' He drank some more wine. 'However, I also have these.' Fordham placed a bundle of white five- pound notes onto the table, 'and this.' He tossed the small cloth bag full of sovereigns towards him. 'The whole amount is five hundred, which surely, Sir, will keep you going until you return to the big City.'

Belington, seethed, he had expected to receive his first full payment now, and his angry, disappointment was visible for the repulsed man to see.

His, Lordship's scowl deepened, when Fordham put his hand inside his jacket pocket for the wallet, which contained the signed marriage lines. Red faced, he watched him open a deep drawer within his desk, place it inside, lock it securely, then with the key held tight in his hand, he disappeared into a small area obscured from his view.

Several seconds later he returned, lifted the chalice to his lips, and downed the contents.

Belington banged his empty pewter hard onto the wooden table, then he reached for the flagon, and refilled it. He drank thirstily, wiped his mouth on the back of his sleeve and sneered.

'Well, Sir, if this is the measly amount, I am to get for now, it will have to do.'

The notes and the bag tucked safely away on his body, he collected his hat and turned back to the man. 'But I warn you, Arthur Fordham, and you best heed it. The next time I want a substantial amount of money from you, I expect, to receive what I have asked for, immediately and in full. Do you understand me?'

The man nodded as he whispered beneath his breath. 'Yes, yes, to hell with you, you bastard.'

'Now, I must bid you farewell, and be on my way.'

'You what, what did you say, your, Lordship? You are about to leave here, but why man its' your wedding night; surely you wish to bed your bride. And we have food, music, and more wine.

'Believe me, Sir, this time, I promise you, I'll not be away for too long of that you can be sure.'

Fordham slouched in the chair, finished the liquid, and sneered. 'Are you not pleased with my choice of daughter for you. Does Isobel's innocence, and beauty which will be yours to feast upon for many a year, not please you my Lord?'

Belington smiled. 'Please me. Yes, of course I am happy with my bride. But tell me, why did you not give me the eldest? I would have taken her.'

'Oh, yes, I believe you would have. But you see, our youngest gone from here is my Ace card.' He swigged more wine. 'Because, with her gone so far away, well, it will drive my wife insane.' He laughed and refilled his tankard. 'She will either, wither up and just die, or return back to Cornwall, where I found her.' He leaned back in the seat and closed his eyes.

'You see.' he continued. 'Once she'd given birth to her precious Isobel, she bolted the door on me, and still does to this very day.'

Belington scrutinised his hosts ugly face from over the rim of his goblet. Then he answered.

'You should have kicked the door down, for I certainly would have.'

Fordham smiled. 'Well, that's not quite true, I had found a new mistress, who took so much out of me, when I was with her, that once back home, I was glad to just sit, and drink.' He laughed. 'No, I'd had enough of her by then anyway, she was never any fun and would always fight against me when I took her. No, I just never wanted to bother with her again. So, it suited the two of us.' He stared at the man, who today had become his son-in-law, and sniggered. 'No, now, I just want her gone, gone from here, and out of my life for good.'

'Well, I hope my new wife doesn't get ideas like that, because it won't work with me, of that you can be sure.'

'Exactly, so if I had given you my eldest, I think you would be only too glad to have her bolt the door on you.' They both laughed loudly.

'Now what about a few games of cards, who knows, perhaps I might win some of my money back from you.' Fordham suggested.

'No, I'm away. It is urgent business that calls me.'

Fordham, his drink finished, wiped his mouth with his sleeve. 'But wait, I do not understand you, sir. You have a bride that awaits you up the stairs in her room, and you want to leave.' He stared at him hard, 'But why, man, why,'

'Because I have some urgent business in town, I told you about it. So now I must leave.' Fordham refilled his tankard. 'And what about the coach, I have arranged to collect Isobel from here, in two days' time, will you come back here to travel with it?'

'No, your beautiful, daughter, will have to journey to her new home alone.'

He supped more liquid. 'But tell me, does it bother you that she will be unaccompanied, and be on her own.'

His host frowned. 'Certainly not, but I thought...' He stopped, the chalice close to his mouth, he downed the liquid. 'Assumed, you would stay for a couple of nights here at least.'

Belington his patience thin, gulped the contents, and threw the empty tankard down onto the table.

'We'll I'm sure we will meet soon in London. Now, it is without delay, I'll bid you farewell.' He waited for no answer, and the door resounded, behind him.

Outside in the dampness, he shivered. Eager to reach his destination before darkness fell, he made for the stable, and as requested his stallion was ready for him. The lad held the animal's reins to keep him calm, as the man staggered onto the wooden step, then up into the saddle.

The boy respectfully kept his head bent as he spotted his master's approach.

Fordham looked up at Belington. 'Wait.' He shouted. 'I'll ride with you.'

'No, I'm away now.' The feisty animal reared upwards, as the whip was brought down across its grey flank. Hooves back on the ground, the magnificent creature pounded off towards the long, bridle path, which snaked in and out towards the large wrought iron gates.

Out into the open country lanes, the man gathered great speed. Lord William Belington's desperate hunger for the card tables, and his need for the company of the coarse women of the bordellos, screamed for his quick return.

There was absolutely no way at this time, he wanted to be burdened, with the company of a milksop girl.

His disappointment, about the amount of money secured upon him, would disperse once he had retrieved the full amount.

Also, what Fordham did not know was, this would be the first of many more payments to follow. This man, his father-in-law, would now keep him in money constantly. He would have no more dept, and to always have money in his pockets, would make him a much, stronger man. But it was the thought of never being in dept again, that pleased him, the most. He did not want heirs, he could not care less about his ancestral home, and estate, but if a child, or children came along, so be it.

Also, should Fordham, ever have any thoughts about stopping the money, he himself would gain much pleasure, to rip the uncouth, man's heart from his chest.

Anger, and humiliation, consumed Fordham as he returned to the library. 'Damn the man.' He shouted. 'Not only had he denied me the pleasure of a big social event, upon which all my wealthy, neighbours would have attended. He's robbed me of my desperation, to boast my daughter's noble position.'

He sank into the chair and refilled his goblet. He downed the liquid quickly. Frustrated by the man's hurried departure, which also had deprived him, of some satisfaction in winning some of his money back, the decanter still in his hand, he threw towards the fire opening, it shattered into tiny pieces, which caused him to laugh loudly.

Fordham's mood blackened as each second passed, and the household was about to witness some of his foulest, tempers and outbursts ever.   Mary, when told the news of what had transpired between the two men, had given strict instruction, that on no account was any young member of staff to enter the library. And this order was to be kept in place, whenever the Master was now in residence.

Then the Mistress, sent for Alice to come and see her in her chambers.

Chapter Ten

Isobel awoke refreshed, as she watched the early sunrays creep in through the partially opened drapes, and a mighty dawn chorus filled her ears. With all thoughts of yesterday's service from her mind, her arms stretched high above her head, she kicked the covers away.

Alice still busy with her young Mistress's clothes looked up and smiled. 'Oh. Miss that man, he left last night, he has gone. But you have to travel tomorrow on your own.'

'What... did ...you say?'

'The man, his Lordship, he rode off last night. They say your, father, he be in the most, foulest of moods.'

'I'll go and see, Mama, and find out exactly what has happened.' Her robe tied about her she quickly left the room.

On her return, she grabbed her friend, and they, danced each other around the room.

'Alice, it is true. I am so happy. And, apparently, it has all been changed. I have to leave here tomorrow, and journey to this place called Sussex, on my own.' She smiled at the girl, then continued. 'And, because it is such a beautiful day, I shall go for a long ride after breakfast.'

'Oh, my lovely, it'll do thee good. I'll away and get your clothes for you.'

Dressed in her green habit, Isobel, went to her mother's chambers to check on her, before she left. She entered quietly and again witnessed Mary in a terrible state of distress. But as usual Anna was beside her, ready to help in any way possible. Isobel knew her mama had caught sight of her, and would try hard to ignore the incident, as she pulled the shawl tighter, about her poor, thin body. Anna smiled at Isobel, as she removed the bowl of warm water from the chair, then, she quietly walked off with it.

'Mother you are still so bad. The doctor is coming to see you again today. I wanted him here yesterday, but he could not make it. But he will arrive later today, please, he must, come and check you once more.'

Mary looked at her and smiled. 'Oh, fuddle, duddle, my dear. But, if it will make you feel happier, he may come and see me.' She touched the soft velvet. 'You look so lovely in this colour. But you are so thin, off with you my, darling, get out in the fresh air. It will do you good, or have you just come back.'

'No Mama, I am on my way now, but I could stay and sit with you, if you would prefer?'

'No. Absolutely not, little one. 'It's a wonderful idea; no, you get out there, but please be careful, I know how you love to roam the countryside.'

'I promise I will.' She leaned over and kissed her mother's damp forehead.

Outside in the corridor, her back against the closed door, her heart pounded her chest as she wiped away her tears. That noise in her Mother's throat, was even louder today, so she was pleased the doctor was coming back to check on her.

More composed, Isobel wondered at the stillness of the house as she slowly descended the stairs. She was also surprised, not to have encountered a single member of staff as she made her way to the back of the house, which was a quicker way to the stables.

Tranquil, her beautiful black mare was saddled and ready for her, and the boy steadied the animal, while she stepped onto the wooden box and mounted. She smiled as the lad handed her the reigns. 'Thank you.' She uttered as her feet gently coaxed the creature to trot on.

She rode as if pursued by a pack of hounds, and the warmth from the sun caressed her face as she neared her favourite place.

Oh, how she prayed, that somehow Dune had heard of her delayed departure. Extremely hot and tired on their arrival, Isobel dismounted, and led her horse to the stream, that cascaded over the rocks. The animal drank thirstily, and cooled by the water, she tied him beneath the old oak, with plenty of shade.

Her jacket removed, Isobel sunk down and leaned against the trunk. She smiled as she watched the busy bees fly in and out of the bushes filled with pollen. The warm breeze tantalised her hair, relaxed, her eyes closed. Birds in full song flew overhead from branch to branch, and somewhere in the far distance, a dog barked. Many animal noises at times broke the total silence, up on the top of this hill. She smiled and opened her eyes. She loved it up here and could see for miles. Here, nature was at its best. Below across the many fields there were many cows to be seen happily chewing the wonderful carpets of grass.

Here she always felt at peace, and the chosen spot was not just for its beauty, it was as far away from the house as it could possibly be. Shrouded by the comfort of it all, her heavy eyes closed once more.

A loud noise shattered the quietness, and she woke with a start, and for a split- second Isobel forgot where she was, and why she was there. She stood, and the sight of the dust cloud's approach, caused her heart to race with excitement. It could only be Dune he must have heard that she had not left as planned. Just to be in his arms for a little while, to have him close to her was all she craved for.

Steam oozed, from the magnificent white animal, as it halted beside her, and with his reigns still clutched tight, he descended. Her slim waist, instantly encircled by his free hand, he pulled her tight to his body, and his lips descended. The kiss was long, wonderful, it was perfect. And his beautifully shaped mouth, drew the very breath from within her, as she melted against him. Isobel needed this moment badly, because she knew after today, she would never see him again. He pulled her closer, and the full realization of her life without him, caused all her pent- up tears to fall.

Eventually, seated within his arms, he listened as she told him about yesterday's events.

'The man has gone, and left you to travel all that way on your own?'

'Yes, I leave tomorrow. The coach will arrive at dawn,

and I am due to depart as soon as it is loaded with my trunks. Apparently, it takes roughly nine to ten days to journey to this... place called... Sussex. My poor, Mama, is so very distraught about it all.'

'Isobel, I cannot let you go like this, because I know that I love you. Love you very much my love. So, what I intend to do is this, when you leave tomorrow, I shall follow you from a distance. You will not even know I am there, because I need to know where this place you are going to, will be.' He pulled her round to face him. 'You'll not be able to see me, but believe me when I say, that I will be there to watch over you.'

'You would do that for me Dune.'

'For you, my adorable one, I would give my life. I love you with all of my heart.'

'Oh, dearest Dune.' She sighed, as he drew her tighter to his body.

'I need to know where you will be, because once everything here is settled, I and some of my clan, will travel to this Sussex. We need to know, what Sussex life might offer us once we all eventually, end up there.'

'Dune, my heart is full, I just do not know what to say, except, thank you my dear, dear Dune. It will be such a comfort to know that you will be near to me, whilst on that terrible long journey.'

He held her close to him, and then, they just sat in complete, silence for some time.

It was with a great reluctance she carefully moved away

from him, and he helped her to her feet.

'I am so sorry, but I must get back. Mama is not at all well, and I want to spend the rest of my time with her.'

'Yes of course you must, but remember my words, my love. You will not be able to see me, but I will be close at all times.' He helped her up into the saddle, reluctant to leave him, Isobel lent down for their final kiss, which was too last, until, who knew when.

It was with a heavy heart, and great reluctance, she finally, rode away. She knew he would stand to watch, until she was just a small spec on the horizon.

Isobel returned home at a much slower pace. She was hot, tired, and very thirsty, plus the heat was unbearable. Alice still busy in her chambers, hugged her when she walked into the room.

'Good, ride Miss.'

'Yes, dear friend, and Dune turned up, and we spent a few hours together.'

'Oh, I am so pleased for you Miss Isobel.' She smiled. 'So, right, yes, let us get these cloths off you, and while we have lunch, you can tell me all about him and what he had to say.'

Later sat in a simple day dress, Isobel caught up with the book she was well into, and the cool breeze that skimmed across the room from her open French doors felt good. She leaned back in her chair, and a picture of Dune flashed into her mind, and happiness filled her heart.

Dune's declaration of his love had made her feel, oh so

special and warm inside.

She was still confused over her own feelings, was it love between them, did she love him. Nether-the-less, if it was love, it was totally out of the question of them ever being together.

Her father, would have gone berserk, had he any inclination of what had passed between the gypsy, and his daughter.

Also, there was Dune's clan; they would find a relationship between Dune, and Miss Isobel, impossible to deal with. Their worlds were so different; it would never work out between the two of them. Plus, she was not sure, if it was love she felt for Dune, or was it just a great, pure, friendship on her part. Hopefully, time would tell her the answer.

Regardless of all these reasons, she, pushed it all from her mind because, she still wanted to meet her beautiful Dune, to let him kiss her and speak of his love.

It was early evening, Isobel went to sit with her mama, and she read some more of Charles Dickens, story.

The doctor had visited Mary, that afternoon, but all the man did was to change the liquid for another one, which he felt would be, stronger, for her needs.

When Isobel walked out of her mama's room that night, she never knew, that Mary could no longer digest any solid food.

Chapter Eleven

It was the second day of August 1836. It had been with great reluctance, and heavy hearts, the men of the household had earlier descended the long staircase with the young mistress's luggage. The coach had arrived just as daylight broke, and now fully loaded it was due to set off.

Isobel's father was nowhere to be found. However, her mother insisted, she be helped down to the courtyard to see her beloved child's departure. After a very unsettled night, with her hair combed neat, a warm cape about her shoulders, and red rouge gently rubbed into her pale cheeks, Mary was passable.

Agnes suddenly appeared, and for the very first time ever, she hugged her sister. Members of staff were visibly, shocked to see the older girl's tears, when, she rushed past them, eager to return inside the house.

Mother, and daughter, pulled apart it was time to leave. Their tears fell freely, as Mary murmured. 'Now, my darling you must not let these men ride you around in that hot box for too long. You will need decent breaks to stretch your legs.'

'Yes, Mother. I will insist they do so.'

'Good. You must have stops, like the times we travelled to your Grandma's in Cornwall.'

'I will make sure they do. But, please, Mama, you must not worry about me. Just concentrate on your pledge. That as soon as you are well, you will come to visit, and stay with me for a long, long time.'

'Yes, my dearest one. But, whatever happens, please remember, I will always be with you. Always. Isobel, I will never leave you, ever. Please remember that, and very importantly, you must always keep your wits about you, and permanently, be on your guard.'

'I will Mother of that you can be sure.' Isobel knew the promised visit would never happen, and in her heart, this final embrace was to be just that.

Reluctant to leave the arms that had kept her safe and secure, since her first breath, she stepped onto the box and up into the coach. The man secured the door behind her, then, he climbed back up to his own seat.

The reins raised a slight tap of the whip, and the four chestnut horses trotted on.Isobel still on her feet, waved from the window, and as they rounded the bend towards the tall wrought Iron gates, the distressed figures vanished from her view.

It was quite cool for the moment, but by early afternoon, the coach would be unbearable from the heat it had collected inside. Isobel pulled the two pieces of curtain together, in hopes it might help the carriage to keep cool. Then seated on the hard, wooden bench she whispered.

'I cannot see Mama anymore.'

Tears streamed down her face, and from the arms that pulled her close, Isobel felt love and comfort.

'There, there, Miss, I'm with you and I'll never leave thee.'

'Oh, dear Alice. I think with you by my side, I could face anything life wants to throw at me now. When, Mama, told me you were to leave with me, I was ecstatic. She smiled. 'Is that terribly selfish of me.'

The girl shook her head. 'No, Miss, not at all. You know, I only wish to be with you, to serve you always, is my pleasure.'

'Bless you, bless you dear friend.' She smiled, 'But Alice, you know I told you of that noise in Mama's throat, well, today it sounded louder. I wonder what it can be?'

'I'm not sure, but the Mistress, has had a terrible cough for such a long time now.'

'Yes, she has, I just pray she will get better. Although, I am not sure that she will.' They hugged each other tight, and two extremely frightened girls, so sad to have left the only home they had ever known, let their pent, up tears, fall freely. And both took comfort from each other, as the coach gathered up speed to take them to their new lives, somewhere in Sussex.

Alice, when summoned to see Mary yesterday, had been overjoyed when asked if she would like to leave with her, young, Mistress and move to her new home with her.

'Oh, yes, Madam, I would love to go with Miss Isobel, very much.' But her pleasure had been dampened, because this had been the only home, she too had ever known. Consequently, over the years, through the kindness of this dear, dear lady, she also had a fair amount of luggage to take with her.

'You must take all of your clothes, and possessions with you dear child.' Mary had stated. She had then stood, and taken her into her arms, and as she kissed her hair, the Mistress had whispered, 'you have brought me much joy through the years dear, dear Alice. I pray you will be safe with my Isobel, for this is a long journey you both will embark upon. I pray the Lord will protect each of you, dear child. Be safe, be safe always.'

Alice had been so over-ought, that when her Mistress had released her hold, she had curtsied and hurried from the room.

Mistress Mary's behaviour had always baffled her, but because of it, Alice had grown to love this lady with all her heart, and no-one could ever take that away from her. Plus, she would continue to love this dear lady, forever more.

The Master like every member of the household, she hated, and despised due to his terrible treatment towards everyone, but mostly towards Mistress, Mary. Also, lately she had become very worried by the man's peculiar behaviour, when he was around her, and the looks he threw at her whenever, they passed each other. No, he was, a person to be extremely, weary of, that, Alice knew for sure.

Mary near to collapse, waited until the coach disappeared round the bend before she let the staff gently help her return into the house, and up to her room. Settled back into her bed an instant bout of coughing shook her body, and more and more blood could be seen.

Mary knew her end was near, and much too weak to write the letters for her loved ones, her faithful Anna sat, and wrote her last words.

The first was for her adorable Isobel, she wanted to tell her to keep herself strong, life married to that awful man would not be easy. She was so, so sorry, for what her father had made her do, and that she, herself, had cursed him through all eternity.

It is with a happy heart, I must inform you, that Alice is your half- sister, this, I know to be true. I know you and Alice care for each other deeply, because since small children a strong love has developed between you both. Please accept her now for who she is because, with her by your side you will never be lonely. And I am so happy to know you have a family member with you.

If life with that awful old man gets too bad, you and Alice must travel to your Grandmothers, you will both be safe there, and have a good life. If you do this, please do not even tell Agnes where you have gone.

Lastly, she again spoke of her love for Isobel, and that, she would always walk beside her, and never leave her. Never.

The second was to her dear wonderful, Mother and friend. It thanked her for the woman she was, and how through her life Bella had been there for her. She spoke of Bella's, strength, and courage, and how it had made her a stronger person. She told of her strong love for her, and how she would, always love her dear, dear, Mother.

The third was for Alice. She wrote, how she had always loved her, from the minute she had been born. She said how happy she was, when she and Isobel, had, become, such good friends. And, how grateful she now is, that she will be going to that awful man's estate with Isobel, to start a new life. Also, knowing her child will not be on her own, is a great comfort for her, because her two girls will be together.

She ended, may, 'God bless you,' always dear, dear Alice.

The letters finished; Anna kept them safe until she could go into town to get them posted.

Mary also told the dear lady, she was to book passage to her Mother's home in Cornwall, where Bella would gladly take her in.

Her smile week, she succumbed to another terrible fit of coughing, and blood fell freely onto the bed. She fell back against the pillars and gasped for air. She should have left her barbaric husband years ago. There had been so many times, when away in Cornwall, she had almost never returned to Durham. Still, that was all in the past now.

Somehow, she knew her beautiful Isobel, with dear Alice by her side, would come through whatever ordeals laid ahead. Because her precious one was a much stronger, feisty woman, than she herself had ever been.

Fatigued, her breath, slow, Mary's eyes closed, and the rattle sound in her throat, suddenly stopped. The doctor, who had urgently been called stood, he examined his patient, then shook his head.

Mary, pain free at last, let the peace consume her. She floated upwards, and upwards, the sky was blue, and the Godly silence was beautiful.

Upwards, and upwards, peace, contentment, she was going to her final place to rest.

Anna stood, and gently laid a thin white sheet over her pain free face. One by one, the staff disappeared from the room, but Anna who had come to love her mistress sat and held her cold hand as her silent tears fell.

Chapter Twelve

Isobel smiled at the coachman who helped her down from the carriage. Exhausted and weary, her feet crunched the gravel. Despite the warmth from the day, she shivered.

She could never express enough gratitude, towards her mama's insistence, that dear Alice left with her. Through the horrendous long journey, with those terrible nights spent in taverns not suitable for young ladies, and the people who had occupied them. Her dear friend by her side, had given her added strength.

While the two men unloaded the heavy trunks onto the dusty ground, Alice brushed her long blue dress, and reached for some of the carpet bags.

Isobel, her back to the house was visibly shocked to see the acres of land before her. She saw they splayed to the horizon line, and far beyond. And the tall Poplar trees that stood at the bottom of endless, hills, she thought resembled rows of soldiers.

Her emerald eyes could not make out any shapes or figures in the far distance, but she raised her hand just in case Dune was out there and could see her.

If he had kept his word and was there, he now knew exactly where, she and Alice were.

She had not yet told her friend about his intentions, and, until he arrived, if he did come, that would be the time to tell her.

The men finished, tapped their hats to take their leave. Composed, Isobel returned to their side and held her gloved hand towards them. 'Please, this is for your kindness towards us.'

They took the sixpence, bent their heads and muttered, 'Thanks me lady. Thanks, be.'

The girls stood side by side and watched until the coach rounded the bend and was out of sight. Complete silence filled the air, and still not a soul had come to greet them.

'Well, this be a nice to do, I must say.' Alice declared. 'How dare they treat you like this, Miss Isobel. To be left out here unattended, after such a long trip?' She picked up a couple of small bags that had fallen and placed them back onto one of the wooden trunks.

She looked at Isobel, 'come, Miss, let us get inside, and see where everyone be.' Alice smiled. 'Exhausted, you surely must be.' They turned to stare at the front of their new home. 'It looks a grand place, Miss. Just see how tall it stands.'

Isobel looked up at the parapet. 'Yes, but let us hope, the inside is not as neglected, as the front grounds seem to be.' Coldness ran through her, this mausoleum was to be her new home, and suddenly, she was again very frightened.

'Come, Miss, once we are in there, I'll get you settled, and see about some food for you. You must be hungry?'

'No, not really, I just want a hot drink.' Food was the last thing on Isobel's mind, as she noted the ten brick steps, that led up to the paint, stricken door, were also in desperate need of a good clean.

The door was slightly ajar, and the girls looked at each other, as Alice's hand gingerly pushed it wider, which allowed her to enquire. 'Anyone be there, your new Mistress, has arrived.' With no response, she squeezed Isobel's hand, and smiled.

Both extremely apprehensive, entered the large, square porch-way. Cold musty air gripped them as they ventured further into the pitch, black, eerie, silence. Isobel shivered, and most fearful, pulled Alice closer to her side.

It was then, the girl, silently vowed to stay with her young mistress forever, never to leave her side. (Which, would, become a lifetime commitment)

A sudden small patch of light appeared, and they slowly walked towards it.

Alice reached for the handle of the lantern and held it upwards. The flame flickered, as it allowed them to see the vast, hall they were in. It was extremely wide, long in length, and sparsely furnished. A severely, neglected, stone-built Inglenook, floor to ceiling, centered the room. Alice seeing the stairs to the left of the fire, pointed, and whispered. 'I's reckon those stairs, lead down to kitchen and work- places Miss.'

Isobel nodded. 'Yes. Mama, always called those areas, the heart of the house.'

The girl smiled. 'Well, I think, I need to go down there.'

'Alright, Alice, but I shall come with you. I'll not stay here alone; it is too dark.'

Carefully, and fearfully, they descended to the last step, the light was not strong, and with several long corridors before them, they were not too sure which way to walk.

'I think it might be best if we try this one straight ahead of us first Miss.'

'Yes, but it's so dark down here.'

With the small lamp, they slowly wandered towards complete darkness.

Suddenly they turned a corner, and a glimmer of light could be seen at the end of the passage. The girls, extremely hesitant, walked towards it.

Alice entered the room first, with her Mistress close on her heels. Shocked to the core, neither could believe the horrendous sight that greeted them, or the smell that literally made both, heave.

An extremely, fat woman completely dressed in black was fast asleep, sprawled out across the enormous, wooden kitchen table, filled with stagnated rubbish.

She snored loudly, while chickens clucked happily to and froe, across the rotten, stained floor. The girl stepped forward and shook her, but the smell of beer and wine that oozed from the woman's mouth, caused her to draw away quickly.

Isobel, a hankie to her nose, cried out in horror at the sight of a small boy asleep on a bed of straw, emitting a foul stench. Disturbed, the child sat up and rubbed his eyes. 'Who who... you... be?' The tiny voice questioned.

Isobel's heart melted he was so small.

'Who you, who you be,' Alice cried. 'Why you'd better show some respect lad.

My Mistress be your new, Lady Belington, that's whom my, Ladyship, be?'

The girl's sharp manner did not suit her, and Isobel touched her arm. She just wanted to get out of the repulsed hovel.

'Alice it's alright, he's too young to understand who I am.' She fought back her tears. 'Let us get out of here and take him upstairs with us.' Isobel smiled at the fifthly child, who was no more than three or four years. 'Could you show us some of the rooms up there?' She asked.

He jumped down, and with a big toothless smile, and dirty streaked face, he answered.

'Be me--plea-sure lady, follow me.' His wee fingers struggled to try and lift the large lantern from the floor.

'Give it here,' Alice scoffed. 'This light be as big as you boy. Catch yourself on fire you will.' She grasped the handle, 'now, come on with you and show your new mistress the house.'

Stunned beyond belief over the conditions of the place, they walked from the room, and Isobel, smiled through her tears as she witnessed, Alice, squeeze, the tiny hand that had slipped into hers.

Back in the large hall, the brighter glow allowed the boy to show them the double ornate doors hidden behind a large, threadbare wall rug. Which, when opened, heralded a dark oak staircase that, twisted and turned up to all four floors.

They made their way up to the first landing, and Isobel was shocked by the length of the corridors each side of her. There were many doors, but again, all was in complete blackness. The trio moved slowly along to enter the nearest room. It was completely stripped of furniture, and the cold, damp, musty air, overwhelmed her. She was mortified, after several more inspections, to find the same results greeted her.

Out in the passage, Alice wiped her eyes. 'Oh, dear, Miss, Isobel, come, I cannot bear to look at any- more. Dear Mistress, what are we to do? You can't possibly live here, it be… it's…'

'Absolutely, unbelievable. Not fit for animals, let alone human habitation.'

'Yes Miss, that's what it be.'

But Isobel's deepest concern, as they returned down to the hall, was where the two of them would sleep that night, which, was now almost upon them.

The boy entered the kitchen first, and the old woman her hand raised, lunged at him.

'There you be…little bastard. Where has thee, been. …I.' But the sight of the two ladies that followed him in, she fell back onto her chair. The little one, quickly hid behind Alice's dress, then, he instantly peered out, to bravely inform, 'these ladies, gona live here.'

'Here. Live here. What do youse mean?' She slurred, as her beady eyes bored into them. 'The Master,' she mumbled. 'He, not be here, so away with you. You cannot stay till he comes back. Go, get out now.'

'*Don't you dare talk to your new mistress in that… tone,
you… you, filthy, tramp.*'

Isobel touched Alice's arm. She, like her friend had
never experienced such anger, but words failed her, because
her thoughts, and concerns, were on the big question. Where
they would sleep that night.

It was then, she suddenly remembered the cottage, the
coach had passed it almost as soon as it had entered the
grounds, so consequently, it was a good distance from the
house. Isobel prayed someone lived in it, and if they did, it
would be fit, for them to stay in.   But how would they get
there?   She truly, could not believe, the disgusting,
deplorable conditions of William Belington's ancestral
home.

This nightmare, she and Alice had entered in-to was
absolutely, unbelievable.

But mostly, she wondered if her father had any idea of
the fate, he had handed her, when she had been sold to the
disgusting old man, so he could gain a status.

The sudden sound of a man's voice echoing the corridor,
fearfully, Isobel shivered.

But to her relief, the person who quickly stepped into the
room was a complete, stranger, who stopped in his tracks at
the sight of Isobel and Alice. His flat cap swiftly removed,
he bent his head, respectively.

'Ah, this here be Ben. Tell um, they can't be here.' The
old woman slurred.

He completely ignored her drunken words, and humbly stated. 'Your Ladyship, I am, Ben, and I beg you excuse my intrusion into the house. But, when the coach past our home, I took it upon myself to come up to see if I could offer you any help.'

'Oh, Ben, thank you.' Isobel quickly answered. 'Yes, yes you surely can.'

The man flushed and smiled.

'But first tell me, did you know I was expected, or did you just come to see who had arrived?'

'No, my, Lady, we all knew you would be here soon. News of the master's marriage, is all about Sussex.'

'I see. And yes, Ben, you certainly can be of assistance to us.' Isobel squeezed Alice's arm. 'We are destitute and cannot possibly stay here.'

His facial expression gave him away, and Isobel knew he felt pity for her.

My, he thought, this woman, before me be a mere, child, she be so fair, and incredibly beautiful. But his face turned bright red, when Alice, smiled at him. And you be pretty and Bonny to Miss, he thought, as he gazed at the dark-haired girl, with the lovely creamy skin, and deep, brown eyes.

'Please Ben.' Isobel's words broke the silence that had descended. 'Could you possibly take us to a local Inn for the night?'

'Lady Belington. Mistress. I be sorry, but there are no Inns around here. And if there was, we could not travel now, because the roads are not safe after dark. All I can offer you is my humble abode, which I share with my sister, Florence.'

'Florence your sister, will she mind us descending upon you both?'

'Not at all, she told me to offer you our home if you needed it.'

'Oh, I see. Well, we will be forever, grateful for your kindness, for this night, and tomorrow we will have a chance to survey our options.'

The trunks and bags stacked inside the hall Ben turned to Alice. 'Miss, can you please show me what you'll need for your, Mistress, and of course yourself to take with us for now.'

Alice thought his mop of unruly blonde, hair, deep blue, eyes set nicely above rosy cheeks, in not a handsome, face, but ruggedly, pleasant, most attractive.

'Mm, oh, yes. Those three, brown carpet bags, there please. And I think that large black leather one, just there.' His smile made her feel funny, but she added. 'Also, Ben. It is Alice.'

He looked at her strangely. 'My name, it be Alice.'

'Ah, and a pretty one it be.' He stated.

Isobel outside in the fresh air, replenished her lungs, and marveled at the strength she had mustered, to verbally, dismiss, the old woman. She wanted her gone by the next day. Ben helped her up onto the long wooden seat, and ready to leave, they waited for Alice, who had returned to the kitchen to find the boy.

She had found him fast asleep again on the rotten straw, and with no sign of the foul woman, she caressed his forehead, until his dark eyes opened. 'All, been a wee bit too much for you me lovely, come on.' About to gather him to her, Ben walked into the room. She smiled coyly. 'My Mistress, she's not happy about the little one here on his own.'

He smiled. 'I know, come on lad.' The child securely in his arms, and with Alice close on his heels, they all walked from the room.

Chapter Thirteen

The horse proceeded slowly back up the long drive, till eventually the cottage came into sight. The animal stopped outside the gate, and Isobel as Ben helped her down, thought how neat and tidy the garden was.

The door flew open, and Florence, short and plump, not a fraction, like her tall, slim, fair brother, curtsied on their approach.

'Oh Florence, we are indebted to you.'

'Mistress, you and your lady are most welcome.' She moved to let them enter, then, quickly closed the door.

Isobel's relief was obvious to everyone one, by the big sigh she exhaled as she looked round the plainly, furnished, spotless room. Exhausted, Isobel and Alice sat in the two respectable chairs, and both welcomed Florence's sweet warm tea, and a portion of her freshly baked cake. Once the tray was taken away, she begged her leave to finish her preparation, of the supper.

The lad had been taken straight to the back yard, to be cleaned up, and when the boy eventually ran into the room, all the adults were in awe of the child's beauty.

He had been scrubbed from head to foot and dressed in an old cut down shirt of Bens.

His jet, black curly hair, creamy complexion, long, lashed dark eyes, everyone in the room instantly adored him.

After a meal of rabbit stew with home baked bread, which the youngster demolished heartily, it was time to retire. Florence insisted, the Mistress have her room, and when she entered, Alice was already there with warm water to help her wash and change into her nightwear.

The single hard wooden structure was not at all comfortable, but it felt good to just stretch her body out. Isobel was grateful for the quietness of the night as she lay and listened to Alice's even breaths, as she slept on the wooden chaise, Ben had made for his sister. He and the boy were asleep in front of the warm, embers downstairs, and Florence was in her brother's room.

Numbed to the core, Isobel wondered what on earth she was to do. Her poor Mama must never find out her circumstances. No daughter defied her father, but she could hate him with a vengeance. She knew, there was only one way she could free herself from this terrible, nightmare, and that, was to enter the church. Enter it, never to leave it again. But she had Alice, and Dune, in her life so that could never be the answer for her. She remembered, Grandma Claremont stories of her struggle, when left with a small baby and a business to manage. If she were here right now, she would tell me to be brave, get on with it. Show some back-bone my dear, get it sorted.

Isobel turned onto her side, and through the small window, she watched the stars, shimmer in the dark, clear sky. 'Like you, my dear strong, Grandma, I must find the courage, to survive this ordeal.' She thought of all the money, hidden away for her use from her two special ladies, but was still confused, over what to do next. She knew the sensible thing would be to leave first thing, but it was Dune. If she left almost immediately, and he turned up there, would he realize she had gone back to Durham, no he might, never find her, so for now she needed to stay put.

Isobel decided to wait till the light of day to finally make her decision, should they journey back, or stay to find out, just what did lay ahead for her. One thing she did know, if her beloved Dune stood before her now, she would have ridden off with him to wherever he wanted to take her. And, dear, Alice would have gone with them. Yes, far, far away. Far away, as they possibly could.

Again, Isobel thought of the severe punishment, her father would bestow upon her and Dune, if he had any inclination, that a gypsy boy loved his daughter.

However, what the innocent bride did not know, was the cruelty her Father could unleash was angelic compared to her new husband. Pure, demonic, evil ran through this man when angered, which, she herself would soon find out firsthand.

Signs of dawn's arrival peeped in through the curtain-less window, and she decided the first thing to do in the light of day was to look at the house again. Then afterwards, the whole situation would be reviewed once more.

Her heavy eyes closed, and a troubled sleep finally engulfed her.

Isobel knew it was going to be another, extremely hot day, and after a breakfast of new laid eggs, and fresh baked bread, she with Alice by her side, left the cottage.

Ben was already out there with Florence and the little one, and once they were all settled in the old cart, he urged the two horses to trot on.

The sad, neglected house came into view, and in the full brightness of the day, Isobel was amazed by the vastness of the estate. The animals came to an abrupt halt by the stone steps. Ben quickly jumped down to the ground, he secured the reins, then extended his hands to Isobel.

She smiled, and said, 'thank you Ben.' as she stepped from his arms to the gravel.

She noted, how brightly, flushed his face became as he turned to Alice, whose smile must have made him melt, he cleared his throat, and the moment was gone. He turned to help Florence, lastly, he reached for the little one, who he decided to keep hold of for now. He moved to where Isobel had walked, bent his head, and told her. 'I came to the house early this day, Mistress, and the old woman was still here. I told her plainly, you better be gone when I bring the new Mistress back later.'

'Oh, thank you Ben. Yes, lets' hope she has gone.'

Belington, over the years had completely stripped the place bare. Not one room was livable, and if she stayed, if she stayed, where else was she going to run off to?Isobel knew the task before her would be a gigantic one. So, she was extremely, grateful that money would not be a problem, and possibly work on the house could start almost immediately.

She decided the big hall on the ground floor, should be made warm, and welcoming. Once the Inglenook, was cleaned up and re-painted, and chairs, and a table stood in it the area would be comfortable.

Below stairs, the kitchen, passage- ways, and some of the rooms near to the stairs, had to be cleaned, painted, and furnished.

They were up on the first landing and Isobel had chosen the large room at the top of the stairs. It was ideal, because the door at the back of the room, led into another room, which would make a fine bedroom, then in that room, there was a smaller door on the far wall, that would be perfect for her bath to be kept.

They moved through yet another door, and again the room was large, and as the sunrays bounced from wall, to wall, Isobel questioned. 'Alice, would you like to have this for your use?'

'Oh, Miss, this is far too big for me.'

'No, no, it is perfect, because you will be next to me, which is where I want you to be.'

'Oh, Miss. Well, yes thank you then. Thank you so much.'

Isobel squeezed her hand and smiled.

They decided to check all the other rooms along the corridor, and as they entered the very last one, Isobel extremely puzzled, turned to Ben. 'His Lordship does not seem to have any quarters, or facilities where he can read, or do whatever the man does.'

'No, Mistress. All the floors have been closed for many years. The main hall is where he stays when he's here.'

'Well, he certainly must have his own quarters. I would not want to see him sprawled down there when in residence. I think the hall should be for everyone's use. It will be a nice place to sit and relax.'

'Yes Mistress.' He replied.

Isobel looked round the light airy room and nodded. 'Yes, this will do nicely for the Master.'

Ben simply nodded.

It was a duplicate of the one she was going to have. Like hers it was extremely spacious, it also had a door that led into one that could be the man's washroom. 'Yes, Ben, when the big clean up begins, this will be cleaned and furnished for the man please.'

'I will see to it, Mistress.'

Florence, who had been below stairs with the little one, entered the room as the decision about the Master was made, and unbeknown to the two young girls, she was an extremely wise woman.

'Madam, may I speak with you?'

'Yes, certainly, of course you can.'

'It's just, well I wondered with the Master, away so often, perhaps you would feel happier if my brother slept in the house for a while.'

'Oh. Well yes. I think that's an excellent idea.' She

smiled and looked at Ben.

'Would it bother you to do that? Live in the house?'

He bent his head and answered. 'Not at all, Madam, it would be my honour to do so.'

'Mistress.' Florence continued.

'Mm. Yes, dear.'

'Perhaps, my brother could have a room near to the Masters? So, he can be close to tend his needs when he is here.'

'Oh, that again is an excellent suggestion, and it will be helpful to us all.'

'And, what about the child, your Ladyship, will he remain here with you?' The older woman smiled at her.

Isobel looked at the beautiful boy before her and whispered. 'No, no, he cannot really, not just yet. Can he? Till I know how things will go. Do you think he could live in the cottage with you for a while Florence?'

'Madame, it would be my pleasure. And you, and, Alice, must stay with us until you are able to move in here.'

'Thank you, dear, Lady.' Isobel smiled. 'And, who knows, once we get sorted out with the accommodation, perhaps he can come back to live here with us.'

It was decided, before the journey back to the cottage for lunch, that the room beneath hers and straight across from the main hall, would make an ideal day room. The French doors, needed to be replaced, but once, they had been done, they would open out onto the front lawns. This would allow the cool breeze on long, hot summer days, and nights to drift into the room.

On their return, Florrie busied herself with the food, and drinks, and it was well into the evening, when the first decisions on the big clean up, were finally decided, upon. After a delicious meal of pheasant stew, they all decided to turn in early, because tomorrow was going to be a rather busy day. Isobel's second night on the hard bed was not quite as bad, because she settled down and slept quite well.

The next morning, every- one was up at the crack of dawn. The big clean- up was about to begin. Ben had set off to the nearest village, with his pockets full of money, taken from Isobel's hidden, pile. People were needed, helpers, who would carry out most of the work.

Carpenters, seamstresses, painters, and the local blacksmith arrived within a few days. And it was not long, before, iron lanterns, and candle holders attached to the walls brought much light to the darkened rooms, and areas they needed to work in.

The kitchen cleared of all the rubbish was scrubbed from top to bottom as was the main passage- ways, and all the rooms below stairs.

Finally, all painted in white, the difference amazed everyone. Isobel then, guided by Florence, decided the large square room next to the kitchen with the door that led straight into the yard, should become the wash and laundry area.

Isobel, and Alice both worked hard, and began to enjoy

the task before them. To see life spring back into each room and boast its newly, made furniture was reward enough. Storage shelves lined the spotless kitchen walls, all that was needed was new brass utensils to hang from the nails. Food for the large pantry would be brought, and the new long wooden table, with its six chairs looked grand in the center of the scrubbed floor. The old black grange shone and burnt proudly, thanks to the blacksmith.

Blessed to have, Ben and Florence, Isobel's feisty strength shone through, and grew stronger as each day passed. Now at last, after all their hard work, although very apprehensive, Isobel and Alice could finally move into their quarters.

There had been no news of the man Belington, or any sign of his return. Relaxed and happy at all she had achieved, Isobel was quite content.

Chapter Fourteen

It was the end of September, it was barely light, but the cool Monday morning, was very welcoming as Ben helped Isobel step up into the carriage, she smiled as Alice entered and sat opposite her.

'This be a nice coach Miss, and comfortable. I wonder what the big town is like?'

'Yes, it is call Portchesterton, and Ben said it is near the sea. The cool breeze after the awful heat through August will be very welcomed.'

The journey was roughly two hours, and as Ben helped them down onto the gravel the girls stretched their bodies.

'It was so nice of that neighbor to lend you the horses and carriage, for the trip.'

'Indeed, Madam. Old man, Kingswood, hardly uses it now.'

'Mm, that's interesting. But for now, Ben, you need to show me where to go for the solicitors I seek.'

He steered his mistress towards the section where most trade was carried out, and as the girls walked towards the sea, both welcomed the salt breeze. The office was easy to find, and a loud, bell clanged as they opened, and closed the door behind them.

Isobel smiled, as she walked towards the small man seated behind the desk.

She produced the note of introduction, her grandma had

sent and handed it to him.

'Ah, you're Ladyship, how nice to meet you.' He declared, as he peered over his spectacles.

'And I you sir, Mr. Clements.' she answered.

'The paperwork is all clear.' The little man coughed. 'And there is a large amount of money for you here already, Madam.'

Isobel smiled, but, when told of her monthly allowance, she took Alice's arm for support.

'Oh… I…thank you sir,' was all she could say. Isobel instantly liked the man, who gave her such a warm friendly smile, but felt sheer guilt, as she watched him count out a batch of white, five- pound notes, accompanied by a bag of sovereigns.

This money had been set up with this solicitor for her, from her Grandma, Claremont, and with the house in the state it was, money, was desperately needed.

She smiled at him again, then asked. 'Mr. Clements, I have a couple of letters here to be delivered, is there any chance you could see to that for me?'

'Indeed, your Ladyship no problem.' He took them, they smiled, then Isobel quietly left his office.

The money tucked safely away the girls set about to shop for the items on the list in Alice's bag. They brought candles, materials, new china, books, and Isobel brought the next installment of Pickwick Papers. She also purchased, wide, wine-colored, drapes to hang at the French doors in her new bedroom. Ben also had quite a list, which the shop would get someone to deliver to the house for her.

They found a tea- room on the Quayside, and when seated a young girl took their order and each welcomed the sea breeze that entered through the open door.

'Oh, Mistress, the cake is so nice.' Alice said as she refilled their cups.

'Yes, it's full of Lemon which refreshes.' Isobel smiled at the girl, who had been such a great support since their arrival, and again she, silently thanked her mama for the gift of Alice.

When they left the comfort of the tea rooms, Isobel, saw Ben was already at their chosen spot to meet. He smiled at Alice, as he helped his mistress up the steps.

'I've collected all the items we can manage to take with us today my Lady.

The larger items will be delivered very soon.'

'Thank you, Ben. Now, we just want to get back.'

'Miss Isobel, do you mind if I sit up on the top seat to take the air?'

Isobel smiled, when she saw the look that passed between the girl and the man.

'No. No, Alice, not at all.'

They arrived back in good- time. Ben helped Isobel, alight onto the ground, but she stopped to turn and look at him. 'Do you think the man who lent this to you, might want to sell it. You said he hardly uses it now, is that right?'

'Mistress, I can certainly ask for you. Since, his wife

died, old Mr. Kingswood hardly leaves his house now.'

'Oh, dear, how sad. Well, we could do with a carriage like this for our trips into the big town. Thank you, Ben.' Isobel smiled. The man bent his head, as she walked past him to enter the house, and she made her way to the big hall. The cleaned Inglenook with flames chasing up the large opening fascinated her while she sat and watched them. Her eyes caught sight of Alice as she walked towards her with a tray of tea. The liquid poured, her cup and saucer, placed onto the table beside her, the girl sat back and slowly sipped her own. 'Oh, Miss Isobel here.' She took the letter from her pocket and, smiled as she handed it to her.

'Thank you dear.' She looked at the envelope and was puzzled because she did not know the writing. She opened it quickly and tears fell, as she read the words. It was written by Anna her Mother's faithful companion.

She explained that her Grandma Bella, had had a stroke, and that was the reason, she did not attend her wedding, but the lady was well on the mend now.

Mama, confirmed that Tranquil, would arrive with her soon, but she found it strange, when she had asked her to keep the young lad here with her, if he wanted to stay.

There were, other bits of news, and she smiled as she read it. The letter confirmed that Alice, was indeed her half-sister, Mary knew this to be true, and she prayed, now that you girls have been made to move away, the girl could hold a stronger status, which befits her now.

Isobel was excited about this news but, decided to tell

her sister once they were more settled here in their new home.

She was happy about the letter, and was so pleased, Grandma Bella was getting better. Later, she would sit and write to Bella, and her mother again.

The seamstress was still hard at work, but now she was almost finished. There were, new uniforms, for the few essential staff they had. Some of Isobel's old day dresses, were altered for Alice, and the woman, made several new ones for Isobel. It was because of her new status as, Lady, Isobel, Belington.

Rain had fallen for most of the day, Isobel sat in the big hall, rubbed her hands by the warmth of the fire. A maid suddenly appeared with a tray and the little one was with her. He ran towards Isobel and tried to climb up onto her lap. She smiled, then helped him up, then he snuggled in and fell fast asleep. The girl curtsied and quickly disappeared, just as Alice entered the room. She smiled and moved towards the table. She poured tea into their cups and placed Isobel's next to her on the table.

'Oh, he be tired, he needs a little sleep.' Alice whispered.

Isobel looked down. 'To late he's gone.' She swept his beautiful black curls back from his forehead and, planted a kiss.

'He looks so cute in his new clothes, Miss. The pale blue tunic, over his white shirt suits him so much.' She touched his black buckled shoes, 'and these, Florrie tells me, be a terrible task to get off last night before bed. He wanted to sleep in them.'

They laughed together. 'Oh yes, he is a beauty. But, let me take him Mistress, I'll lay him on those two chairs over there.'

'Thank you, Alice.' Isobel picked up her cup, sipped her tea, and watched the girl place the boy on the chairs. She walked back, sat opposite her Mistress, then reached for her cup.

'We have been here in the big house for almost two weeks, how do you like living here, my dear?'

'Very much Mistress. If you are happy to be here, then so am I.'

'Yes, our improvements on the areas we live in, are great for us all.' Isobel looked at the girl, she was her best friend, and they both loved each other.'

She smiled and reached for her hand. 'Alice, I have something to tell you.'

The girl smiled back.

'I hope this will make you feel happy, like it did me, 'Alice, Mama told me in her last letter that you are my half-sister.'

The wood crackled and the silence was intense. 'Your sister, but...how...are.'

'Alice.' Isobel interrupted. 'You are my sister, and I think it is wonderful.'

'Oh...Mistress...' They stood and embraced, and tears fell.

'Such happy, great news dear, one. From now on you must call me Isobel...'

'No, no Miss, I cannot do that.'

'Look, I think the best thing to do is give you time to digest this information and get used to the fact that you are my sister. Then we will discuss the details between us more, is that alright with you Alice.'

The girl nodded, she was in total shock, she needed time.

It has been almost three months, and still no sign of Belington, and a good routine in the house was well in order, and she felt pleased with all they had achieved. Isobel had written several letters to her mama, and Grandmother Bella, but today it had been Dune mostly in her thoughts.

It was still quite warm, but the weather was beginning to change, and one morning in October, Isobel asked Ben to walk with her to where the decayed stables stood. It was a large area, and possibly at one time, she thought the place might have been well kept.

'Ben, my horse Tranquil is due to arrive any day now. It has been arranged that one of my mother's grooms will bring him for me, and the lad will stay on to care for him.' She stopped and looked about. 'But, as you can appreciate, no animal can possibly be stabled here.'

'No, your, Ladyship. I know of a man who could have these stalls, the work sheds, and the whole area, good as new in no time.'

'Oh, that would be wonderful. Also, do you think a

couple of the younger men might stay on to learn how to muck out, and look after the animals?'

'I'm sure they would Madam. I will see to it.'

'Thank you.' She smiled. 'Ben, please tell me about the little one, it seems so strange that no-one seems to lay claim to him, he's so tiny to be on his own.'

Isobel could not know, this was the one question, he wished she had not asked.

Chapter Fifteen

Mistress, all I can tell you is, that he was left outside by the back entrance near the kitchen in a wicker basket. He was lucky because, the staff were happy to keep him and attend to his needs. There was one particular maid, a girl called, Rosie, who was always happy to care for him, and she did so most of the time.'

'Do you think she might have been his mother?'

'Well, some did wonder.'

'Where is she now?'

'Well, that's the thing, one day she just upped and left, it shocked us all it did.'

'But he has no name, and we cannot keep calling him, little one.'

'No Mistress.'

Isobel shivered, and pulled her shawl tighter to her body. 'Alright then. But if no one comes forward as a parent, we shall keep him here, and give him a home with us.'

She smiled at the tall man, who had done so much for her since she had arrived.

'We will have to let him choose a name though, perhaps we'll give him a few and let him decide for himself?'

'Yes, Mistress, the little mite will surely find that fun to do.'

'Ben, before you go tell me is the Master at home much, or does he usually stay away as long as this.' She was so pleased that awful man, had not yet appeared. But it was now late October, and as much as she prayed, he never did return, she knew, possibly any day now he would.

'His Lordship, he stays away most of the time, he's hardly ever here.'

'Ben, would you like to become the estate manager? You and, Florrie, have been so wonderful. I do not know, what we would have done without you both.'

'Oh, Mistress, it was our honour, to be at your service.'

'Well, I shall be forever grateful to the pair of you. You see, why I would like you to hold the position for me, is because, I feel things left in your capable hands, between us we will keep the place, clean and respectable.'

'Oh, you're Ladyship. I will gladly take on the role. But what do you think the Master will have to say about it?'

'Well, I intend to keep him in money, so hopefully he'll spend his time in London, and not want to be here.' She smiled. 'Consequently, the man will have no idea of what we have arranged for the good of us all.'

'Then I thank you, Mistress. And my first task will be to get the stables ready for your horse, and any others that may arrive.' He bent his head to leave.

'Also, before you go, tell me, do you think, Florence, might be interested to become our cook? She has prepared, some particularly good meals for all of us lately. Plus, she fed all the extra workhands, without any problems at all.'

'Yes, my, Lady. I know she would.

'Good, that's wonderful.' She smiled. He returned her

smile and walked off. Isobel watched him as he moved further from her, she knew the man, would do all that she had asked of him and much more.

From the mount of the hill, Lord William Belington, astride his grey stallion, stared down at his ancestral home in amazement. Oblivious of the dark, storm's encroachment, and the light rain that fell from the late October sky, he urged the animal to trot on. Yellow lights, which splayed from several windows on the ground, and upper floor, allowed him to see clearly on his approach, the front lawns had recently been attended to. Bemused, by all he had seen, he entered the newly, cleaned courtyard and dismounted. The sudden appearance of a lad dressed in blue livery, astounded him, and he questioned.

'Who might you be boy? And what do you want?'

'Your horse, Master, if you please.'

'Well, I don't.' He snarled as his large hands tightened on the leather strap. 'No one ever touches my animal. He stays close to me, at all times.' He pointed to the iron ring, attached to the side wall, close to the steps. 'This is where my beauty stays, and will continue to do so, now be gone with you.' He laughed as the youngster turned to scurry away.

'Wait, wait, lad.' The animal's nostrils flared, and steam, oozed from its tired body as the man steered it towards the long, loose rope. 'Boy, are there any other horses over there in the stable yard?'

'Yes... Sir.'

'Well, tell, how many, one, two?'

'There be one, Lord.'

'What exactly do you do with horses, when, you have them in your care?'

'I feed it oats, water and hay. The bigger, boy rub's and covers it warm.'

'Whose animal, is it?'

'Well, the, Mistress, sometimes rides it, but Ben usually rides him, around the estate Sir.'

A smile quivered, around his dry split lips. 'Her Ladyship, does she ride often?'

'No, sir. But her own horse be here soon, and we got to look after it for her.' Belington's, last recognition of this neglected, disused yard was the reason, he had started to leave his animal tied by the steps. And in extreme bitter weather, he would lead the horse up into the warmth of the great hall. The man stared at the lad, hard. 'Here take the reins.' He crabbed the arm, that reached for them, and the boy winced. 'I care very much for this four -legged creature,' his grip increased, as he made his ultimatum clear. 'Should any harm befall him, and you will answer to me. Do you understand?' The man slackened his hold, and tears welled as the lad nodded. The straps eventually, held very securely in his small hand, the young boy hurried back, toward the stables. Belington took the stoned steps slowly, he noticed all were well scrubbed, and the double, thick wooden, ornate doors, had been re-painted. Shocked by the great glow that splayed from the porch, he stepped inside to see all the heavy, dark panels had been removed from the sides, and ceiling. Consequently, the thick glass that now replaced them, allowed the endless iron lanterns attached to the wooden beams, to flood the entrance with light.   He continued through to the main hall and stopped in disbelief, at the scene before him. Throughout, the flagged stone floors were spotless, and the inglenook was banked high and glowed. With all signs of the many years of neglect, gone, this, his favourite place, welcomed him, with brightness and warmth. Everything overwhelmed him, and the sight of the long scrubbed, wooden table that centred the floor, with two carvers and eight chairs to match pleased him. But it was the two silver trays sat in the middle, with decanters and goblets on, he was instantly drawn to. Delighted, to find both completely full of red wine, Belington filled a challis, and thirstily, consumed the liquid. He wiped his mouth, freed a chair, and dropped onto it. His booted feet up onto the table, his bloodshot eyes searched the room. He marvelled at the long paisley, heavy, brocade drapes that covered the two sets of ancient French doors, which opened out onto the front lawns. Several large paintings looked back at him, from the brick wall he faced. The room filled with light, felt completely different. He downed more wine and rubbed his forehead.

'Where would his bride be?' He quietly muttered. He stood, and his chair crashed to the floor, it was time to seek her out, because he'd been away, far, far, too long.

The money Fordham had given him, plus, what the man's bank had handed over, had kept him at the card tables in London, far longer than anticipated. All of August, September, and into October, consequently, it was definitely- time for him to claim his nuptial rights.   From the big hall, he walked slowly down the long corridor, that eventually led to the South wing. But, suddenly, with the light so poor, he instantly realised, she would not be in that part of the house. 'No, no,' he babbled. 'Her chambers would be up there, up the now, immaculately, cleaned stairs.'

Again, the transformation, when he reached the first floor was truly unbelievable. Large gilt framed mirrors, and painted pictures, hung on the newly coloured red, walls of the long passage. Several tables with Candles lit, showed the long corridor to the left of him, now had a long, brown carpet runner that centred the vast scrubbed wooden floor.

The man was drawn, to the double ornate doors, directly in front of him at the top of the stairs. He lunged at them, and almost fell into the room. Sure enough, he saw Isobel drop her material to the floor, as the colour drained from her lovely face. He staggered to the chair opposite hers, flopped into it and declared. 'Well, here you are my dear wife. I hope you are pleased to see me, for I am delighted to be home.' With the decanter in his hand, he refilled the goblet clutched in his other. Then, he looked at her hard. 'My, my, but you have been busy, my Lady, haven't you?'

Isobel, like a statue, never moved, she just stared ahead.

'And for a snippet, I must declare what you have achieved has my complete approval.' He sipped more wine. 'I cannot believe, the difference you have made in what, a couple of months.' He smiled. 'I believed on your arrival, you would have refused to live here, and would have returned straight, home.' He drank slowly and still she never spoke.'

'This is a cold house my dear. Because way back in the eleven- hundreds, my ancestors tried to produce a stately castle, but as you can see it never worked out.'

His red eyes watched her as he drank more liquid. 'Consequently, there is too much flag, and flint stone, inside. Eventually, when they gave up, they had to build my ancestral home, around what they had started.' He refilled the goblet and, sat back.

'Mm, you must have used quite a great amount of money, to have achieved what you have. I know your father, would have sent you away with pittance, so my dear where did it come from?'

She did not move, neither did she speak.

He consumed the rest of the wine, stood, and staggered towards her. 'Will you not join me in a toast my dear, here.' He offered her the decanter. Isobel's mouth was dry, her hands sweaty, she tried desperately not to show her fear, although it was hard. She leant down, to retrieve her material and continued to stare at it has, she pulled the cottons to and froe.

'I assume, dear, wife, I have a room prepared for me,

somewhere in my castle?'

Isobel's hand shook, as she pulled the cord, and the call was answered immediatcly.

'Ben, the Master, is home,' was all she said.

'Yes, my, Lady.' The man bent his head, then, turned to the man slumped in the chair.

'Wine, I want more wine and food, but plenty of wine, *now, I want it now.'*

'Yes, your Lordship, let's get you to your room first sir, and I'll fetch you plenty of it.'

Isobel heaved a great sigh at Ben's smile of reassurance, but still uncontrollable tears fell, as she sat and stared at the door, he had quietly, closed behind them.

Alice rushed into the room, and took the shocked Isobel, into her arms.

'Oh, for a while I managed to forget the reason, that brought us both here. But my heart breaks, for us to be back with Mama.'

'Yes, Miss. I know, I to miss Mistress, Mary as well.'

'I have enjoyed all we have achieved, but now, Alice, I'm so frightened.   The man is absolutely repulsive.'

The girl embraced her, then they sat and stared at the flames that roared up the chimney. Seated together Isobel whispered. 'I dread the thought, of that hateful person, coming, anywhere near me.' She looked at Alice. 'Also, I am, really, frightened, I know something awful has happened, and I cannot get Mama, out of my mind.'

'Yes, the Mistress, was not at all well when we left

home.'

Much later, Isobel, alone in her room, looked about her. Wine, coloured drapes hung floor to ceiling, over the French doors that, opened out onto the balcony. Here, she loved to stand, and drink in the spectacular, views of the countryside. Acres, and acres, splayed out for her to see from where she stood. All the dark wooden, panelled walls had been washed, and repainted to their original status. The warm, colourful, carpet that covered the cold stone floor, helped to make the room feel warmer. The pale, blue Damask two seat sofa, and the two straight- backed chairs, matched each other, and both, had been placed close to the heavy, granite fireplace.

The tiny photo frames of her mama, Agnes, and her grandma, she had, stood on the thick white lace pelmet, that covered its mantle, shelf.

The glass domed clock, which had been a present from her mother, she had rested in the centre of it. Isobel was an ardent reader, and loved her four- tiered, dark wood bookcase, which was now filled with her books. The beautiful, hand carved desk, made by a local carpenter, stood on the back wall near her bedchamber door. And, the small round table covered, with a cream cloth, with two carver chairs, beneath it, finished the room. Everything was nice, but it would be perfect if her beloved, Mama and Dune, were, there with her.

Chapter Sixteen

Isobel could not concentrate on the next chapter and, looked up as Alice knocked and entered. 'My dear, whatever is the matter, you look so pale?'

'Mistress, I am so sorry, but he's sent word. He wants to eat in the big hall and, says you must join him there.'

'What. But this cannot be, he was full of drink. I thought surely he'd sleep well into tomorrow.'

'Ben said, he was in a very deep one, then, he just opened his eyes and demanded his dinner in the hall, and, that his wife joins him. But it be late Miss, surely you don't have to?'

'It's alright Alice. There will be times, when I must be in his company, better now than later. I will dress and eat with him.'

'Come my lovely, I'll help thee.'

'Thank you, dear, what would I do without you?' Isobel's cream, high collared, long sleeved blouse, nipped the tiny waste of her full green skirt as it swished the stairs on her slow descent. Flaxen, hair braided on top heightened her beauty. Her sad, emerald eyes sought the slouched figure at the end of the table, and she shuddered as Ben seated her. Florence, due to the lateness of the night, excelled herself, and provided an excellent meal.

Isobel, played with her supper, and cringed at the sight of Belington, as he filled his mouth, with endless forkfuls of food, washed down by goblets of wine. The man was drunk, and as one of the young maids tried to serve him, he pulled her down to his lap and fondled her breasts. Outranged, by his insolence towards her, Isobel stood and drained emotionally, she turned, and walked from the hall.

Alice already in her bedroom, asked. 'Mistress, are you alright?'

'Yes, I'm just, tired.'

Isobel, motioned Alice to stop, when, she picked up the brush. She did not want her hair brushed, and neither did she want the room tidied.

'Please go to bed, I will not need you any more tonight.'

'But, Mistress, it will calm you.'

'No. No, not now. I am fine, do not fret. I will call you if it becomes necessary. I promise.'

'So be it Madam. Good night then.' And the girl quietly left the room.

Isobel knew, as she climbed into the cold sheets, that Alice was concerned about her, and, she prayed very, hard, that the man, Belington, would not come anywhere near her this night. She thought of Dune, saw his beautiful face, and willed him to come to find, and rescue her. Held tight in his arms on horseback, together, they would ride with the speed of the wind towards the sunset. Finally, to end up so far away, not a thing or person, could ever hurt or harm either of them again.

She eventually slept but, was woken in the early hours as her nightgown was ripped from her body. With the weight of the repulsed man on top of her nakedness, she struggled and fought, with all her might. His hand over her mouth, he punched her face so hard, she was almost knocked out. Dazed, and completely at his mercy, he repeatedly, violated, and abused her young virginal body.

Dawn crept into the room, and Isobel tried to open her swollen eyes. She was crouched behind one of the long, velvet, curtains, but, had no recollection of how, she had ended up there. She froze, as she heard the door open.

'Mistress, where are you?'

Isobel managed to move the heavy material, and Alice's scream as she knelt before her, pierced, the great silence of the house. Ben dashed into the room, just as she covered Isobel's nakedness with a blanket.

'Alice, whatever be the matter girl?' But he could not believe his eyes, as she moved to let him see the state, his dear, sweet Mistress was in. 'Dear God, what has that awful man done to you, my dear Lady?' He whispered.

Alice was inconsolable as Ben carefully lifted, the beaten Isobel to her bed.

Her beautiful face was swollen, and she kept going, in and out of consciousness.

Ben stayed close, and on hand for a couple of hours. Then knowing Belington had gone from the estate, he went off to go in search of the old herbal lady, known for her knowledge of herbs, and remedies, that helped to heal.

Isobel had sustained, some terrible injuries. The man had even bitten into her left shoulder, and the bite mark was extremely red and weepy. The man had severely, bruised her arms, neck, and there were some marks around her young breasts.

Ben returned with the elderly woman, who straight away tended the outrageous wounds, and she constantly gave Isobel the juice from a specially, heated herbal leaf. Which, she told them, would help to keep her hydrated, and settled in a sedated sleep. She reassured, Alice and Ben, the cream with the pungent odour, if applied almost every hour, would heal the black, and blue wounds over her body.

The old woman stayed, to treat their Lady for two days, and now her work was finished, she needed to leave. It was late at night, when Ben, carefully helped her up onto the wooden, seat next to him. But it was her words, before she had left the room, that had caused Alice to worry and shudder. Her elderly eyes, drawn to the bed, had sought the beautiful, sleeping girl, then, she had whispered. 'The young Mistress could be with child after this man's treatment, but only time will tell.'

Isobel slept soundly for the next forty- eight hours, and never once was she left on her own. Alice, Ben, and Florrie between them, kept a constant vigil by her bedside.

The watery, November sun, shone into the room as Isobel's eyes fluttered open. The pain in her body had eased a great deal, but her head was still muzzy, and it ached.

'Oh, my dear sweet, Mistress, at last you are awake.' Alice cried, as she tried to help prop her up against the pillars. Isobel cringed, her arms were sore, and she was quite vacant as to what had happened. Eventually, comfortably propped up, she smiled as she watched her dear Alice, fuss about her.

'Miss would you like a nice cup of sweet, tea?'

'Yes, that would be lovely thank you.' Alice took her hand and kissed it, 'I'll be straight back.' Then she was gone. Isobel's eyes searched the room, and she tried to remember, what had happened, but her head was very, light, and woozy.

The girl returned with the tray and placed it near the bed. She poured a cup of tea and handed it to her, and Isobel drank with a great thirst. Also, the little finger sandwiches, filled with soft cheese, she ate, with a hearty hunger.

'Oh, that feels much better. I was ready for the food. Can I have another tea please Alice?'

'Yes Madam, yes.' The girl smiled and refilled the cup.

Isobel's head suddenly cleared, and her bruised fingers let the handle slip from her grasp. She watched the contents spill out over the bed, and uncontrollable tears fell.

Alice quickly on her feet, sat beside her and, pulled her close to her body.

'Oh, Alice, Alice, what that man did to me was horrendous. I...remember... he... was like an animal. Although, I think they possibly would have behaved, far better than he did. His smell, his breath, the way his hands grabbed, and clawed at my body...I'.

Alice held her tight and, allowed her own tears to fall

upon her golden hair.

'There, there ...but... Mistress, why did you not call out for me?'

'Because it was the pressure of his body on top of mine, that woke me, and he'd already placed his hand over my mouth. I tried hard to scream and push him off, but he hit me so hard across the head, it made me weak and giddy.' Isobel closed her eyes. 'Oh, but, Alice, the terrible things he did to me...were...oh no...he disgusts me.'

'When I found you in the morning you were in a terrible state. But thankfully, the man was nowhere to be found. The boys at the stables told, Ben, he'd gone to collect his horse before daylight and ridden away.'

'He must have found some of the money.' Isobel lifted, her painful arm and pointed to the set of drawers on the far wall. 'There should be a small brown leather bag in there, please bring it to me.'

Alice moved from the bed, to do as she asked. 'It's not here Madam.' She, replied, as she turned undergarments over to search.

Isobel sighed. 'There had been a large amount of five-pound notes in there.' She wiped her eyes and stared towards the window. 'Still, Alice, to be rid of him, is worth every penny he has taken.'

'Yes, dear, Miss Isobel.' The girl sat down again by the bed and took her hand. 'Miss after we found you, Ben went to find, the old herbal lady. He told me, she is an extremely, wise old woman, who treats folk, with her herbal remedies.'

'Really, was she frightening.' Isobel squeezed, her hand and smiled.

'No, no, but she was dressed all in black, and she kept putting drops of a heated herb onto your tongue, and you slept for a great deal of time. She was also here, for two, whole days working on you. And her instructions when she left, were for you to rest and heal, slowly.'

Two weeks had passed since the terrible attack, and ordeal. Now up and about, seated by the warmth of the fire in her room, Isobel, shuddered, as the grey skies of winter, approached more rapidly with each day that passed.

She had also been told, the boy and her horse had arrived safely. Now, almost herself again, she was extremely eager to go and visit Tranquil in his stall.

Alice entered with a maid, who had more logs and coal for the fire. She shivered as the warmth of the room embraced her. 'It's absolutely bitter outside Mistress. I think snow will come early here.'

'Yes, you could be right. Although I would like to get some fresh air, will you come with me to the stables so I can see Tranquil, please Alice?'

'Do you feel strong enough Miss Isobel?'

'Yes definitely. Please help me dress, then you go and wrap up warm.'

Forty minutes later, arm in arm they struggled against the bitter wind as it whipped swirls of fallen leaves and threw them high into the air. It was bitterly, cold, when they entered the open entrance, and the sight of the three lads sat around with blankets tight about them, troubled Isobel. Tranquil in his stall, became restless and made a noise as she approached him.

'Oh, my lovely, how I have missed you.' Her hand caressed the shiny black head that nudged her shoulder, in hopes the tender rub would continue. Isobel turned to the boy she recognised,

'Have you settled in alright here, lad?'

He stood and bent his head. 'Thank you, me, Lady, I have.'

'Tell me.' She spoke to all three now. 'Where do you sleep at night?'

The oldest of them stood and lowered his eyes. 'Here your Ladyship.'

'Here? But it is so cold. And it will get even worse as the winter progresses. No, we cannot have this.' She looked along the six stalls and asked. 'Where exactly do you lie to try to keep warm, then?'

The same boy answered. 'In beside the old estate horse Mistress.'

'Well, I shall talk to, Ben. These stables, must become closed in to keep the warmth in for the horses, and from tonight you lads, will be housed inside.'

The look on all the young lad's faces, was reward enough, but he answered. 'Thank you, Mistress. Thank you so much.'

Isobel smiled, then walked back to be with Tranquil a

little longer, then cold right through, she and Alice returned into the house.

Chapter Seventeen

It was lunch time, and since her ordeal, Isobel's appetite had been minimal. Ben came to see her after lunch, and when told of what she wanted carried out for the lads, and the animals, he left to put her request into immediate action.

In her chair by the banked- up fire, Isobel's heavy eyes tried to read the book in her hands. The knock woke her, and she smiled as Alice entered with their afternoon tea. Sat opposite each other, they enjoyed the sweet shortbreads fresh from the oven, with the warm liquid.

'Mistress, I need to tell you something.'

Isobel looked up and smiled. 'Yes, dear, what is it?'

'Well, it's... something ... the old woman said just before she left.' The girl looked at her hard. 'You have been through so much. I just wanted to spare you. But I feel you should be told.'

'Well, come on do tell me.'

'Her words were... you could be with child, because of what he did.' The silence was so intense, only the noise from the logs infiltrated it.

'I...I... oh no. But... Alice, what am I to do?'

The girl knelt, before her and took her hands. 'She did say, only time would tell. Do you feel any different at all?'

She shook her head. All cried out, she closed her eyes. Surely, it was not possible to have an innocent little one inside her as a result, of the despicable, degraded way, the...the...man had treated her body. She looked at Alice, 'would you please ask, Florence, to come and sit with me for a while.' The girl collected the china, picked up the tray and answered. 'Yes Mistress, straight away.'

Isobel hoped this kind woman, just might be able to give her the answers, she sought.

Florence arrived with another pot of tea, and some more of Isobel's favourite biscuits.

Now, seated opposite her Mistress, it was obvious, she had no interest in either of them.

'Florrie, has Alice, spoken to you about the old lady's words before she departed?'

'Well, no Madam. But I know of them, because I was in the room, when they were spoken.'

'Tell me please, could I possibly be with child after what...he did to me. And, if I should be, how will I know?'

'Oh, I see, my Lady. Well, Mistress, since you have felt a little better from the terrible ordeal you suffered, have you had any queasiness or sickness?'

She shook her head.

'Or perhaps you have missed, one or more of the bleeds, you experience every three to four weeks.'

'No, none of that has happened. My, Mother is an extremely private person, she told me about kissing, and some things that happen between a man and his wife, but she never really explained it in detail.'

The woman smiled at the beautiful naive girl before her.

'My Lady, what the Master, put you through that night was horrendous, and completely wrong. A woman should never be treated in such a way at any time, especially by the man she is married to.' She touched her hand.

'What he did to your poor, young body was cruel, and unforgivable.'

She sighed. 'Also, because of his assault upon you, you could indeed, possibly be with child.'

'Oh, dear Lord. No. Surely that's not the way a child is made.'

'No, it is not the way a baby arrives. What I mean, oh Mistress. I am not sure how to explain what happens. I...I... would you mind if I tell you how it happened for me, Madam?'

'Please, Florrie. I would.'

'When I was seventeen, my, father, gave me in marriage to a local farmer. For several nights he let me sleep alone. Then, he eventually, came into the bedroom and got into the bed beside me. He was very gentle, as his hands carefully, touched every part of my body. From that moment, I just pleasured in everything we did together. The man was elderly, but what a wonderful, gentle, and loving person he was. Every time thereafter in our bed, we were as one, and yes, I was soon with child.'

'Oh Florence, you make it sound wonderful.'

'It was. It can be.'

'What happened to your husband, and where is your child?'

'Joe, his name was Joe. He was killed in an accident.' She held her hand, to her mouth before she could continue. 'He'd gone to feed and clean out the Bull's pen. But, unbeknown to him, the long rope, that allowed the animal to wander, around with unrestricted movement, had worked loose. When I realised something was wrong and went to find him, I found his broken, body face down in the mud.'

'Florence, I'm...so... so… sorry. Oh please, do not speak of it any- more. You will become upset.'

'No Mistress, truly if I can help you by my story, then it will make me feel far better.'

'Well, all- right, if, you are sure.' Isobel wiped her eyes and waited, for the woman to continue.

'The horns had ripped the life from him, and through the shock of his death. I lost my baby before its birth.'

'I am so sorry about your sad loss. Oh, Florence I really am. But thank you dear, for sharing your story with me. Tell me, did you love your Joe?'

'Indeed, my lady, I did eventually. With the right man, love between two people can be tender, enjoyable, and most pleasurable.' The woman looked at the young, innocent girl before her.

Isobel sensed the woman was distressed. 'What is it, Florrie. What troubles you?'

'Mistress, please, I must...I must...I.'

'Florence, please, what is it you need to tell me?'

'Well, you see men like his Lordship, who are the Masters, of their own large, estates can treat women exactly

135

how they want to. Sometimes, their behaviour towards a woman can be good, and gentle. But then, there are those like the Master, that are extremely vile.' Florence stopped, and took the empty cup from Isobel's hand. 'Would you like another one Miss?'

'No, no thank you Florrie.'

'Consequently, the terrible things such as you experienced, sadly, not one person can intervene, to try to stop it from happening. Especially, if the help offered comes from a mere servant, who desperately wanted to protect his mistress.' She smiled and reached for the bewildered girl's hand. 'Dear Miss Isobel, I am truly- sorry, but this is how it stands with the people who hold the higher status above us mere servants. They can treat ordinary folk exactly how they want to.' She stopped and gently rubbed the hand she held. 'I had no idea the Master, would or could treat you in the way he did. He is despicable, and evil, and would not hesitate, to kill a servant, who tried to stop him from, hurting you, again, dear Mistress.'

Isobel squeezed the hard -worked hand and murmured. 'Thank you, Florence, for your story and your words of wisdom. I know exactly, what you are telling me, please do not worry.'

The woman stood, smiled, collected the tray, then, quietly, walked from room.

Isobel knew exactly, what Florence's words had meant, and how true they had been. The upper glass, people with wealth, and position, did not give a care about the poor folk who worked for them, day after day, year after year. They would tread on them, beat them, and even kill them if the need arose. She remembered her father; he was a good example of how you treat the folk beneath you. So, no way could Ben step in to help her at any time, if the man were a wife beater, she would have to tolerate it, because the consequences for him a mere servant could be fatal. True, they had no idea of the man's behaviour pattern, but if this was his way, then she must just lay and let him violate her body. God what a terrible life she will have. Although, she strongly, prayed, he would not repeat those actions or beat her like that ever again, because dear Lord, how would she survive if this were to be her lifestyle, in the future.

She thought of Dune and closed her eyes. She knew, he would try to protect her no matter what the consequences, and oh, how she longed for him to be there with her. The physical pain within her, hurt, but no tears flowed. Although, he followed her to this place, she wondered if he would ever return there, because now, she really ached to see him and be with him.

December arrived with a vengeance, and heavy snow covered the far-off hills, and life settled down nicely in the house, until Belington suddenly returned.

'Miss Isobel, he's back.' Alice gasped.

Drained of colour, she let her book, slip to the floor.

'I what… what did he say...do you know.'

'He wants you to join him in the big hall, he...commanded it,' the girl whispered.

'Please tell him, I am indisposed, with...a great sickness.'

'I will try, Miss, I'll try.' And she quickly left the room.

Isobel stared into the fire. She had prayed on her knees, when she knew for certain there was no child from his evil, violation of her body. What would she do if he came to her this night? Ben had not taken her into Portchesterton for some time, so her resources were really, low. The small amount she had left was secured away in Alice's room.

The door opened, and to her relief it was the said girl who entered. 'Mistress, he be so drunk. Ben said he's passed out at the table.'

'All- right, please fetch me the money you have. If he comes to my room, I'll give it to him.' She saw her friends' concern. 'Alice, it will be fine. Please get it, then go to bed.'

'Well, Miss. Ben, says, he will keep watch over your room all night.'

'No, no. No. This must not happen. He must stay away please; both just go to your rooms.' She smiled. 'I will be fine, but, promise me, you will tell, Ben, under no circumstances, no, circumstances, can he intervene, between, the Master and myself.'

Isobel saw the sadness in her friend's eyes. 'Alice, please, for his own good, and safety, he must not come anywhere near us. Please tell him to stay in his room, if he does not do this, he will have to move back with Florence.'

The girls' confusion showed, but she would explain it all tomorrow, now she just wanted every-one to go to bed.

'Yes, it will be as you say, Mistress.' Alice turned, wiped her eyes, and left the room.

Alone in her bed it was Dune who filled her thoughts. She reached for the pillow soaked with her tears and cuddled it close. Sleep eventually claimed her, until the man's large hands, again, began to desecrate her body. Isobel never moved. She lay still, like a statue.

Disgust for him filled her with every movement he made. Blood flowed into her mouth from the imprint of her teeth as she bit deep into her bottom lip.

With no incident this time, the man dragged his naked body from the bed and left. Cold and numb, Isobel collected the blanket up from the floor, and walked towards the fire. Huddled in the cloth's warmth she sat by the dying embers. She heard the door open to her relief Alice walked in and quickly moved towards her.

'Mistress, are you, all right?'

'Yes.'

'Can I get anything for you?'

'Yes, you can please, Alice. I would like to have a bath.' Through the gap in the drapes, Isobel could see it was still pitch- black outside. Nevertheless, in no time all, the staff appeared, the water was made ready, for her tormented body to ease into, and her bed was remade with fresh clean sheets.

Chapter Eighteen

Snow fell heavier, as each day passed. The Master cooped up inside the house, drank him-self into a deep, drunken stupor. Consequently, his night visits became less and less.

Eventually, the weather eased, and, although the snow was thick on the ground, Isobel astride Tranquil, rode with Ben to Portchesterton. She desperately needed to visit the solicitors to replenish her money. On their return to the house, Ben found Belington, and handed him the envelope from the Mistress.

Then, to everyone's delight, he instantly mounted his horse, and left for London. With the roll of white five-pound notes on his person, hopefully, he would be gone for many months.

Belington's disappearance, once he had been refurbished with more money, kept Isobel sane. Although, she did wonder, why the man never asked her where the money came from.

The fact, she could just ride off and return with it, he never questioned. But Isobel, did smile because, hardly two words had ever passed between them.

January came and went, and February was an awful month, but now in the middle of March, this morning had dawned bright with a lovely clear blue sky. Isobel pushed the covers away, her long legs over the bed, she tried to stand. Nausea, and a fuzzy, head forced her to sit again, she felt awful.

Alice just entered with the breakfast tray, moved quickly to her side. 'Oh Mistress, what ails thee, you be so white.'

'I just feel so queasy, light- headed, and out of sorts. I expect its lack of fresh air.

Today, I will wrap up warm, and go for a little walk.' Isobel heaved, as she saw the food laid out onto the table. Alice worried by her lady's distress, and paleness, ran into the washroom and fetched a round bowl. But no sickness came. A little later, Isobel managed to eat just a small amount of the food, and each morning after, the same symptoms occurred, but by lunchtime, she would be herself again.

Alice, frightened that her dear friend, might be ill, had confided in Florence, so today both women entered with Isobel's breakfast tray. The sight of the Mistress's head over the bowl brought a smile to the older woman's face.

'See.' Alice whispered. 'See how poorly; my Lady, is?'

'Oh, your; Ladyship;' Florrie uttered. 'I think you might be with child.'

Isobel looked up. 'A child.' Her voice was husky.

'Yes, Madam, possibly within you, there is a little one.'

She rested, her hand on her stomach, and stared at them both. 'But if there is how will I know?'

'Perhaps, Mistress, Ben should go and find the old lady again. If he can bring her here, she will soon know if you are.'

'Please, Florence. I really need to have it confirmed.

141

Then if I am not, I need to find the reason why my body reacts like this every day.'

The woman smiled and left the room, and Alice moved across to sit beside Isobel on the bed.

'A baby. Oh, Miss.' Alice comforted Isobel and both cried together.

It was dark when Ben returned with the elderly woman in tow. Taken straight to the Mistress's room, after several examinations, she confirmed her Ladyship was indeed with child. Isobel repulsed, at the thought of his flesh inside her, was physically sick.

The sickness lasted for a few weeks more, and the sight of her thickened waist in the mirror; confirmed; there was indeed a life within her. With the queasiness gone, and still not sure how she truly felt about the infant she carried, Isobel wanted to get her life back to as normal as it could possibly be, under the circumstances. So, she decided to start teaching Edward, for that is the name the little one had chosen for two days a week, until such times as a tutor could be thought about. He learnt quickly, and he was so happy to learn. Alice having been taught with Isobel, could already read, and write very well, but Isobel did smile when the girl slipped back to her strong northern accent.

It was almost time for afternoon tea, and today they had all gathered in the great hall.

Sat in the chair near the inglenook, Isobel smiled. With her old life cruelly, severed from her, she wished her beloved Mama, could be here now, and see her new family.

She would be so thrilled to greet them all. Florrie and Ben looked after her so well, and Isobel had developed a great fondness for them both.

Young Edward, they all gained much joy from, and dear, Alice, her sister, friend, maid, and confidant. Without her by her side, she really wondered what the outcome of the past gruelling months; might have been.

She was extremely, grateful, to have all these happy and wonderful people in her life.

Belington returned in the early hours, several nights later. The man made straight for his wife's bedroom, her nightwear torn from her body, his hands roughly raped her. Isobel, frightened his weight might hurt the child, raised her arms upwards towards him. Consequently, in his fury, he knocked her from the bed to the floor. When he had finished, he stormed from the room.

In his descent down the stairs, the man demanded at the top of his voice; 'Food, I want food, and wine, plenty of it. Port, I want port, now, immediately in the great hall.'

Amongst all the commotion, Alice entered her mistress's bedchamber, and to her horror, found her in a pool of blood, and naked on the floor. She covered her with the blanket and whispered, 'Oh no. Dear Miss Isobel, what has that beast done to you again.?'

The herbal lady returned to treat the wounds and bruises, but this time it took quite a while for their Mistress to heal. Isobel had lost the baby through his brutality, and now she hated the man with a dark, black vengeance, that even shocked her.

Alice opened the door and smiled at the young maid. The girl entered and walked slowly past her towards the table. Once the tray was placed down, she took a white envelope from her apron pocket and handed it to Alice. The boldly written words brought tears to her eyes as she turned to declare, 'Mistress, look, look, a letter, hopefully from home with news.' She handed her the envelope, but Isobel just sighed. 'This is the same writing that was on Mama's last letter.' She opened it and read, but suddenly the papers left her hand and slid to the floor.

'Miss, whatever is the matter?' Alice enquired as she bent to retrieve them. 'You be as white as a sheet.' She held the letter out towards her.

Isobel, unable to speak, ignored the outstretched hand and shook her head. 'You read it please Alice.'

The girl did, and her tears fell freely, and again the correspondence dropped to the ground.

'Oh, dear, sister, I'… the girl knelt beside her. 'I'm so sorry, the dear lady was so kind to me all my life. She was a wonderful person.'

'Yes, she was. Apparently, Mama, passed quite soon after we had left. My poor, Mother, had suffered from my father's terrible abuse, and behaviour, for many years. But at least he never beat her, well not to my knowledge he did. Isobel wiped her eyes. 'I do pray, she is at peace now, and in a lovely place.

'As do I, Miss. As do I.'

Isobel tried to get out of bed. Alice rushed to help her. With her shawl about her body, the girl helped her to the chair near the fire. Isobel stared into the fire, although shivers ran through her thin body. A smaller envelope, which had been tucked inside the big one, had fallen out onto the floor, and Alice bent to pick it up.

'Miss.' The girl held it out towards her. 'This was also with the letter.'

Isobel took it from her and tore at it angrily.

'It's just a note from Grandma. She says, Anna is now there with her, and if you, and I, wish to leave here, we could journey to Cornwall. She has offered us both a home with her.'

'Miss, I will go anywhere, anywhere, you wish to go.'

'Thank you, Alice, you are such a comfort, but we are settled here now, but perhaps we might visit her soon.' But Isobel could not consider this move, in case Dune did arrive, if she left, he would have no idea where she had gone.

In the weeks that had passed, since the news of her beloved Mother's death, her miscarriage, and Belington's return to the house. Isobel had become almost a recluse.

Consequently, Alice, Ben, and Florence, were all extremely concerned about her.

It was true; Isobel, would never see or feel her mama's closeness again. Yet, just two nights ago, she had woken to the strangest sensation of a special nearness, and was positive, she heard a quiet, gentle voice, say. 'Be happy, sweet, Isobel, the evil, that surrounds you, will soon be gone. You are loved so much, cherished, and always will be, dear one.' The thought of possibly hearing these words brought her much comfort.

Then last night, something had woken her, and as her eyes searched the room, she had inhaled, scented rose water. The strength of the odour was so strong, she had reached for her robe and left her bed. She walked towards the window, and, below a star- filled sky, she saw many shadows. Tears fell, as she raised her hand. Rose water was constantly used by her mother, and from this experience, she knew her Mama, was finally at peace, and in a restful place.

Isobel returned to her bed; contentment, filled her. Mama had told her, she was with her, and would be close to her forever. A peaceful, sleep cocooned her, something that had not happened for a long, long time.

The next morning when Alice entered her room, Isobel was already up, and out on her balcony. 'Morning, Alice, it's a lovely morning; I shall have a little breakfast, then I will go for a ride.'

The girl smiled. 'Yes, Mistress. Wonderful, I will away and get your food, then I will get your green riding habit for you.'

Isobel reached for her hand. 'I am sorry. I know you have been worried, but I do feel a great deal calmer about things now. And yes, you are right, poor Tranquil needs a good ride.'

'Oh, Mistress, we have all been so worried for you. Your mother, my sweet mistress was a wonderful lady, and we all loved her very much. But you know, she would not want to see you so, so sad.'

'Yes, and at least now, she will never find out about the condition the estate was in when we first arrived, or the hellish things we have endured over the last months. I know the shock of the nightmare we entered in, would have done her no good at all. And, if she had any idea of the way the brute of a man has attacked me.' Isobel, shuddered. 'No dear Alice. I feel Mama is now at peace and protected.'

'Oh, yes indeed, Miss.' Alice smiled. 'But.' the girl declared, 'I am so happy you are now back with me.' Alice moved towards her, and they hugged and cried together.

Isobel loved her daily rides, and always returned invigorated. She galloped towards the far-off hills and revelled in the warmth of the sun in the clear blue sky, and her eyes drank in the beautiful countryside around her.

Chapter Nineteen

Trees were all fully leafed, and she breathed the clean air deeply into her lungs.

Like always, she searched the distance in hope and despair; that Dune may be there. The man was constantly in her thoughts, but now she hungered and ached for him desperately. Where was he? Did he ever intend to return? Isobel knew if he ever found out what Belington had done to her poor body; he would not hesitate to kill the man. She just wanted, no, needed a sign, or indication, that he had not abandoned her. She rode quite a way and enjoyed every moment of it, and when she returned to the stables, she felt a great deal calmer and stronger.

She rode every day after that, and a week later, Isobel almost at her destination, caught sight of what looked like another rider in the far distance. She came to a complete halt, and as the risen dust brought the horse closer, her heart somersaulted, and silent, tears fell down her face.

Dune smiled and she almost fell into his outstretched arms. His kisses rained over her beautiful face, as he whispered, 'My darling, darling, Isobel.' He pulled her tight to his body and kissed her full on the mouth.

'Oh, how I have longed for you and this moment. Oh Dune, for such a long time.'

'My lovely, adorable, sweet one. I also have longed for you.'

'Please hold me tight, Dune, and promise to never, never let me go.'

Isobel's joy bubbled inside her, and later, held tight in his arms, seated on a blanket, beneath a tree, Isobel asked, 'where have you been it has been so long, almost a year.'

'Yes, my darling, I know, but my father was taken ill again with his back, I had to go back to Ireland. I was there for almost six months with him, otherwise I would have been here sooner. And of course, there was no way of letting you know.'

'My Mother died. Did you know that Dune?'

'Yes, my dearest, I did hear of it. I am sorry, she was a kind, beautiful woman. She always reminded me of my own Mammy.'

'Oh, do you know you have never spoken of her to me. Is she here or in Ireland?'

'No, she passed, when my baby sister was born, and I was small; Nana Rosa brought us both up.'

'Dune, please tell me about them.' She snuggled closer and smiled at him.

He bent and kissed her hard on the lips, then said, 'well, where shall I start?'

'From when you were born of course, silly. I want to know all about you, my lovely Dune, Everything. Oh, Dune if you only knew just how much I needed to see you, feel you, hear your beautiful Irish voice.'

He pulled her close, and she snuggled into him. Her happiness brimmed over, and every thought of despair evaporated. Lost in his wonderful arms, she heard him begin his story.

May 18th, 1814. Leah, aged seventeen, tall, slim, with long black, hair down to her trim waist was a real Romany beauty. It had been her first year in the fields on Fordham's estate as Tom O'Malley's wife. Her back breaking, legs hardly able to move, two elderly ladies carefully guided her away from the dusty, stifled air that surrounded the fruit bushes.

Her labour had begun well before dawn, and both women knew it was almost her time.

Amongst the sand dunes she was helped down onto a blanket. In the quietness of the moment Leah heard the constant waves lap the shoreline, she welcomed the cool breeze, which floated around and over her sweaty, anxious body. Eyes, dark as coal focussed on the white seagulls as they circled overhead in the cloudless, deep blue sky. Through much pain and despair, eventually a cry filled the air, and her first born had entered the world.

Tom knelt and tenderly kissed her sweat, soaked brow. She handed the baby to him, and tears filled his dark eyes as he held the infant close.

Work in the fields stopped. His family, friends, and the rest of the travellers gathered close to watch him lift the new- born upwards to the sky for all to see. His voice emotional, he declared; 'This here be our first son.'

Cheers, laughter, and Irish jigs erupted on the grass edge.

Appropriate to the birthplace, Tom looked at his wife, and with much love in his heart, he announced; 'and this day, I say, me boy be named; Dune. Dune, O'Malley.'

Leah loved his chosen name. Exhausted, she smiled her approval towards her handsome man.

With no complications at the birth, after only one day's rest, she was back in the fields hard at work. Dune was just four, when he too became a fruit picker. Pittance though it was, he now earned money.

Always on the 1st first day of June, the travellers were pitched in the area Fordham allocated for them. Hats and scarves about their heads, their wicker baskets would be filled before the red streaks of dawn, were half- way across the sky.

Dune grew into a beautiful child, and his Mammy, and Da, loved him deeply. With thick black hair, and eyes that mesmerised you, he strongly favoured both parents. Tom, unlike most of the men who sat round the fires on chilled nights, drinking and chatting, preferred to spend time with Leah and the son; he was so proud of.

It was his sixth summer in the fields, when he had first seen the very fair Isobel. The rabbit he had been after, went through the bushes and ended up in the main garden of the house. Dune had fallen through a hedge border onto the grass, where Mother and baby sat on a large blanket. His sudden appearance had caused the inquisitive Isobel to crawl towards him; once she reached him; she pulled herself up and rested her tiny hands on his dirty knees. Stood by him, she smiled, babbled, then clapped her hands, but as the Mistress stood; to walk towards them, Dune carefully sat the white- haired beauty back down and was gone in a flash. From his first encounter with Isobel, Dune always found ways to watch her grow, through the summers that followed.

'And our second encounter, my darling, was when I found you quite a distance from the house with a cut knee.' He smiled and kissed her upturned face. 'I did try to clean your wound. If I remember clearly, I spat onto the dirty cloth I used to wipe the sweat from my face when I worked in the fields.'

Isobel sighed. 'Oh, Dune, it's a lovely story, and you told it so beautifully. I was so young when we first met. Did you love me then?'

'Questions, my Lady, so many you ask. Yes, I have loved you from the very first time I saw you. But it was when I tried to tend to your blood-covered knee; that you first took notice of me. I was eleven and you were six.' He gathered her close and the kiss was long and wonderful.

'Do you think this is a beautiful spot?' She saw his nod. 'I chose it because it reminded me of our place back home.'

'Yes, my sweet love. It's quite similar.'

'Where are you camped? I hope it is not too near the house. Are you here on your own, or with some of your people?'

'No, there is quite a few of us, because we want to see

what the land and fields are like in this part of Sussex.

'Dune, when I received the news of Mama's death, I was relieved. Because of my father's continuous cruelty towards her, I feel now she is at last free, and at peace.'

'It is the right way to think, my lovely. This is our way also. We are saddened by their loss, but also happy for the quiet; peacefulness they can now be embraced in.'

'Oh, Dune, I cannot believe you are here with me, you have taken so long to return to me. But you had to go to your poor papa, I understand that.'

'Also, my uncle and I have started to breed these special horses. We gypsies use them all the time, they are called Cobs, and Vanners. Our clan's use them to pull their large, caravans, across the countryside. They, are beautiful, reliable creatures, with extra broad backs.'

'Oh, they sound quite special.' She snuggled closer to him, and he kissed her nose.

'Yes, they are, they are handsome creatures.

Consequently, because I wanted to be here with you as soon as I returned from Ireland, there is a great amount of work that needs to be done. Once it is all completed, we will all return, and I will be here with you forever, my darling.'

He pulled her tighter to him and kissed her hair.

'Dune, Dune my darling, I am so happy, that you are here with me now. But we must be so careful, this man I am married to is, well he is a demon. We must always meet far, far away from the house, much further than we did when we were back at home. This man frightens me, I think he is pure evil, so darling you must be careful, so careful at all times.'

He held her tight, then looked at her beautiful face. 'My darling, please do not worry, we are camped a great way from here, he won't find us.'

She sighed and whispered. 'Good.'

'Will I see you tomorrow, Isobel my darling?'

'Yes. Yes of course you will.'

His kiss melted her, and with great reluctance, both made ready to leave their new special place.

Reluctant to leave each other, they eventually, rode away in different directions. Isobel on her return dismounted in the stable yard, and the sight of Belington's grey horse in his box, unnerved her. Dear Lord, she thought, why now, I was so happy and now the despicable man is back. But to her relief as she walked into the big hall, there was no sign of him sprawled about anywhere.

She climbed the stairs slowly, emotionally drained, and very tired after her wonderful encounter with her beloved Dune. All she wanted was a nice soak in the bath, a light supper, and go to bed and read. She opened the door and the sight of Belington slouched in her chair caused her heart to almost stop, then pound hard in her chest.

Dry mouthed, hands sweaty, she stood in the doorway and could not move.

'Ah, dear wife you are back, come in my dear.' He gurgled. 'After all, it's your room.'

she did not move.

I said, 'come into your room now.'

In a trance like state, Isobel moved just a little further in.

'Yes, that's it. Now pull the cord, I need some wine.'

She did as he asked and was relieved to see Ben enter.

'*Wine, I want more wine, now, man.*'

'Yes, my Lord.' He bowed and left the room.

Complete silence descended, and Isobel stood and stared into the empty fire- place. Ben, on his return, knocked and entered with the silver tray in his hands. He walked towards the small table next to where the master sat, but before he could place it onto the surface, Belington grabbed the decanter, the top instantly removed, he lifted it straight to his mouth. He gulped the red wine, and Isobel cringed as she witnessed much of the liquid cascaded down the front of his tunic and stain her blue chair. Ben bowed and turned to leave, luckily her husband did not see the look that passed between Mistress and servant.

Belington, with little left in the decanter, clutched it tight in his big hand. He burped, loudly, wiped his mouth on his sleeve, and looked at her. 'You have some money for me dear wife?' Isobel still had not moved, but now she walked through to Alice's room and opened the drawer where her bag was tucked away. She was so thankful, that when they had gone into Portchesterton to replenish her cash recently, the kindly man, had put it into two big bundles. Consequently, now she returned with one of them, and held it out to him. He snatched it from her hand, and without another word, stood and waddled very unsteadily towards the door. His hand on the handle, he stopped and turned. 'By the way, Madam, your father is dead. He was found with his throat ripped out, in some dark alley in a back street of the Bordellos.'

Chapter Twenty

Isobel shivered. His bloodshot eyes bored deeply into her as he continued. 'There will be no more cash from that quarter now, so I do hope you can continue to keep me well replenished in the future.' He downed the last dregs from the decanter, once emptied he threw it down onto the carpet, 'and, of course, my dear, you will have to raise the amount a great deal higher now he's gone.' The vibration from the slammed door, shook the room, and Isobel to the core.

She was so relieved after he left, tears began to fall, but not one was for the man she had always called Father. However, she did shudder as she pictured his lifeless body on the filthy ground, covered in his own blood. No, these were happy tears, Dune's face was before her and joy filled her heart.

Alice rushed into the room. 'Are you alright Miss?'

'Yes. Yes, I am fine thanks Alice. But just look what he has done to my lovely chair.'

'Oh, that's awful.' She collected the decanter from the floor. 'Luckily, the carpet is not stained, I will ask Ben to come and take the chair away, I be sure he will get it fixed for you.'

'Yes, I expect he will. Good old Ben, I truly do not know what we would have done without him, always being around here to help us.'

'No, and Florence, they certainly are special people.'

The girl smiled. 'I'll away and get our super, and I will speak with him.'

'Thanks, Alice.'

There was a light knock and Ben entered. 'Oh, Mistress, what a mess. I'll take it away and get it done for you.' He smiled, opened the door and one of the young lads from the stables walked in, he bent his head, then moved towards the chair. Between them, they lifted it, then, they manoeuvred it through the door, and down the stairs.

'Thank you, Ben.' Isobel said, as he turned back to close the door.

She knew by tomorrow night it would be back in its rightful place, as good as new.

Later, seated by the fire, her thoughts were of the wonderful afternoon spent with Dune, and now she hungered for his presence beside her. She wanted to feel his hands on her body and his perfect lips caress her face and neck.

Isobel sighed loudly. She had still not mentioned Dune's arrival to Alice, and for the present, thought it better not to speak of her gypsy love to her or anyone.

For the second time that day, Isobel shuddered; Belington, would indeed need a great deal more cash from her now her fathers had dried up. Utter panic gripped her. She would have to continue to keep him well stocked, because if not, his returns to the house would become more frequent, and that, she could, and would not endure.

This, she must avoid at all costs. It hurt Isobel deeply,

when she thought of the way, she was forced to use such vast amounts of her beloved Grandma's money. But, without the cash to give him, her life would become unbearable.

She sighed and reached for her book. Still, at least this night he would not seek her bed. Hopefully, with all the cash, he now had in his pockets, he was already in London.

But to Isobel's shock and horror, Belington entered her room in the small hours, and again took her with much force. She put up no fight, she laid like a statue if she wanted to see Dune this day, she dared not have the slightest mark about her. The smell from his body odour, his breath close to her face, the way his hands grabbed at her, caused her heart to pound in her throat. Also, she must not bite into her lower lip, like other times, no, Dune must have no idea of what she went through at the hands of this evil man.

It seemed like hours before he clambered off, and instead of his quick departure, his naked body lingered by the bed. His hand snaked down, and grabbed a handful of her hair, he pulled up towards him, and sneered. 'Stupid, little girl with your childish ways, you will never beat me. Never.' His eyes never left he face. 'For you dear wife, there will never be any reprieve. You are mine till you leave this world, and never forget it.' His laugh, as the door banged behind him, echoed in the room.

Isobel stifled a scream, as Alice entered and quickly reached her side. 'Oh Mistress,' she whispered, and held her close.

It was five a.m. The bed had been stripped and changed. Bathed, and now in clean nightwear, Isobel climbed back into it. Alice returned with their tea, and together they sipped the welcome liquid in silence.

Isobel looked at Alice, then took her hand. 'There... there is something I must tell you.'

The girl frowned. 'Oh, yes, Miss, alright.'

'Dune is here. He is camped far away across the hills.'

Alice stared, then quietly, mouthed, 'Dune, here... how, I mean... have you seen him?'

'Yes, yesterday. When I went for my long ride and, did not return till late.'

Isobel saw her deep concern. 'It's alright, truly, you need not worry no one else knows he's here, and no one would connect him with me.'

'But, Mistress, how did he find you... us? Oh, Miss, that man... the master, please be careful of him, there is a great deal of evil in the man. Ben has told me some horrific stories where he is concerned.'

'Well, hopefully, he will be gone soon, if not already. He has a great amount of cash on him now.' She smiled and hugged her. 'Listen, dear friend, when we left on our journey to travel here, Dune followed us from afar, because he needed to know where we would both be settled.' And she continued to tell the girl about his journey to Sussex, while keeping them both close to him.

'How wonderful for him to have done that for you, Mistress, and yes I am pleased that he is here for you, but I can't help to be fearful for you, actually, for you both now.'

'Yes, I know, but please it will be fine if we are both really, careful.' She smiled, 'And now with Dune here, oh, Alice, I am so, so happy, and I do, I love him. I really do. I was not sure back home how I felt about him. I was so young. But yes, I love him with all my heart. With this long absence, I was not sure, but to see him today, to be held close and kissed. Oh, Alice, I adore him.'

'Ah Mistress, I know, you do, you always have, that's for sure.'

Isobel noticed the serious worry on the girl's face, and she knew she was deeply concerned; even when they were children, she showed her worry over Isobel, and Dunes secret meetings.

The birds were in full song; when Isobel eventually pushed the covers from her and sat up. She saw the French doors were wide open; her long legs over the side of the bed, her arms stretched above her head, she yawned. She slipped her feet into satin slippers, pulled her wrap about her shoulders, and walked out onto the balcony. The view from there always took the breath from her, she inhaled deeply, then returned inside. Alice entered with their breakfast; the tray placed onto the table. She stated. 'It be a beautiful day, and you have slept quite late Miss.'

Isobel smiled as the girl pulled the chair out for her, and together they ate the delicious home- baked rolls with the soft- boiled eggs, washed down with warm, sweet tea.

'Are you unsettled about; Dune?' Isobel, asked.

'Oh, Mistress, no, how could I be? He makes you so happy. I'm just concerned over your welfare, and safety, from that terrible man.'

Isobel smiled and took her hand.

'We will be really, careful when we meet, we will keep as far away from the house, that we can.'

'Yes, Miss, I know you will.'

'Belington informed me, our father is dead, apparently, he was found somewhere in a bad part of London. His throat, had been cut.'

'Oh, Mistress, I'm so sorry to hear that for you.'

'Well, I cannot shed one tear for the terrible man he was, but I do hope wherever he is now, he might find some peace.'

Alice stood and began putting their used plates, and utensils back onto the tray.

Isobel looked at the girl and asked. 'Alice please sit down for a moment.'

The girl sat and Isobel took her hand. 'I want you to be my sister now, really be my sister. Because we can train one of the younger girls to become my personal maid, and I want you to have one also.'

'No, no Miss Isobel, I'll not have that. I want to serve you, serve you always.'

'But Alice, you are my sister, and you were born for this status.'

The girl shook her head, 'no Miss, I want to serve you.'

'Well, you are my sister, companion and you can spend more time with me socially if we employ a couple more maids. How does that sound dear?'

'It's your choice Miss, yes, but I still want to serve you.' The girls laughed and hugged.

'So, now Alice, you must call me Isobel, we are sisters, no more Miss or Mistress. Understood?'

'Isobel, that will seem so strange for me to do, but yes, I will try, and thank you Miss... sorry, Isobel.'

She went on to tell her about her concerns now that Fordham's money had ceased, and the last thing they needed, was for Belington's long absences from the house to stop. Consequently, it was up to her now to keep him in money.

Alice laid out the green habit for her mistress's ride and helped her dress. Isobel, ready to leave, hugged her tight, then hurried from the room, and as she skipped down the stairs, Alice sank to the floor.

So, Fordham was now dead. The man who had fathered her, and senseless tears fell onto her clenched hands. She was very tiny, when she noticed the man, who crept into their bedroom in the dead of night to lie with her mama. Mother had always told her, she must be still and silent in her small bed, whenever he appeared.

Since she had received, and read her letter from Mistress Mary, many questions from her young days in the masters, house had been answered. And the only reason her mama had endured his attention, was, because she was fearful of what the awful man would do if rebuked. Alice also realised, just how much she had been protected by mistress Mary, and her tears fell again. She stood, and quickly retrieved the pages from the letter, deep within the pocket of her dress. She threw them onto the warm embers, and silently whispered, as she watched them slowly burn. 'That all be in the past, and Miss Isobel, will never hear one word, about those nights from me.' Composed, Alice collected the tray and walked from the room.

Chapter Twenty-One

After all she had endured since her departure from the only home she'd ever known, Isobel never dreamed it was possible to feel such happiness, and contentment as she rode to meet the man, she loved so deeply. Puzzled to see he was still mounted as she reached her destination, she eased Tranquil to a slower pace, and stopped beside him. His arm reached out, and she was pulled tight to his chest; the kiss was long and left her breathless.

'I have found us a different spot to be together,' he uttered into her ear, while his lips caressed her lobe. Eventually his hold slackened, she smiled as the strong pent- up emotion, he aroused within her, threatened to explode.

'But I will still wait here for you as usual, to lead you through the bushes to the spot. Will that be alright with you darling?'

Mouth slightly parted, Isobel nodded.

'Good, now follow me closely. He let go of her reins and urged his horse forward.

As they entered the bottom of the hills, Isobel saw the track was indeed very narrow. She was enthralled by the scenes of nature at its most beautiful, as they weaved in and out of trees, bushes, and many tracks that led off in different directions. Eventually, they emerged from beneath an aged willow, whose abundance of long leaves danced in and out of the stream that ran beside it.

Isobel's sudden loud gasp, as she inhaled the beauty of the scene, and the clear blue skies above, why, the place was magnificent. She smiled; this was to be their own wonderous secret place.

Dune dismounted and helped her down. The animals led to the water, drank heartily, then, tied carefully beneath a tree's shade, both grazed contentedly on the grass.

'It is a place of sheer wonderment, is it not, my lovely?'

'Indeed. It is perfect.' Hot and dusty, Isobel bent and, put her hands into the cool stream that cascaded over the rocks. Her eyes feasted on the magnificent, carpet of wildflowers as she walked to where, Dune was sprawled out on the big rug. His eyes were closed.

She knelt, and kissed his beautifully, shaped lips. He smiled, and pulled her onto him, and in the next instant; he turned, and was on top of her. The return kiss, and his body pushed into hers, aroused her, and she desperately felt the need of him.

Florence's words suddenly, tumbled into her mind. 'Oh, Mistress, it can be so wonderful, when the man you love and adore, tenderly shows you his physical love.'

Isobel gently eased him off her and looked into his black eyes. 'I love you so very much.' She whispered.

Since her farce of a marriage, her body had been so brutally violated. Consequently, at this precise moment in time, she needed to know, how it felt to be gently, and sincerely loved by the man who had her heart.

Isobel wriggled, and Dune stood to help her to her feet. She took his face in her hands and kissed his lips tenderly, then, unable to reach the buttons on the back of her blouse, she turned away from him. His hands shook as she pointed to them; he fumbled, then the loose garment slipped from her arms to the ground. Then the skirt followed, undergarments removed, her lips parted, unconcerned, she turned back and stared at his face. Isobel saw tears well, as his eyes dwelt upon her nakedness.

'I adore you, my love. I love you so much. For you, I would readily give my life,' he whispered, as he picked her up, she clung to him, then he tenderly laid her back on the rug. He removed his own clothes and lay down beside her. His hands moved very, slowly over her body, and each touch thrilled her to distraction.

Birds fluttered, back and forth overhead in the deep blue sky. And, only nature's sounds filled the air, as Dune took her to a plateau. A plateau, she had never experienced before, and a wondrous contentment, engulfed her as they became one.

Eventually in each other's arms, sleep claimed them. Held tight and secure, it was extremely late, when with a great reluctance, they pulled apart, dressed then rode off in their different directions.

And thereafter, Isobel could not wait to ride out to be with him. Cocooned completely in his passion, her joy and happiness blinded her slightly from the real world.

Ben, who had managed to buy the carriage, and the

horses from old, Mr. Kingswood was ready to collect Isobel, Alice, and young Edward. Isobel had promised to take him with them the next time they went to the town. It was not quite light, and the journey to Portchesterton was quite pleasant. It was June, and Isobel had just turned eighteen the day trip was for her birthday.

Ben parked the horses and carriage, then, went off to collect some of the items the main house needed. Metal candle holders, the blacksmith had made, needed to be collected, and he had quite a list to collect from other shops.

Isobel, and Alice, went along to see the solicitor, then when replenished with more money, they brought some materials, papers, and some bits for the kitchen. Then Isobel purchased a new book, a pack of white paper, and some paint brushes, for the boy, who had started to paint and draw.

Ben had been invited to join them in the café by the sea, when he was finished, so he had dressed smartly for to-days trip. But Isobel ordered lunch, and they had lemonade, then when this was all finished, they had their usual pots of tea, with lemon cake.

After a good three hours in the café, it was time to leave. Ben helped, the ladies up into the coach, then the sleepy youngster was handed up to Alice, Edward who was tired laid his head on her lap, and instantly fell asleep.

The journey back was uneventful, and on their arrival, Ben lifted the lad out and Alice took him into the house.

'I need a nice cup of tea it's been a tiring day.' Isobel

said as she sat down next to the Inglenook. 'But we brought all that we needed. Didn't we Alice?'

'Yes, indeed we did, Miss, and it was a lovely day. And this is for you.' She smiled then handed her something wrapped in a nice pink soft paper.

Tears gathered as Isobel undid the gift. It was a new book for her to read, and she was delighted. 'Oh, dear Alice, this is wonderful, but you should not have brought me anything.'

'Yes, I should. I love you dear sister so very much.' Both stood and hugged tightly, and tears fell freely.

Molly came up the back stairs, with a tea tray in her hands, and as she laid it on the table, the little one opened his eyes, he slid from the two chairs to the floor and ran towards his Ma. But Alice stopped him, and he was lifted high in the air, and his giggles and laughter filled the room, then he sat at the table, to eat a fresh baked cake.

Tea and cake finished, Isobel said. 'Well young man come with us, I brought you a present today.' He smiled and held both their hands as their climbed the stairs.

Handed his book of white paper, pencils, and paints, his pleasure was wonderful to see.

'Fank… thank…you.' He flew at Isobel, climbed up onto her lap, and smothered her in kisses.

'Oh, you lovely lad, oh you are my beautiful boy, Edward.'

There was a knock, Alice opened the door, and a young maid stood there.

'Please, she said, 'I have come for master, Edward. It be his supper time, then bath, and bed.' The girl smiled.

Isobel stood and placed his feet onto the floor. 'Goodnight my darling. Tomorrow you come up here with me, and we will draw and paint together.' More kisses were reigned upon her. Then he moved towards Alice. After many kisses and hugs, he smiled and left with the young girl.

They both laughed, he was such an adorable boy. 'He has been calling me Mama for some time now, Alice, do you think he should?'

'Yes, Miss, sorry Isobel. I do, it sounds lovely to hear him call you that.'

'I agree, and I intend to let him because, I get so thrilled when he calls me by that name. Mama.'

'He certainly is a lovely boy, and we all love him.'

'Very true, Alice. Absolutely true.'

November loomed, which meant the weather would start to interfere with her daily rides. Also, Dune would soon be away, to seek a camp for the long winter months ahead. Today as Isobel approached their special place, despair filled her, for there was no sign of him, and he was always there first. She dismounted and sat on a rock to wait. She was very anxious, and it seemed an age, before she witnessed distant dust as it moved extremely fast towards her.

She stood, and smiled, through her tears of relief as he quickly dismounted, she fell into his arms and whispered.

'Darling, I was worried. Is everything alright?'

'Yes, and no, my love.' He pulled her tight to him and kissed her hard on the lips. 'No, I am fine, I am indestructible.' He winked. 'Nought will happen to me, my love. But I am sad and sorry, for I must leave for Ireland immediately.'

'Leave. But Dune, why, what has happened, tell me?'

'I have received bad news about my father, once again. One of the horses they were working with went mad, and it fell, sadly it fell on my father's legs. He is very poorly. They fear his back has completely gone.'

'Oh no. Dune I am so sorry to hear that.' She saw the sorrow in his face and pulled his head onto her breast. 'Oh, my love. When do you leave?'

'Now, just as soon as I return to the group.' He lifted her chin. 'Darling I will be back, I promise.' The kiss, as always, she did not want to end.

Isobel's moist eyes searched his face. 'Dune, what will I do, with you, gone from me again?' She snuggled into him, and his arms pulled her tight, and he kissed her hair.

'I will return just as soon as I can. This I swear, my dearest.'

'No, my darling, you must stay with your poor father, until he is good and well again, and, Dune, perhaps you might bring him back with you when you return.'

'Yes, that's a good idea, but he is such a stubborn man, he might not want to come. But I will return as soon as I feel he's on the mend.'

171

She moved slightly away from him and took his hand. 'Please, my love, love me once more before you go.'

'But my darling it be too cold, it's almost winter.'

'Well, are there any glass houses near here, do you know?'

'Yes. There are several, that are not far from here.'

'Can we go there, darling, have you got time?'

'My darling Isobel, for you I have always got time, and my love.' He kissed, her, then, helped her to remount, and together they rode off towards them.

The sky was very dark; Isobel hoped a storm was not on its way.

It was not long before they came into view, and they both chose the smallest one to enter. There cloths were slightly damp from the light rain that had fallen, but now thunder, lightning, and an extra, strong, wind was crashing across the sky.

'Just look at the rain is thrashing down. I am glad you put the horses in that one next to us.' She uttered.

'Let's, hope it soon passes,' Dune muttered, as he laid the blanket down on the ground. He reached for her and she melted, in his arms. He was gentleness itself, and she felt so much love for him, that her chest hurt. How she loved this most adorable man. Again, and again, while the thunder crashed about them, he took her to their special place, and she was completely in heaven.

'Dune.'

'Mm.'

'It must be quite late now. I think we should leave because, you have to be away for your journey.'

'Yes, my darling, see what you do to me.' He helped her up, they both dressed, he folded the blanket, and they walked outside.

'Well at least the rain has stopped; here let me help you up, my love.'

'Thank you, Dune, what a wonderful afternoon,' she muttered. He kissed her hard, then, once she was mounted, he took hold of the reins. He insisted on riding some of the way back with her because she was not sure of where she was; also, the sky was still very dark, and the wind was strong.

It was a risk, but neither cared; he rode a good distance with her. Finally, after many kisses, Dune eventually left.

Chapter Twenty-Two

Isobel's spirits exceptionally high, she entered the stable yard. She smiled when the lad came and took Tranquil, 'Thank you.' She said, then turned and walked towards the house.   She entered the big hall and was relieved to see it was empty. She quietly walked up the stairs and entered her chambers. Relieved to find just Alice in her room, she smiled, but straight away sensed something was wrong. 'Whatever is the matter, Alice? You are so pale. What has happened tell me?'

'It be him. The master. Came in the house, black as thunder, told Ben, to round up as many men he could, because he'd found a gypsy camp on the estate. Oh, his anger. Mistress. It fair made me tremble, it did.'

'Oh, no, has he hurt any of them or did they elude him?'

The girl wiped her eyes. 'He... he, found two, tied them to his horse, then rode like a madman. He brought them back to the courtyard and let them drop to the ground like stones.' She dapped her eyes. 'Miss. Ben, says, he beat them unmercifully, and he thinks one if not both might be dead.'

'Dead, oh no. I pray not, how terrible. Tell me, do you know where the poor men are now?'

'Yes, they have been taken to the herbal lady. The master rode off with some men to look for more, that's when Ben, and the stable lads, put them into the cart so he could go and try to find her.'

'So, do we know where Belington is now?'

'No, Miss we don't.

'Alice, as soon as Ben returns, please ask him to go out and look for more camps, and if he finds them, he must tell them to move far away.'

'Yes Miss, I will ask him to do this as soon as he returns.'

'Thank you dear.'

'But Isobel, you have been gone so long, what about your bath and some food?'

'Alice, later, I am in no hurry; please, go and find Ben first.'

The girl smiled and quickly left the room.

Isobel pulled the cord, the young girl knocked and entered. 'Molly, I would like a bath please, can you organise it for me.'

'Indeed Madam.' The girl smiled, bent her head, and quietly left.

Alice, returned, and was surprised to see Isobel had, had her bath, was changed, and ready for her supper.

'Oh, Mi…sorry Isobel, you're ready to eat.'

'Yes, Molly was very- good, she can see to my bath times now, I will talk with Florence. It will be one job less for you to do. But tell me what happened with Ben.'

Alice, smiled. 'Well, he did find the lady, thankfully. Then he found several more camps. He told them what had happened, then with them having to move on, he told them to travel over the large hills, because there was no land there, only glass houses, and they would be safe.'

'That's good Alice, but we must pray for these poor people, and hope Belington does not find any-more of them.'

There was a knock on the door, their supper had arrived.

Alice, hummed, while she, helped Isobel, get ready for her bed.

'I saw Dune this afternoon, and we found a glass house to shelter in while the storm was so bad. He leaves for Ireland tonight, because his father is very un-well again.'

'Oh, I am so sorry to hear that. He might be gone for quite some time then Miss?'

'Yes, Alice I think he will.' She smiled and took the girl's hand. 'Alice, I think Ben taking those poor men to the herbal lady, was an extremely kind, and caring thing to do.'

'Yes, I to thought this. Do you need me anymore tonight Isobel?' I am reading one of your old books and it is really good.'

'Oh, I am so pleased. No, you go dear.' They hugged, and the girl closed the door behind her.

Isobel thought it really, strange, when Belington did not return that night; in fact, it was many weeks later, before he was back at the estate.

Months passed, and now deep into their second winter in Sussex, Isobel sat by the inglenook playing with young Edward, smiled when the young, maid appeared. The girl bent her head. 'Mistress, it's time for young Edwards, lunch.'

'Thank you, Molly.'

Edward, screamed, with delight, when Isobel tickled his tummy, 'Come on young man, your lunch is ready. Now, go with Molly, and behave yourself.'

The lad threw his arms around her neck and kissed her. Isobel's heart melted; he was such a loving, beautiful boy. He waved bye, his hand in Molly's they disappeared down the stairs.

The fire was in full glow, and the heat from it was wonderful. She gazed into the flames and thought of her beautiful Dune. Puzzled, she frowned, and wondered why she had not received, a single word from him, since he'd been gone. Isobel knew, he could write, so why not just a note to say all was good with him. Also, she wanted to know how, is father was.

He had been gone, for almost five weeks, and she missed him so much.

December, and it was their second Christmas there. With no one actually, knowing young Edwards, age Isobel decided to make Christmas day his birthday.

The long table in the big hall where the Christmas tree stood, was covered with food and drink and under the tree there was quite a few gifts for the lad, from his mama.

Isobel pulled him close to her and whispered in his ear; 'I think you are six today, so we are all here to make it a happy day for you.'

Dressed in a brown, velvet tunic, trousers to match that finished at his knees, white tights, dark brown, buckle shoes, he looked beautiful. His black, curly hair constantly shone these days, and his skin glowed.

Edward had been thrilled, and blindly ran into Isobel's arms, 'thank you, mama. Thank you.'

Florence made a sponge cake, tiny sandwiches, and there was fresh lemonade, and through much laughter and joy, he received a little gift from everyone. But despite everything, when the Master was in residence, they took no chances, and the lad was kept well out of sight until he had left.

Belington's visits back, and forth to the house, became less frequent as the long winter settled in around them. Nevertheless, when he was there, and entered her room, Isobel bit hard on her lower lip, and pretended, she was with Dune. She thought of how he took her to their special place, and how wonderful her body felt beneath, his.

Pent up in the warmth of the house, time passed slowly. Two days ago, Isobel and Alice had ventured up to the second floor. With the lantern held high above them, their eyes searched the long corridors that led off to the east and west wings. But, through the black abyss, all that greeted them, was a bitterly cold, eerie silence. Consequently, they had quickly returned to the sanctuary of Isobel's room.

But there was still so much of the old mansion Isobel wanted to explore, and when Ben offered to escort them, although apprehensive, she agreed.

Shocked and surprised by the vast number of spacious rooms again, all empty, on the second floor, Isobel decided; the third and fourth ones could wait to be investigated, once the hot summer days; and long, light nights arrived. There were so many cold, dark passageways, seeped in dampness, which had sent a chill of uneasiness, right through her.

Isobel caught up with the books she had set aside to read and wrote several letters to her grandma.

It had been dark for most of the day and, as she sat close to the fire a sudden knock startled her. 'Enter,' she called, and little Edward, followed by Alice scurried into the room. He ran straight into her welcome arms, climbed onto her lap, and snuggled tight against her.

Isobel kissed the top of his dark head. 'Hello, little man, what have you been up to?'

'Come to say night, had my dinner with Florrie and Ben. So now I go to bed.'

'Mm, you've had your bath. You smell delicious. Would you like me to read you a story before you go to sleep?'

'Yes please, please.'

'Come on then, let us get you settled.' Edward giggled as Isobel tickled him under the chin. Sat on her lap, they waited while Alice went to get the night- time book.

Unlike her father, Belington showed absolutely no interest in anything to do with the house when he returned from his trips. He always used the big hall, to sit and drink from the decanters of wine, constantly filled on the long table. From there, he usually crashed into Isobel's bedroom, and once he had his way with her, and his pockets were again full, he was off back to London. Consequently, the quarters allocated for the Master were never used, and because of this, the child had been brought from the cottage, to live in the house.

Inside Alice's large bedroom, there was a small dress room, which was where the little one slept on his new wooden bed. Isobel felt much pleasure when she had furnished it for him. The set of four drawers was filled with many new clothes. A carpet covered the cold, flag, stoned floor to allow him to play on it with his wooden toys, and on each visit to Portchesterton, she returned with something new for him.

Blind to the fact, he could have been fathered by her husband, Isobel adored him, as did Alice and the whole household. The beautiful boy constantly told her and her companion, just how much he loved them.

Edward Claremont is the title he now owned, and Isobel had purposely given him her grandmother's name, because if in the future his identity was ever questioned, she would simply say he is related to her.

Signs of winter suddenly began to disperse, and very slowly signs of spring began to rear its head in the vast fields and lanes. Then thankfully, the long hot days and nights, settled in. There was still no sign or word from Dune, and now Isobel wondered if he had just, simply, abandoned her.

Life had to continue, and with the help of several farm hands, she worked on the gardens at the front of the house. She had also started to have some restoration work done on several more ground floor rooms. The largest, Isobel decided, would be for guests when they came to the house to visit, which she felt certain would happen sometime in the future. The second when completed, was going to be for Edward's lessons, because it was time for her to see about a tutor for him.

Today Isobel, was extremely happy, she had received a letter from her grandma, who was feeling so much better, that, she hoped to visit her later in September.

Ben held out his hand, and Isobel smiled as she stepped onto the box to enter the carriage. Alice followed, and smiled lovingly at her man.

'Oh, Alice, it's going to be another, ridiculously hot day, so if you wish to sit up beside Ben, that's fine with me dear.'

The girl blushed. 'No, I think I'll keep inside in the cool for now.' She sat opposite Isobel, her eyes searching the carriage, she stated. 'Miss you were so lucky when Ben got this for you. It has been kept so clean and in good state.'

'Yes, it certainly was a good buy for me. Ben said poor Mr kingwood, was himself in bad health now. So, he would have no more use for it. Yes, I am pleased with it.' She smiled.

'Oh dear, do you know Alice the heat is going to be quite unbearable, so it's just as well, we will have shopped and returned before noon.'

Chapter Twenty-Three

The sun was up, but it was still very- early when, they rode through the iron gates and galloped along the road to Portchesterton. July and the start of August had brought such heat, Isobel had not ventured outside until quite late in the afternoon, and she would sometimes take her ride in the evening.

The animal's trotted slowly, and a slight breeze swirled occasional through the two square openings of the compartment. The two- hour journey was uneventful, and Isobel was relieved when she eventually stepped down onto the path. Both women breathed in deeply, as the salty wind from the sea greeted them.

'Mistress,' the man tipped his hat. 'I will find shade and water for the horses first. Then I'll away to fulfil the list you gave me.' He looked at her and smiled.

'Thank you, Ben. We will buy what we need, then when we have all finished, say in one hour, you must come along to Quayside café, again for our tea and cake.'

'Ah, I thank thee your Ladyship, but I not, be dressed for it.'

'Ben, you look perfectly, respectable to me. So, we will see you there, in just over one hours' time.'

'Thank you your, Ladyship. It will be my honour.'

The girls left him, and walked towards, the office of the solicitor. The man was such a charmer, and Isobel always, enjoyed her long chats with him. But she always felt guilty, when handed the money, she wanted to explain about Belington's gambling, but, she knew, that was a story, she could not tell.

Her business complete, they went into several shops, and brough some material, six china cups, several news- papers, Isobel brought several new books to read, then for Edward she purchased, more pads of white paper, pencils, and several books for children.

The welcome breeze, ventured through the open doors, and windows of the immaculate tea rooms, when she and Alice entered and took their seats at a table.

Ben was not far behind them, and together they enjoyed the special tea, with the usual refreshed, lemon cake.

It was time to leave, and after the long hot journey back, Isobel was quite exhausted and extremely queasy. 'Oh Alice, I feel a little sick.' She declared, as the girl helped her up to her room. '

'Yes, Isobel it could be that awful heat, mind you, I do think the carriage seemed to rock more on our return trip.' She opened the door and steered Isobel towards her bed.

'Miss, why don't you lie down, and rest for a little while, and I'll go down and fetch you some cool, fresh lemonade.'

'Yes, thank you Alice. I will.' With most of her top clothes removed, Isobel sank into the cover. She curled her tired body into a ball, and sleep claimed her instantly.

The heat from August gone, September brought forth, more wet and windy weather. Isobel walked out onto her balcony, and stared at the hundreds of acres before her, this had become a morning ritual for her, because she loved to stand and drink this scene in.

She returned into her room, and Isobel saw her blue habit was already laid out for her usual daily ride, but, she hesitated, and took a deep breath. She ran her hands over her flat stomach.

She was sure she might be with child again. If she was, although this child within was not made from love, such as the kind she shared with Dune, at this precise moment in time, she felt extremely vulnerable, and very alone.

Always full of empathy, and love for those in need of it, she wanted someone, constantly by her side to receive it. Her hands still on her small tummy, her decision was made.

'Alice. I shall not ride Tranquil today. Nor will I in the weeks ahead.'

'Oh... yes, Mistress, very well.'

'No, you see dear sister I think I might be with child again. So, I do not want to chance it, if I am, I do not want to endanger it in any way. She smiled. 'And, when I ride my body is shaken, and crashed about quite a bit.'

'No of course you don't. Oh, you think you might have a little one inside you, are you pleased Isobel?' The girl pulled out the chair and smiled.

She walked towards it and sat down. 'Well yes, I just hope and pray I can carry the wee one until it is time for it to be born. Mm, thank you dear, fish for breakfast, nice.' She smiled.

'I do like the way Florence steams this fish.'

'Yes, Flo is a great cook. Do you want some of her fresh bread, or a soft roll?'

'Mm, one roll please.' She watched the girl put two rolls on her plate. '

Isobel smiled. 'Do you know what Alice?'

'No, Miss I do not.' The girl replied and grinned.

'I feel quite hungry, and I have hardly any sickness, like last time.'

'I'm pleased. Let's hope it stays like that. How many bleeds have you missed now?'

'I believe it to be two.' Isobel ate most of the food, because she knew, she must keep her body fuelled for the baby's sake. 'Alice, in Mamas last letter, when I eventually read it, she told me how her life changed once I was born. She said, because I had been another daughter, my father had treated me with the same attitude, he had dealt Agnes. He had shown, absolutely no interest, in either of us, he wanted sons.'

Isobel pushed the plate away and frowned. 'So, if I am with child again. I want to nurture this tiny one inside me, and please God, I will deliver this baby safely. And like Mama, in her own words, I will have my own precious little one, to protect and love. Also, he or she will belong to me, just me always. Does that sound selfish Alice?'

'No, sweet Isobel. After what you have been through. No, not at all.' The girl took her hand and kissed it. 'But what if you have a son. Do you think the man will act differently?'

'No.' Isobel shook her head. 'I feel this man, Belington, to be completely, filled with his own esteem. He will not give a single care, about what happens on this estate, after his demise, or what happens to me, or any child, he does father.'

She pushed the chair away and left the table. 'You see Alice, Belington has no companies like my father had, he has no interest in anything other than his cards, and all the wine he can drink. She returned to her chair and sat down. 'Also, I think, he goes with a great deal of women. No, he has no interests, the poor man, is to be pitied, really. Really, pitied.'

'You are right, Isobel, he has no love or friends. He has no one, so sad. So sad.'

'Yes, Alice, so true. But, on a happy theme. I never told you about the page I kept aside that was in my grandma's last letter. It was about your mother.'

'Really, Isobel.'

'Yes, and it was written by my mama before she had become too ill to write.'

'Oh.'

'Yes. She says, that when you were born, my mother, learnt a great deal from yours.

She used to go down to the kitchen area and sit with her in the tiny room she had been given and watch how she looked after you, Alice.'

'Miss how wonderful.'

'She, said when I was born, she had gained so much from Nellie, that she was confident when she had me in her arms. She told me, she adored me, she loved you, and she also loved your mama.'

'Oh, Mistress, Miss. Your Ladyship, I can honestly say, Isobel, I will call you that now with a most happy heart.' They hugged, and cried for their lost Mothers, who had loved them both very much.

The day dawned wet, bitterly cold, and very- windy. No one ventured out unless they really had to. The horses needed to be seen to daily, and wood and coal had to be collected and brought into the house, but other than that, every-one stayed put.

Isobel sat in her room with a book, could not concentrate, because the baby was very- busy with its arms and feet, and she was extremely uncomfortable.

Alice knocked and entered, and a young maid followed her in, she had come to make up the fire. Her job finished she turned curtsied then left the room.

'I have coffee with biscuits, Isobel, do you want them there or will you come to the table?'

'I will come over to you, but the baby is so busy, he or she has not stopped kicking me.'

Their drinks finished, Isobel stood and moved about the room. 'I have more news from Grandma, her letter arrived two days ago, did I tell you Alice.'

'Yes, you did Isobel. How is she now, it was such a shame she had another stroke.'

'She's still not feeling too good, and the doctor has said, she cannot think about traveling anywhere. But, once this baby is here, and a little bigger, perhaps we shall go and visit her.'

'Oh, yes, that would be lovely. I remember our trips there when we were small. I always enjoyed them.'

'Yes, Alice, we will go. I miss Grandmother so much.' She smiled and held her tummy.

'Oh, she also informed me, that my father's brother has inherited the house and all that went with it.'

'Oh, really, did you know him?'

'Well, no, not really, but I do remember he came to the house once when I was small. Father had a sister, and another brother, but I think this one must be the eldest, so he has naturally inherited it all.'

'Is that how it works with the folk that have houses, money and are high up?'

'Yes, my dear, sister, that is exactly how, it all happens.'

'Isobel, Miss Agnes, you said she had gone into the church, is she to become a nun, then?'

'Yes, she told me, when we were small, that was what she wanted to do.'

The hard winter's punishment was felt by everyone, snow fell night and day, week after week, consequently, it was impossible for anyone to get outside. But thankfully the stable lads walked the horses up and down the concrete base inside the stables for hours at a time, which gave them some exercise.

Isobel well into her eighth month stared into the fire, her thoughts were still very much full of Dune, but now with the baby to think about, his absence did not seem to hurt quite so much.

The little one was restless, and its continual movements made her back ach terribly.

She stood and walked around the room, she stopped by the far window and gazed out into the pitch blackness. Sheep usually roamed all over those yonder hills, and she could normally see them, but now in the sheer darkness she whispered, 'I hope you have found shelter, from the severity of the bitter, wind that blows out there, dear sheep.'

Alice sat near the fire looked up and answered. 'Sorry did you speak.'

'Yes, I cannot see the sheep, they are always out there on the hills. I just hope they are all under cover out of the bitter wind.'

'Oh. I see. I'm sure they are.' The girl looked over to where she stood.

'Please come back to the fire, and warm yourself, it is always quite cold over that part of the room.'

Lost in deep thought Isobel did not answer or move. The girl stood, brushed her hands down the sides of her blue dress, and walked towards her. 'Please, Isobel, come back to the warmth, it be bitter this side of the room.

'Yes alright.' She held Alice's arm and slowly moved towards the fire, back in her seat, she watched the girl return to close the heavy drapes across the window.

There was a light knock and Florence entered with a tray in her hands. 'I brought soup and fresh baked bread for you and the Mistress.' She whispered to the girl.

The baby kicked hard, and a sound, left Isobel's lips.

'Mistress, are you alright?' Both women concerned, rushed back to her side, both saw the anguished on her face. Isobel gently stroked her large, round tummy and smiled at them.

'Yes. Yes. I just feel so very uncomfortably. Mm, Florrie, you have brought us our food?'

'Aye, My Lady I have.'

'You are so good to me, and all the household staff, for which I thank you so much.'

'Oh your, Ladyship, it be my pleasure. Truly it be.' She smiled and quietly left the room. Outside in the corridor the woman wiped her eyes, the love she had for her young Mistress was so obvious for all to see.

Chapter Twenty-Four

It was bitterly cold outside, but Isobel needed some fresh air. Wrapped up warm, she made her way to the back of the house where the ground was very flat and safe. Movement for her now was very restricted, but at least the baby seemed to have quietened. She walked towards the bushes free of snow and glanced up at the watery January sun. There was no warmth from it, but still she closed her eyes. The screech of the gales overhead dispersed, and a tense silence shrouded her. She opened her eyes, and her breadth caught in her throat.

There, high on top of the hill, a man astride a black horse stared down at her. The baby suddenly kicked hard, her knees buckled, and she clutched the thick bush for support. She managed to straighten, and slowly walk back to the house. 'Dune,' she whispered. 'Was that you up there after all this time?'

She entered the big hall, and Alice ran towards her, 'Isobel, you be as white as a sheet and you are frozen; come to the fire and warm yourself.' Led towards the flames and carefully seated, Isobel uttered no words.

'I'll away and fetch you some hot tea.' The girl smiled and hurried, towards the stairs.

Isobel felt certain it had been him she had seen. She stared at the red flames, and the guilt she had first experienced, over the little one inside her returned. If it were

Dune, she feared his reaction to the sight of her condition, which, she could never tell him was the result of one of Belington's many drunken rapes.

Ben came up from the kitchen to light all the lanterns scattered all over the house, but when he saw the mistress, he turned to retreat down the stairs.

Isobel caught sight of him, and called, 'Ben no, stop, please come back.'

He walked towards her and bent his head.

'Tell me, since that last terrible episode with the master, have you seen or heard of any gypsies camped locally?'

'Yes, Madam, there be a big camp of them. But they are well hidden; the Master never rides out where they be.'

'I see. Thank you.'

He bent his head, smiled, and walked away.

She stared into the fire and silently muttered. 'Oh, dear Lord, will I ever be able to forget this man, who haunts me so?'

Alice looked up and smiled when Ben entered the kitchen. 'I've just made Miss Isobel, some hot tea. Is she alright?'

'Yes. She asked if I'd seen any gypsies.'

'Oh. And have you?'

'Well yes. It quite surprised me, because after Belington beat those two almost to death, I didn't think they would come back this way.' He poured tea into his battered mug. 'Why? He asked. 'Why does, the, mistress, talk of the travellers, with such emotion?'

Alice sunk onto the wooden chair. 'I…I…. Ben.' She looked into his light, blue eyes as he knelt before her. 'I fear so much for my Miss, Isobel. I truly do, and I pray hard, that she might let him go.'

'Who, who should the mistress forget?'

'Dune O'Malley. A devilish handsome gypsy boy, my beautiful lady gave her heart to when they were both really small.' Alice wiped her eyes, 'when he left, I hoped he would never return.'

Ben stood. 'He was here, when?' He looked at her hard, 'when?'

'Mm, last Summer, I think. Look, I must take her tea up. I will explain it all to you later when we are alone. I promise.' She moved towards the table, but his hand stopped her.

'My love. Do not fret about our sweet, Mistress, because no harm will befall, her with us to look out for her.' He drew her close, and their lips brushed. 'Just to see you, makes my heart sing,' he murmured. He picked, the tray up from the table and handed it to her. Her face aglow, she quietly left the room.

Once back in the big hall, she placed the tray onto the table. 'Here, my lovely, it's nice and hot. I made it fresh for you.'

Isobel smiled, but refused the offered cakes.

Edward, seated with his toys on the rug, clambered up and begged. 'Can I please have one?'

'Yes of course you may.' Alice declared, as he settled at the table. 'Here you are, little one.' The plate placed before him, she ruffled his dark hair, and his giggles filled the air.

Isobel blurted. 'When I went for my walk just now, Alice, I saw a man who was high, up on the big hill; he was astride a horse.'

'Oh, Miss, could you see who it was?'

'No. I felt. I thought, it might...it might have been Dune.' She looked at the girl. 'If it was, what will he think about my baby?'

'Dear, dear one. Anyone who knows you, knows, you are good through and through. And your heart is pure, pure in every way. If the man you saw was him, he knows this to be true, so true.' She took her hand. 'Dear Isobel. No one could ever, ever say a bad word about you. You are the most caring, kind person I know.'

Isobel smiled. 'Oh, my dear sister, you are so sweet.' They laughed and drank the tea.

'I am really tired, Alice.' Isobel said.

The girl pulled the cord, and they waited for the young maid to come and take the tray and Edward back to the kitchen.

'Come on, Miss, let's get you up to your chambers, so you can have a well needed rest.'

'Alice helped, her climb the stairs, and, once in her room, she removed some clothing and was helped over to the bed.

'Ah, that's better, I just hope I can have a little sleep.'

'Yes, hopefully, the baby will lay quiet for a while, for you.'

Isobel, settled back, and was in asleep in no time.

Alice arranged for the young maid to sit with the Mistress, while she slept. On the understanding that, if Miss Isobel woke, she was to pull the cord and Florence would come straight up to the room.

With the mistress settled, Alice quickly returned to her own room. She pulled on strong laced, boots, wrapped a thick, long, grey wool cape about her body, then, opened, her door quietly. She hurried out, and down the stairs, she took one of the lanterns from the porch, then she, silently left through the main entrance.

The bright, light was tightly, gripped in her hand, while it guided her safely along the icy stones under foot. The wind was bitter, has it whipped through her body. She made her way to the back of the house, and the bushes at the bottom of the hill.

It was not quite dark, and to keep warm, she walked up, and down as fresh snow fell.

She pulled the cape tighter about her, and the raw coldness made her shiver. A sudden noise caused the birds nestled close by to fly out and away.

'I know you're there, Dune O'Malley.' Alice declared. 'Show yourself!' The coldness took her breath from her.

'No, no, my dear. It's me. Ben.'

She turned and fell, into his welcoming arms. 'Ben, what are you doing here?'

'I saw you leave, so I followed.' He took the lantern from her hand, and placed it onto the ground, and the large grey blanket, she saw over his shoulder, he wrapped tight about her cold body.

Suddenly, the whimper of a horse broke the eerie silence as it neared them, and the person beside the creature, they saw, was covered in snow. Ben picked up the light and held it high, and Alice's big sigh was lost in the wind as Dune halted in front of them.

Hands on his hips, the handsome devil whispered. 'Alice. Alice me darling, how might you be on this bitterly, bitter cold night?'

'Dune, Dune O'Mallery,' she declared. 'Why, oh, why, did you have to come back now?'

'Will you not, come and give me a big hug, then girl? He laughed.

'No, you keep your distance.' Her voice quivered, and she looked at the man next to her.

'This be our Ben. He be the estate manager. He and his sister, Florrie, treat my Lady, wonderfully, with their care and love.'

The two men shook hands, and Ben said. 'Quick, let's get in some shelter, follow me.' He took Alice's hand, and guided her to an extremely, well-hidden outhouse.

'Ah that's much better,' the girl said as she watched the door close behind Dune, who had brought his horse into the dry as well. She turned to Ben. 'This is a big place, what was it used for?'

'I know not, but I remembered it was close by.' He smiled.

'Dune, was it you, Miss Isobel, saw up on the hill earlier?' Alice asked.

'No. No, my lovely, it be one of our group. He needed to look for somewhere to camp.'

'Aye, but you cannot be here,' Ben declared. 'This be much too near to the house, and the, master, he must never find any of you here on his return. He vowed, after the last time, he would run his sword through the next gypsy he sets eyes on.'

'He did and would.' Alice agreed. 'Also, you will put my, Lady, into so much danger, plus the disgrace if it is known, who you seek out.' She looked at his handsome face. 'When you left her the last time, Miss Isobel was inconsolable for weeks and weeks, she missed you so much.' Alice shivered; she was so cold. 'But, when she found she was again with child, she vowed this time to protect it while it was within her. Consequently, she has been quite content, because she has the wee one's, arrival to look forward to.' She wiped her eyes. Dune, his face serious nodded in agreement.

'It is almost her time now.' Alice continued. 'And if anything should happen, to endanger her baby now, I truly fear it will finish her.'

Dune walked over and took her into the comfort of his arms. 'You have always been a good friend to my true love, and I know your love for her is has strong as mine.' He kissed her hair then, returned to stand next to Ben.

'But nevertheless, she is still very miserable, and

197

unhappy. But the wee one does give her new hope, because as a Mother, she prays the love she gives to the child, she will receive back, and that he or she, will be beside her for a great deal of time.'

'My word, dear Alice, I would never do anything that could bring my Isobel any harm.'

'No. No, I know you wouldn't, but when she saw the man, it frightened her. She thought it was you, and because she is so near her time, she feared about your thoughts on her condition.' The girl looked at him hard. 'You see Dune, the man she was made to wed is absolutely evil, and repulsive, and we all hate him with a vengeance.'

A silence followed, then Ben asked. 'Are you here alone?'

'No, there's several small groups of us, but please do not worry, for we'll keep as far away from the house as possible, and definitely out of sight.'

'Where is your camp?' Ben asked.

'It's way over the hills.'

Ben nodded. 'I see, well if you ride, over the two double hills, at the bottom of the last one, there are many big outhouses like this. In them you can light fires, or light them outside, because that area, does not lead to any place, so no one ever rides that way. There you will all be safe.'

'I thank you Ben, this is good news for my folk. Because a great deal of them, hate to be inside any buildings, no matter the weather. But I'll away and find the glasshouses as soon as I can.' Dune took hold of the girl's hand. 'I will keep my distance, until well after the birth. And I'll await you or my beloved to seek me out when ready. This I promise.' He smiled and kissed her hand. 'Also, dear Alice. I know very well, just how these, Masters treat women, whether it be their wives, Mistress's, or women in their kitchens. I truly know what these men can do and get away with.'

Alice leaned forward and planted a kiss on his cheek. 'Thank you, dear Dune. Thank you very much. We must keep Miss Isobel safe at all times.'

'Absolutely. Absolutely.'

'But tell me, when did you get back here from Ireland?'

'Just three days ago, but the weather has been so terrible, I stayed at the camp.'

'Oh, I see. Well, I better get back to Isobel, she was asleep when I left, so I best leave.'

Outside in the snow, the men shook hands once more, and Alice, snuggled close to her man watched the gypsy with his horse close by him, disappear from their view. Then, hand in hand they quickly returned to the warmth of the big house.

Chapter Twenty-Five

Isobel was extremely uncomfortable, and all she could do was cat nap. A sudden sharp pain in her abdomen woke her. She saw it was now night, and tried to stand, but it was not possible.

Alice now back in her room, stood and walked towards the bed.

'Isobel, what is it? Is it the baby?'

'I'm not sure, can you please pull the cord I need Florence. Hopefully, she may know what it is that ails me.' But, by the time the door opened, and the woman rushed in towards them, Isobel's painful contractions were for all to see.

'Oh Florrie, do you think the baby is ready to be born?' Alice whispered.

Isobel cried out, has another sharp pain racked through her.

'I'm not sure, but my brother must go and seek, the old woman out just in case. Because   I fear it be too soon, for the little one to come.'

'I'll go and find him.' Alice whispered. 'Please, stay with the Mistress.'

The woman smiled as she watched the girl hurry from the room. Florence squeezed out the cloth from the tepid water and wiped the sweat that oozed from Isobel's face and neck.

'When did the sharp, pains begin my Lady?' She queried.

'I have had twinges, on and off for the last few days, but today they have been more severe. But, Florrie, the old woman said my little one would be born, in February, or possibly March, and it's only just the end of January.'

'Babies sometimes decide they want to be with their mama's much sooner.' She smiled and looked towards the door as it opened, and Alice, quietly slipped back into the room.

'I asked the kitchen staff to keep constant hot water ready in the laundry room, and the linen and towels, we boiled and stored away, are ready for our use, just in case.'

'Did you find Ben, Alice?'

'Yes, he left straight away, I just pray he finds her.'

Florrie looked at Isobel as a pain caused her to throw her body from side to side. 'Yes, dear, I feel the baby is definitely on its way.' She whispered.

The contractions became more frequent, and while both prayed for Ben's quick return, the two of them did what they could, to help make Isobel, comfortable. Many hours passed, and when he did finally appear, thankfully, the elderly lady was with him.

She immediately took over in the well- lit room, and with the fire built high in the grate, the woman began to deliver Isobel's first child.

The long labour continued, and still no baby arrived. She gave her patient quite a few mouthfuls of the sedative herb, which at times allowed Isobel to lie quiet and still. But as the sweat poured from her, the desperate need to bear down took hold. Although the voice she heard in the distance, repeatedly asked, 'no, no, not yet, my Lady, please do not push.'

Alas, the sudden urge, out of her control, and overwhelmed by the pain that thrust down through her body, a loud scream filled the room. Then mercifully complete oblivion took her.

The only sound that broke the deep, silence was from the fire as it roared upwards to the chimney. Florence, and Alice, worked quietly as they washed and cleared the blood -soaked sheets, from beneath where their Lady had lain. Isobel, weak and exhausted from the hard, long labour, with the help of the sedative herb, was finally in a peaceful sleep.

Through their tears, both women looked towards the cushion, where their Mistress's stillborn son wrapped in clean linen, rested.

'I cannot bear to think what this will do to our dear sweet, Miss, Isobel, now.' Alice cried. 'I fear this terrible loss she will never recover from.'

Florence nodded in agreement and wiped her eyes.

The old woman seated by the fire, stood, and walked to where the lifeless bundle lay.

She carefully gathered the child to her breast and muttered. 'Ben, when he comes to find me, I just return from a birth, but the Mother, just a wee girl herself, did not live.'

She looked at the women. 'Cause, now with no Mama, the new- born needs a Mother's milk and warmth.'

Alice wiped hcr eyes and stared at her. 'Where...was...this...and what's happened to the...little one?' She whispered.

'I say no more. Decide quickly, speak to Ben, and if it be yes. I take him with me.'

She carefully placed the child back onto the cushion and returned to the rocker.

'Oh.' She looked across at them again. 'Do not concern yourselves over the Mistress, the herbs as you know, will heal her, plus allow her to sleep for a great length of time.' She smiled, which was something she rarely did.

The two bereft women hurried from the room and down to the kitchen, where they found Ben seated near the fire with a small tankard of ale in his hand. He stood as they entered, and the terrible news brought tears to his eyes. 'Oh no. But, yes, you are right, Alice.' He sighed and shook his head. 'This will surely finish out beautiful, Mistress.'

They told him of the old woman words, he dropped back into his seat, and stared up at them both.

'Well, what must we do then. Florence?' He muttered. 'We have to make a decision.'

'No, no.' Alice sobbed, as he stood and took her into the comfort of his arms. 'No, we cannot do this. What if... what if Miss, Isobel, ever found out the awful truth, she would never forgive me, forgive us. We are all she has now. We are her family.'

'Yes dear, I know.' Florence answered. 'But I know how I felt when I lost my little one. True it was my husband as well, but the loss of the baby, well I cannot explain how it makes you feel.' She took the girl from her brother's arms. 'Our sweet Lady needs to wake and find she has a child, and the old woman can give her that. Wants to give her that. And most importantly as well, the little one needs to be nursed, and fed on a Mother's milk.' She kissed Alice's forehead, then looked into her eyes. 'If you allow this deed to happen, it will be purely for the Mistress's happiness, and welfare, for that is our only concern.' She smiled. 'Plus, there is the child. You know our Miss, Isobel, would take the wee one into her bosom without a care.'

'Yes. Yes, she certainly would do that. Look, how she loves young Edward.' Alice whispered.

The woman smiled and hugged her. 'Believe me when I say, for many years now, the old lady has carried out many, different acts to help people. It is also well known she never tells of any.' Florrie wiped the girl's eyes. 'And' she continued. 'Every secret charged to her, she has declared, will go to the grave with her.' The woman smiled, then continued. 'Yes, the herbal woman can be trusted, and on her many visits here, over the last few years, her admiration for our Lady, has grown, and it be there for all to see.'

The decision made, they walked from the kitchen, and made their way back up the stairs. Thirty minutes later, Ben and the old lady quietly left the room, and disappeared out into the bitter black night.

It was in the small hours, when the house was still and silent, that Florence opened the bedroom door to Ben's rapid knock.

'Come we must go quickly.' He murmured to Alice, who, stood over the tiny, covered bundle, was hesitant to pick him up.

'Here let me.' He moved towards her.

'*No, no.*' She looked towards the bed and continued in a whisper. 'Sorry Ben. I will carry him. She lifted the blanket carefully, and tucked it beneath her shawl, and total silence filled the room as she followed him out into the hallway.

He manoeuvred her towards the corridor on the left. They moved slowly, and Ben held the lantern high to allow the light to guide them through the pitch blackness of the long passageway.

He suddenly came to an abrupt halt in front of a thick wall carpet, and Alice watched as he pulled the heavy brocade to one side to reveal a strong, metal door, for which he produced a key. It was hard to turn, and he cursed as he tried to open it. Then suddenly it moved the lock and the door opened.

'There be a great deal of stairs that turn down and around to the flagged floor below, so make sure you hold the rail tight.'

'Yes, I will Ben, thank you.' She smiled and gave him her hand. He carefully guided her through the opening onto the small platform, she sighed, and stood very still. He let the rug slip back and secured the door.

With the bundle held tight against her, and her free hand on the slimy rail, she carefully descended the round, wrought iron staircase. Curtains of musty damp, mildew clung to the walls, and the stench air caused Alice to heave.

'Oh, Ben, the smell makes me feel so queasy.'

'Aye, this place has not been used for years, it be locked up tight all the time now.

Many years back it was a smugglers haven.' His feet at last on solid ground, he turned to help her down the last few steps. 'Stay here don't move, these stones be very wet and slippery.'

She nodded, as he turned to rest the lamp onto the wide shelf above an extremely small door. His hand retrieved another rusty key, but ironically, this one turned quite easily, but one of the top bolts refused to budge, eventually freed, gusts of cold air lashed in towards them.

The old herbal lady shuffled in. The tall man, who bent himself in half to enter, close on her heels, was Dune.

Not one word was spoken, and silent tears fell, as Alice handed the mistress's tiny, lifeless son to an elderly, gypsy, lady. But the deadly silence was suddenly broken as the discoloured cloth, produced from beneath Dune's long coat moved, and started to cry.

He lifted the bundle to his lips and kissed it, and Alice, witnessed his tears as he held the little one out for her to take.

The deed finished, cold air swept in as the trio, vanished back out into the bitterness of the night, and not one word had been uttered. The door locked, and secured, Ben walked carefully behind his love, while they slowly returned up the stairwell.

The warmth, from the baby snuggled tight to her chest, made Alice smile.

Glad to finally be back in the passage- way, she carefully removed the little one from beneath her cape and, hurried towards her Mistress's chamber.

Before she entered, the girl opened the cloth, and looked down at the tiny face, and tears threatened as she saw the dark, eyes that stared back at her. 'Look, Ben, the baby has put its tiny hand to its mouth to suck upon.'

'Aye.' He said as he lifted her chin upwards for his kiss, then he quietly, descended the stairs and was gone.

Florence walked over to the bed and smiled, Miss Isobel is much cooler, this be a good sign. Well need to wean her from the herb, because the baby needs to be fed from the milk, she will soon have.'

'Florrie, the little one, be quite fair for a gypsy's child.'

She looked towards the crib near the fire. 'Hush, careful, no one must hear. Why do you think a young gypsy girl mothered her?'

'Well, because I told you it was Dune, who gave her to me. I thought she must have been born from one of his own.'

Florrie walked towards her. 'No sweet girl, this little beauty is our dear, Miss Isobel's daughter, and we never speak again of that terrible night.'

The baby's tiny hand went up to her little mouth, and they both smiled.

'I can't believe how contented the wee one is or, how she sucks upon her tiny fist.'

'No neither can I.' Florence declared, as she reached into the crib to pick the bathed, bright eyed bundle up into her arms. 'Also, sweet one.' She continued, 'to have been born for two days, and not yet had your mama's milk, you be so calm.' She walked towards the table and sat down.

'I know not what, babies need.'

'Well, my dear, I will tell you this, once this beautiful little one, has sucked the Mistress's milk, she will scream the house down, when ready for the next, and the many more, feeds that will follow.'

Mesmerized, the girl watched, Florence, spoon, tiny drops of tepid cow's milk into the eager tiny mouth.

Chapter Twenty-Six

Lanterns lit the darkened room, and a fire burnt high in the grate. Isobel her body still very painful, opened her eyes.

'At last sleepy head, we thought you were going to sleep forever.' Alice declared.

'I heard a baby cry.'

'Of course, you did my lovely, your beautiful, daughter is extremely hungry.'

'My, did... you... say daughter?'

'I did, Miss Isobel, you have a beautiful, tiny daughter.'

Alice helped her to sit, and with the pillows propped behind her, and a warm, shawl wrapped about her shoulders, Isobel, watched her walk towards the fire, where the wooden crib, Ben had lovingly made stood.

A cry left her, as Alice collect the small bundle up into her arms, and slowly returned towards the bed.

Tears gathered, and the lump in her throat made it hard to swallow, but as the pure white blanket was carefully put into her eager arms, Isobel let them fall freely.

The baby she held was perfect, and she smiled as the tiny arms suddenly splayed upwards. She tenderly grasped, her two tiny hands and drew them tight within her chest. Never had she known or felt such joy. Emerald eyes feasted on her daughter's beautiful face, and she lifted each tiny, finger to her mouth. 'My beautiful one.' She crooned. 'I will love and cherish you always.'

Isobel absorbed completely in her own happiness, never noticed Alice walk to the other side of the room to hide her flood of tears. She stood by the window and stared out at the torrential rain as it fell from the thick, grey sky. 'Please, this guilt. Please, dear, Lord let me be rid of it.' She silently asked.

'Oh, Alice is she not wonderful? And she is your niece.' Isobel declared as the girl walked back towards her.

'Indeed, she is gorgeous, just like you, her precious, Mama.' The girl's lips trembled as she wiped her eyes.

'Tell me what happened. I can only remember the terrible pain, but not much about her birth.'

'Ben fetched the old herbal woman, and she tended you very well, also you have slept for almost two days since baby arrived.' The girl pulled the cord. 'Florrie said she will show you how to feed her, she can get very hungry.' Alice smiled, and stated, as she looked at the beautiful, dark eyed baby, held safely in her mama's arms.

Florence knocked, entered quickly, and smiled as she moved towards Mother and child.

'Oh your, Ladyship. Is she not the most adorable little one you have ever seen?' Overwhelmed, the woman kissed her mistress's hand.

'While you tend to your daughter, I'll go and get you some tea, and food, you must be hungry Isobel?'

'Yes please, Alice. I am and very thirsty.'

The girl smiled but stood to watch as the woman lifted the little one up to one of the Isobel's breast. The tiny head moved rapidly from side to side, then, suddenly it remained very still, and the noise as she sucked the milk, broke the intense silence of the room.

All three women laughed through their happy tears. But it was the sight of the tiny pink, fist under her chin, while she fed, and looked up into the joyful eyes of her mama, that confirmed to Alice. The right decision had been made.

Ben seated at the kitchen table stood, and opened his arms, and Alice walked straight into the comfort of them.

'Oh, dearest, I am so exhausted. She muttered against his shoulder.

'I know my love, you must be, and my sister Florrie also.' He kissed her forehead, and she snuggled in and let her tears fall freely.

'Oh, my love. I have never seen my sweet, Miss Isobel, so happy. Her joy when she held the wee one for the first time, was wonderful to see.' Alice looked into his eyes. 'After what I have just witnessed, I know for sure we did the right thing for her.'

'My dear sweet, girl, we did, and as Florrie says, it must remain our secret.' He turned her to face him. 'Promise me you'll forget it all, all of it.'

She whispered. 'I promise.'

He lifted her chin, and her lips trembled beneath his long, tender kiss. Eventually released from his hold, he continued. 'It was a complete hell, hole here before you and the Mistress arrived, and between us all we have achieved so much.'

He poured tea into a cup and Alice sat and sipped it.

'Now with the little one's arrival, she will bring much happiness back into this big old house.'

'Yes. She certainly will.' Alice agreed.

Ben knelt, pulled her close and kissed her hair, but she never heard his silent prayer. That Belington, never learnt, of what was entrusted to the three of them now.

'I must make some fresh tea for the Mistress.' Alice reluctantly left his arms and walked towards the range.

'Aye, and I need to away and milk the cows. I'll see thee later.' He winked and walked from the room.

Alice extremely tired, called one of the young kitchen maids to take the tray up to the Mistress, and seated in the rocker by the fire, she enjoyed a quiet moment. She dunked her biscuit into the steaming tea, and, sighed, as she felt the warmth from the range,

Florence looked around, everything was neat and tidy, and with her Ladyship, and the baby fast asleep, she smiled at the maid and quietly left the room.

The sight of the dear girl fast asleep in the chair, Florrie crept towards the large teapot and quietly poured a well needed cup. Curled up in front of the warmth, she looked across at the young woman who had stolen her brother's heart, and within seconds her heavy eyes closed.

Alice woke with a start and stared about her. She stretched her arms high above her head and smiled at the sleeping Florence. She eased herself from the chair and quietly moved towards the door, but her hand caught the handle of a pan, and she cringed has it crashed to the floor.

'Oh, Florence, I'm so sorry I didn't mean to wake you. You must be so very tired. When did you last sleep in your own bed?'

'I'm not sure my dear. But I needed this.' She held out the cup, yawned, and finished the cold liquid. 'Where are you off to?'

'Back upstairs, to be with Miss Isobel.'

'No need to yet, because the young maid you sent up with her tray, she be staying with her, with strict instructions to pull the cord when she wakes.

'Okay. That's good. I'll make us another fresh pot of tea then.' But before she moved towards the kettle, she bent down in front of the woman's chair.

'I want to thank you for all your help through, Miss Isobel's labour.' She reached for one of Florrie's rough hands. 'You are so like her mother. Mistress Mary.' Alice uttered.

'When my mama, suddenly passed the wonderful lady, practically brought me up. Her kindness towards me was, well, unbelievable.' She gently rubbed the hand she held and smiled into the watery blue eyes.

'Oh dear, dear child. No, it is I that should thank you. Since you and her Ladyship's arrival, you have brought so much love and happiness to me and my brother.'

'No, no Florrie, without you and my Ben here to help and guide us, I truly fear of what might have happened to the two of us.'

The woman ran her free hand, over the head that now rested on her lap. 'So young and vulnerable, you both were to have been sent away, to endure who knows what, on such a long journey.' Her voice halted, and the girl moved to look at her. Florrie took the pretty face into her hands, as she continued, 'plus all the sadness, and the terrible cruelty thrust upon our dear Lady, once here.'

They embraced each other. Alice kissed her cheek then whispered. 'I just want you to know, you are a wonderful lady, and we love you very much. And now, you sit there, while I get you your freshly made tea.'

Alice returned to Isobel's room, she thanked the young girl, who curtsied and quickly left.

Her Mistress was still sleeping, so she picked up the beautiful pink, bundle and sat in the rocker near the fire.

Isobel woke, sat herself up, and reached for her wrap, then she smiled towards Alice, and asked. 'Is the baby, okay?'

The girl stood and walked towards the bed. Isobel's eager hands took the beautiful bundle and again her tears of pure joy fell. 'Oh, Alice, dear Alice, I am so happy, is she not the most beautiful little one.'

'Dear Isobel, yes indeed she is, a real beauty.' The baby opened her eyes, and her fist went straight into her tiny mouth. The girl smiled, 'she is wanting her milk again.' Alice declared. And together they managed to get the baby to Isobel's breast so she could feed again.

Florence, came to sit with Isobel and the baby, because Alice needed to go somewhere with Ben. The girl rushed into her room, wrapped up warm, then hurried down the stairs where he was waiting for her.

Outside he helped her up onto the wooden seat, wrapped the blanket about her, climbed up next to her, then they were off to see if they could find Dune.

It was now February, and still bitterly cold, and after roughly an hour they saw several campfires.

'See, that be good, because they are all well out of sight. I think they be pretty safe, where they are now.' Ben uttered.

He helped Alice down from the wagon, then hand in hand they walked towards the warmth of the glow.

The gypsies, all stood at their approach, then three broke away from the group and walked towards them.

'What do you want here,' a gruff voice enquired.

'We be sorry to turn up like this, but we are looking for Dune, Dune O'Malley. Anyone here know of him.' Ben asked.

'Why. Why, what do you want of him.' The voice was from a woman sat in a large wooden rocker close to the fire's heat.

Alice stepped forward. 'It's me, who wants to speak with him.'

The woman looked her up and down. 'And why pray do you need to speak to the lad?'

'It be for my Mistress. Mistress Isobel Belington.

A man walked towards the old woman, he bent down and

215

whispered something to her, she nodded, then looked back at Alice. 'Yes, we know of you and your Lady, can you come back tomorrow, and we will have hopefully, got word to him.'

'Oh, thank you so much, I really need to speak to him.' Alice smiled. 'Thank you.' Then she turned and walked back towards the wagon.

Ben took her arm. 'We be grateful.' He called to the men, as he helped her back up on the seat, covered her with the large rug, then walked back towards the group.

He returned, climbed up beside her, and the horses were made to trot on.

'What did you go back and say to them Ben.' Alice murmured.

'I told them to move over across the far hills, where they would find all those large glass-houses I told Dune about.'

'Ah, bless you Ben, they'll be thankful to know that.'

'Yes. But listen I will go back and see them, you only want to let Dune know, the Mistress is happy and getting well again.'

'Yes, that be it. Thank you dear.' She snuggled up to him, and without another word, they journeyed back to the house.

Chapter Twenty-Seven

Seven weeks had past, and her beautiful Mary, named after her beloved Mama, once fed, and changed would settle down and sleep. Isobel, and Alice, absolutely adored, her, as did the whole household.

She was a very contented little one who hardly ever cried, and Edward loved to sit by her crib and talk to her. Plus, he constantly thanked Isobel for his baby sister.

Isobel knew her poor body had been through the mill, but thankfully, she was now up and about, and it was the beginning of April, summer was on its way.

Today was Isobel's first day to ride since her little one's birth.

She made her way to the stables and smiled at the young lad, who had Tranquil ready for her.

She climbed up onto the box, and seated in the saddle, she smiled, and beckoned the boy closer. She held out her hand, 'I want to thank you lad, for exercising my horse while I was unable to, the boy moved nearer, he saw the sixpence in her hand.

'What is your name?' she asked.

'Bert, Mistress.'

'Well Bert, please take the money, you are a good lad, and I want you to have it.'

He bent his head. 'Mistress. I thank thee, very much.'

'No, it is I, who, thanks you. You have cared for him

really well, so thank you.' She smiled, the lad touched his hat, then he stood and watched her ride away. Isobel, the reins gripped tight, felt the sun caress her face, as she rode with great ease.

The countryside looked lovely, and signs of spring could be seen wherever you looked.

Although it was early April, the day was quite warm, and Isobel welcomed the slight breeze as she rode towards the hills.

Suddenly, she pulled the leather tight, and slowed her pace, then, she abruptly halted. Her heart pounded her chest, as her eyes stared straight ahead to rest upon another horse and rider. Tears blurred her vision, and she stayed perfectly still as the other creature moved slowly towards her. Strong, hands reached for her, and she was gently pulled across the saddle into powerful, arms, but still she never moved.

'My beautiful one,' Dune whispered, as he pulled her closer to his chest and gently cradled her. 'My darling Isobel.'

She stayed perfectly still, held close and safe to his magnificent body. Time passed, and as he continued to hold her, she eventually opened her eyes, and turned to looked up at him.

His lips descended and her heart almost stopped. He helped her down, tied the animals to a tree and laid the blanket onto the grass.

Isobel moistened, her dry lips as she pulled him down beside her, again the kiss was long as he tenderly, held her close. 'It be to soon.' He whispered. And Isobel nodded her agreement.

Neither said much, and they laid together for some time. Eventually, they both sat up, and Dune walked over to fill his tin cup with the clear water that ran by the tree. Isobel drank thirstily, then he sat again. 'You had a daughter I hear my darling?'

'Yes. Oh, yes. She is gorgeous. So beautiful I have called her Mary after my beloved Mama.'

'My love, I...I... think, that, be a wonderful name for her.'

Isobel knew the time was late, and the baby would need to be fed. 'I must get back.' She whispered more to herself as she left the rug and walked towards the stream where Dune was refilling his metal cup. He handed it to her, but she shook her head.

'My love. I must go. Will I see you tomorrow?'

'Yes, yes. And the next day, and the day after, and for evermore.' He laughed.

'Dune, I am so sorry, how is your poor father. Did he come back with you?

'No, my love, sadly he died, and I had a great deal to do after his death, because I told my clan I was moving here to be near you. And, Nana Rosa, now being here makes life a great deal easier for me.'

'She is here, your Nana, Rosa.'

'Yes, she came back with me, which I am so happy about. Now I can look after her, she is a wonderful woman, my love. I wish you could meet her.'

'Dune, who knows, perhaps one day I will.'

'Yes, hopefully, my love.'

'But darling, I am sorry about your father, but I am so happy, that your back here with me.'

They kissed, and he helped her to mount. Although they knew it was a risk, they rode side by side, until the dirt road to the stables came into view. Isobel knew he would stay back out of sight, until she had entered the stable yard.

The baby fed and settled, Isobel had a long welcome soak, then sat by the fire, she watched the flames disappear up the chimney.

The door opened and Alice accompanied by a young girl entered with several trays.

'Supper is ready my, Lady.' The young girl said with a smile. She pulled out the chair for her Mistress, then she curtsied, and quietly left the room.

'Oh, Alice this looks lovely, Florrie is such a wonderful cook isn't she, and she always seems happy about doing all the meals.'

'Yes, she's certainly a wonderful lady, and tonight she has made us a stew of lamb, with vegetables from the estate gardens.'

They ate the succulent meat, washed down with their usual glass of lemonade,

The plates and utensils returned to the kitchen, Isobel looked across at Alice, who looked like she was deep in thought, as she stared into the red flames of the fire.

'Alice.'

'Mm. Sorry. Yes, Isobel.'

'Dune, has returned, he met me in our spot today, oh, it was so good to see him, and be with him. She smiled. 'He also told me, about, when he met with you and Ben, when the snow was thick on the ground.'

'Yes, it was the day you saw the man on the horse, way up on the hill behind the house. Remember you thought it might have been him.'

'Yes. Yes, I do. It was just before Mary was Born.'

'Yes, that's' right, and yes, we did meet up again after the baby arrived.

He promised me, he'd not try to see you, until you were up and about again.'

'Oh, dear Alice, well he kept his word, because today was the first- time, I have seen him since he left for Ireland, when his father had his fall.'

'Yes, he's very, good where your concerned, Isobel, there is no way he would go against, any decision, you or I make about him. And yes, how is the poor man, hurt his back badly, didn't he?'

'Sadly, he passed.'

'Oh, Isobel, I'm so sorry, to hear that.'

'Yes, it was sad. But Dune, said he would not have wanted to live if he could not walk. He said it was very quick at the end.'

'So sad for him though Miss. So, Sad.'

'Yes. But he seems okay, he brought his Nana Rosa back

with him, and he seemed quite excited about that.' She reached for the girls' hand. 'Alice, I love him so much, so, very much.'

'I do understand how you feel, the girl replied. 'What I mean is, that since I have met, Ben, I truly know, what it feels like to have the love of a man. I just worry about you, because of who he is.'

'Yes, and I appreciate that, but one cannot help who they give their heart to.' Isobel said.

'No, with that I agree. I promise, I will do everything in my power to help you and the handsome Dune spend time together.'

'Thank you, Alice, Thank you. That means so much.'

Little Mary cried out, and Alice off her seat was instantly beside the crib. She lifted her into her arms and took her to where her mama sat.

The baby fed, changed, and settled back down, the girls huddled round the fire, because the nights in the great Manor House were extremely cold, whatever, the weather.

'Alice, when I told Dune, the baby's name today, he said he liked it and how it honours Mama.'

'Yes. That be so true, so true.'

'He also asked me, if he could find a piece of land so they can build special stables for the horses they breed. He said they are called Valour and Cobb horses.' She smiled at the girl's puzzled look. 'They are specially bred for the gypsies to use. These animals have an extraordinary, broad back, which allows them to pull their heavy homes from place to place.'

'Yes. I see. Yes, you can certainly understand why they would need such an animal to heave those, heavy caravans, from one place to another.' Alice muttered.

'Consequently, this means, he will be here, perhaps forever.'

'Yes, it all sounds wonderful, and you will have him close,' The girl smiled, 'and I'm happy for you both.'

Isobel shivered, suddenly, she felt cold. 'I must speak with Ben he will know the best part of the estate Dune will be able to use.'

Life was good, Belington had not returned since he had found out he had a daughter and had been gone for almost five months. Consequently, with Dune so close Isobel was extremely happy. Time passed, and the summer heat came in with a vengeance, sometimes, it was far too hot to move.

The part of the estate the gypsies have chosen to build their pens for the animals was almost ready for use now, and Isobel's life was wonderful, and her happiness far exceeded anything she could have ever dreamed of. With her beautiful daughter, Dune, and her new family, she never thought such happiness would be hers again.

She spent every stolen second, she could with her gypsy love, and Alice, true to her word, did all she could to help her.

Christmas arrived and the house was lit up with lots of lighted lanterns. Little Mary, now eleven months, could now walk a few steps, but she mostly wobbled and fell to the ground. It was Christmas day, and young Edward was to celebrate his seventh birthday.

The whole atmosphere was happy, as they all sat at the long table in the main hall, eating all the lovely food, washed down with lemonade, or tea.

The main door crashed back against the wall, and to Isobel's horror, Belington staggered into where they all sat.

He looked like a snowman, and it was obvious, he was frozen to the bone.

Ben stood and rushed towards the Master, and to everyone's relief he managed to get him up the stairs and into his own quarters. Bowls, of heated water, were quickly taken up, and after his warm bath, Alice informed Isobel, he was fast asleep in his own bed.

But in the late hours of the night the man fumbled into her chambers, and took her with extremely, unnecessary, force. Then to her disgust, the naked man stayed very still and fell asleep next to her.

Sick to her stomach, Isobel edged her bruised body very carefully to the end of the bed, she reached for her wrap to cover her nakedness, then stood and walked from the room. The terrible, weather, kept Belington trapped in the house for far longer than anyone wanted, all the man did was sit in the big hall, and literally drink wine, day and night. But, considering, the man was mostly drunk, he still sought Isobel's bed nightly, putting her body through sexual hell.

Also, with him around, Isobel could not meet up with Dune. There was absolutely no way they could ride together either, because of all the thick snow, scattered, everywhere. Consequently, most people had to stay indoors.

Chapter Twenty-Eight

Alice quietly in the room seeing to Mary, looked up when Isobel returned from the wet room.

'I feel quite sick this morning.' She informed her.

'Oh Mistress. Do you think you might be with child again?'

'Possibly, Alice. Possibly. Considering the amount of time Belington was here.'

This continued every morning for the rest of that week, which confirmed she was indeed, going to be a mother again. But this time, she could not be too sure who the father would be, consequently, she could no longer meet her love for fear she might lose the little one.

In the first years as Belington's wife, Isobel had suffered several miscarriages. The man never cared, what he did to her body, or, in what state he left her.

She was not sure how she felt about being with child again, but, if she were, she prayed, the baby would stay, safe within her, until it was due to be born.

'Isobel. My darling.'

She stirred and smiled. 'Dune… Dune, no what are you doing you cannot be here, he is still here. No, no, you must go.'

'No. No, my sweet, he's gone.' He pulled her close. 'Its fine. Belington has gone.'

'Dune. But how…how did you get here, and how do you

know he's gone?'

'Because, I met Ben, he told me the man had left last night, he's keeping watch for me now. He will come and tell me, should the man return.'

Isobel was in heaven. 'My love, are you really here with me?' Happiness filled her, as he pulled her tight to his body, his kiss was long, and she gladly, let him tenderly show her just how strong his love was.

Dune climbed from beneath the covers and dressed, 'where's your baby, Mary, darling?'

'She will be with Alice, sometimes she take her from her cot, down to the kitchen for her breakfast. Why, did you want to see her?'

'Well, as I was here, I did think it would be nice to see your beautiful, little one.'

'Go and hide in the bedroom because the maid will come in here.' Isobel pulled the cord, and within minutes, the girl, knocked the door.

'You rang, Madam.'

'Yes, Molly. Could you please ask Alice to bring Mary back up to the room please?' The girl curtsied and closed the door.

Alice knocked and walked in carrying the baby. Isobel held out her hands and, Mary fell into her arms, smiled, and clapped her tiny hands. The baby spotted Dune, he held out his hands, she looked a little wearily, then fell into them. The two women were speaking to each other, so Isobel never saw the loving way Dune, kissed and cuddled the little one.

'I must away now, so do you want to take your beautiful daughter back, darling.'

The baby's fingers in her mouth, she cooed, and smiled as she was returned to her mama.

Dune, ready to leave, kissed Isobel, then the little one. Alice opened the door, then, she closed it quietly behind them both.

His visits became more, and more, frequent, and Isobel was in heaven every time, he came to lay with her.

Mary was one year old and in the big hall there was a lot of activity. The table was full of jellies, there were finger sandwiches, and Florence made a lovely jam sponge. She had many gifts, and she adored her new dolly with a tiny pram to push her about in.

Life was good, and as her waist got thicker, Isobel decided to hire a nanny, and a tutor. The room just pass Alice's was now ready to become a nursery. Edward's room downstairs had been ready for his teaching for some time.

Isobel interviewed several gentlemen, but the one she chose, was possibly in his fifties.

He was nicely dressed and spoke extremely well. Plus, he had taught in a school for many years. Isobel liked him and took him on immediately. His name was, Mr Charles Turner and once he moved into his accommodation, the teaching began. And he and Edward got on from the start.

The young girl for the nanny position, Rosie, was a spinster, who had been working in London Town. But she hated the town and wanted to move to the country. She settled very well, and loved the baby, and Edward.

The months passed quickly, it was the end of May and Isobel wanted to go into Portchesterton, she needed more money. They took Edward again, and her precious Mary was also with them.

It was an enjoyable day. She brought some new toys for the baby, and Edward who loved to draw or paint, she brought paper, pencils, and paints. He was delighted and threw his arms about her. She purchased more materials, books, and some papers. Lastly, they went into the beautiful, sweet shop, situated near their lovely café, and brought several varieties of different flavour sweets, to take back home with them.

All the shopping completed they were all seated at the table in their usual café. Edward and Mary were eating a dish of ice cream, while Isobel, Alice, and Ben, had their usual pot of tea, with the lemon cake.

'My little angel, you are such a good girl.' Isobel pulled her close. 'Look at your face.' She wiped her clean, then the baby cuddled into her and fell asleep. Edward busy drawing in his big new pad of white paper, smiled at them both,

'Isobel, she is so adorable.' Alice whispered.

'Yes. I feel very blessed.'

It was time to leave, Alice collected Mary, and they all walked to where the horses and carriage waited for them. Ben helped Isobel up into the seat, then when everyone was aboard, he started the journey back.

It was quite late when they returned, Isobel was tired, and went straight to her room. But when she opened the door, Belington was sat there drinking wine.

'Ah, my dear, so you are here, where have you been?'

Oh, dear Lord, Isobel thought, he has never spoken to me like that before. So, she walked to the table, placed her bag onto it, then faced him. 'We have been to Portchesterton.' Was all she said.

'Good, you will have some more money for me, then.'

Isobel walked to the table, took a ward of notes from her bag, and held them out.

With his hat in his hands, he moved towards her. 'Thanks that will do nicely.' He walked towards the door, then turned, 'By the way, when is the baby due?'

'In July.'

The door slammed, and he was gone.

Isobel smiled, and thought of Dune, who, if Belington had left the estate, would come, and see her later.

It was very warm, and she was extremely uncomfortable, she had taken to going out into the garden in the cool of the evening. She knew her time was near, there had been some niggles, and was walking up and down, and her back ached terribly. Alice came into her room with their afternoon tea and placed the tray on the table.

'Alice, dear. I think the baby might be coming.'

'Oh, Miss you think so.'

'Yes, I have been getting a few twinges, since yesterday, but an hour ago I think it was a definite sharp pain.'

'Do you want your tea first, then I'll away, and get ready with Florrie.'

'Yes, I will have a cup of tea, but I will drink it while I walk about.'

'Yes, fine Miss. I'll get these back to the kitchen, then I shall come straight back.' Alice gave her the cup, then she gathered everything back onto the tray and quickly left. '

In the early hours of the morning, another beautiful baby girl was delivered, and Isobel named her Victoria, after the young girl, who was soon to become England's Queen. Again, she was exceedingly happy, because once more, Belington would show no interest in the new addition.

Mary, and Edward, loved their new, tiny sister, but Mary could not understand, why she could not lift the baby out of the crib to play with her.

Belington had not returned for almost two months, and Isobel's happiness was for all to see.

The baby was four weeks, and Isobel's body felt good, so she had just started to ride again. She had just left the courtyard to go and meet Dune, when a young stable lad rode out and stopped her.

'Mistress. Mistress. The Master is back, and he wants you home, Madam.'

Not too sure, she smiled and nodded. Then, she turned her horse around, and followed the young boy back to the stables. She dismounted and entered the house.

Belington was in the big hall sprawled out drinking wine, and as she entered, he screamed at her, 'more money woman, now I need it now. Go and get it.'

Isobel hurried, up the stairs and went to the drawer where it was hidden. Belington followed, and Isobel, turned and gave him the envelope.

'How much is in here?' He demanded.

Isobel could see he was quite distraught, 'There is about twenty Pounds.' She answered.

'About twenty pounds. Twenty Pounds, is that all?'

'Yes. But that's a lot of money surely.' She held her head high.

Belington grabbed her, and went completely mad, he picked up items and threw them across the room, frightened and fearful, Isobel, tried to open the door, but he lunged for her and ripped her clothes from her body. He was unmerciful, as he repeatedly raped her, and when he had finished, she was naked, and unconscious on the floor.

Alice opened the door, and, screamed as she moved towards Isobel's still body. Ben rushed in and declared. 'Dear Lord.' He knelt beside Alice, who had covered her nudity, then, he lifted the dear woman up to the bed.

'What has that evil man done to our beautiful Mistress, yet again.' He muttered.

'Ben, you must go and find the herbal lady, quickly as you can.' The girl cried.

'I'll away now. Be as quick as I can.' The door closed behind him, and Alice gently washed her Mistress, then sat and held her close to her body.

Dune concerned about Isobel not turning up to meet him,

had ventured quite near to the estate. He caught sight of Ben as he steered the cart through the large iron gates.

Without a thought Dune cut across the grass to greet him.

'I, Dune. I must go and find the herbal woman. The Mistress she be in a bad way, the Master came back, and that man has beaten her something awful. She be very hurt.'

'Where is he now Ben, this man who thinks to beat his young, beautiful wife is okay.'

'He be gone back to London, he left about half-hour ago, he did.'

'You away and find the woman, and I'll deal with this Bastard. I will kill him I surely will.' Dune rode off like the hounds of hell were after him, towards the lanes that led to London.

Chapter Twenty-Nine

The woman arrived and worked on Isobel for many hours, and in between she sat by the bed and silently muttered words.

Two days passed, and still no improvement. It was almost midnight on the fourth night when the woman stated. 'Yes.' She raised her hands then looked at Alice and Florrie. 'Yes. At last, her temperature has broken she is going to be good.' Then she sat down on the rocker, lit her clay pipe, and stared into the flames.

Dune was back at the estate, he was in the big hall, and Alice kept going down to let him know how Isobel was.

Late on the fifth day, Dune took the old woman back to where she lived, and she told him of the Mistress's horrific injuries. But she reassured him, that she would be back to normal in a few weeks. Now, all she needed was rest and care. Four weeks passed, and Isobel a great deal stronger, was sat next to the fire when Alice came into the room.

'Mistress. Dune is here, can he come and see you?'

'Yes. Yes, please.'

He walked into the room, and moved towards Isobel's chair, he knelt, took her hand, and kissed it. There was a knock, the door opened, and Alice, Ben, and Florrie, entered. Dune stood and smiled as they all found a seat.

'Good your all here. Right. What I must tell you all, is that Belington is dead.' Loud gasps filled the air, and he pulled Isobel up from her chair and held her close to his body.

'Do you remember Ben, when, I went off after the man that afternoon. You were off to find the herbal lady.'

'Ah. I do, Dune I do.'

'Well, I found him, he was so drunk, he'd fallen from his horse and his neck was broken. Although he was not dead, it gave me great, pleasure to sit on the grass next to him, and tell him about all the things, Isobel, and I had done. I never left any detail out. I sat there until he took his last breadth. Then, I mounted me horse and rode away.'   He smiled and turned, to look at Isobel. 'So, my darling, you are now free of that awful, vile man. She was shocked, and began to shake, Dune, gathered her close and tears fell, she sobbed her heart out. But they were tears of happiness, she was so happy. Happy she wanted to sing and dance, because now, she was free. Free as a bird.

The house settled down, and everyone Isobel encountered smiled at her reassuringly. Belington's body had been found, and after much paper- work it had been returned in a coffin ready for burial. Also, with no kin or a will, everything he owned, according to her solicitor was now hers. Which was the great mausoleum, being the house, and the acres and acres of land that surrounded it. The estate was extremely large, and she was not sure what she was going to do with it all.   When it was all finalised, Isobel felt sheer relief. But now he had been sent home, where was she to put him in the ground?   Isobel sent for Ben and sat by the fire in the big hall, she smiled as he approached her.

'Madame.' He bent his head.'

'Ben please sit down.'

A young maid brought coffee and biscuits, they both stayed quiet while she poured for them. Isobel offered him a short bread, but he shook his head.

'The Masters' body has been returned for burial, Ben as you know. But I have no idea of where to put him, because there is no burial ground around here, consequently, I do not know what to do.'

'Mistress. We could build a church and bury him near it.'

'Build a Church. But...where… how?'

'Miss Isobel. Here on this land, there are mines that are full of Flint stones. These stones are what men use to build cottages, and the big houses like we see in Portchesterton. I'll not, be sure, but I would think there must be money you could earn from the stones if you allowed the mines to be opened up.'

She frowned at him and, was trying to digest what he was saying.

'Open these mines. Ben, I do not understand what you speak of, please explain with more detail.'

'Mistress, sorry. Mistress, you see, these mines I speak of are all over this large estate. To open them up would be a good thing, it will give the local men work, and at the same time bring money in for you to have.'

'Really Ben. But if these mines are like you say, why did

his Lordship never open them up?'

'Because I truly- believe madam, he could not be bothered with it all. Then after many years, I believe he forgot they were even on the estate. He would have had to go out and find the men to work the mines, then their wages would have had to be found and made up weekly. And I should think, there could possibly be a lot of paperwork to do.'

'So, Ben, there is going to be a great deal for us to do, if I decide to open them up.'

'Yes, Madam. Yes, indeed. But if you do decide to do this, we could build anything you wanted to. I know many men who use these stones to build, houses, churches, and other buildings.'

She frowned. 'No, what…I mean Ben is, how would you start this kind of work you are speaking of?'

'Oh, I only have to go to the next village, to the Inn, where the men gather, I would have a group of men in no time. The Church, would be up for all to see very quickly.' Isobel, unsure about what to do, or what to think, decided to leave her answer till the morning. Ben had really given her a great deal to think about.

'Well, thank you, let me sleep on it. Come to my office about ten in the morning and I'll tell you what I have decided.' This man, she was so fond of and a couple of his men, had made another one of the smaller room's downstairs into an office for her, which Isobel loved to go and sit in. Especially on warm nights, she would rest by the

236

French doors, and take in the wonderful air. The man stood. 'Thank you, Mistress.' He bent his head and quietly walked away. Later after supper, she went along to the nursery to feed and hold her beautiful little one, and she loved to sit and watch Mary sleep. She sat with Victoria for over an hour, then she kissed them both and walked from the room. Isobel reflected over Ben's earlier conversation. She had no idea such worthy stones, could be mined on the vast land, she now owned. It would be a really good idea to open the mines to make work for all the men who wanted it. Also, any extra money would be good, because there was a great deal she wanted to do to the house, over the coming years. Plus, she could ask her Grandma, to stop giving her so much money. Yes, to open those mines would be a great thing to do. She decided to go to bed, Dune would not be back tonight, because he was away trying to sell some more horses. Isobel already knew, what her decision would be when she climbed into bed and blew her candle out. Ben knocked on the door at two minutes to ten, the next morning, his hat in his hands, he smiled as he sat opposite Isobel,

'Ben, you were right about us needing to have a church near the estate. I have really missed going to the Sunday services, so it would be nice to have one near us.

'Yes Mistress.'

'So, yes open the mines, open as many as you can. Get the men here to work them and then between us we will sort it all out. We will go in the big town so I can speak with my solicitor, who will explain, what we have to do, once the mines are up and going.'

'Yes Mistress, I will do as you ask, and get things started. And yes, I be sure your man will help you all he can.'

'Thank you, Ben, but I shall also be guided by you.'

'Mistress, he nodded. It will be my pleasure to get all this up and started for you.'

'Oh, Ben that will be wonderful, wonderful. But I want to get involved as well.'

'Yes, Mistress, once we have them all up and going, you will learn a great deal, if you wish to.'

'Good, Ben that will be good. But first I need to discuss the church with you.' She smiled. 'I was thinking the large area of ground as you come in through the wrought, iron gates is where the church could be built. If we remove those gates, it can be built there. What do you think?'

'Madam. I think it be a grand idea. It will be a perfect place for a Church. Especially now, with so many folks making their way here to live.'

'Yes. But then, I thought, we could build some small, cottages around and near the church, for the men who will do the builds, to bring their families to live in.'

'Oh Mistress. This be a wonderful idea, and hopefully, we can sell the stones to the many men who will then go off to build in different parts of Sussex.'

'Yes. Yes, Ben that will be good. Also, what I have decided is that the Master should be buried down in that aera now, so the Church can be built near to where he will be.

Because we will need to have a cemetery in the grounds.'

'Yes. Mistress a perfect idea.'

'Fine. Ben, can I leave all of this in your capable hands.'

'It will be my pleasure to get all of this going for you, Madame.'

'Good, just let me know when you want the money to start it all off.'

'Aye, Mistress, that I will. That I will.' He stood, bent his head then walked from the room.

Lord William Belington was buried, and only Ben, and a couple of farm hands new where he was laid. Then, Isobel knew it was with a happy heart, he began to start the venture with the mines. Where in time, it would benefit everyone on the estate. Isobel went along to the nursery, Mary happily playing with some toys, ran towards her and laughed as her mama picked her up, and swung her about. The little one cuddled her mama's neck, as they walked to where Victoria was asleep in her crib. Nanny sat in the rocker stood and walked towards her. 'Hello Nanny. I am taking Mary back to my room for a while.'

'Yes, Madam. I will collect her when her lunch is ready.'

'Thank you, nanny, but, when you come for Mary, would you please bring Victoria down to me for a few hours.'

'Certainly, Madam.'

'Perfect, nanny, thank you.' Isobel smiled, then they were gone. Victoria was wide awake, and was bouncing on her mama's lap, Mary would be in bed asleep by now, so it was lovely to have the baby to herself. Tired now, the baby cuddled in tight to her mama's chest, Isobel sat in the wooden rocker by the fire, moved it back and forth, and the baby cooed.

She was very blessed, she had been given two beautiful daughters, and Edward, who she loved deeply. Yes, she was indeed very blessed.

Ben had indeed been terribly busy, there were a great number of mines opened, and many men working them. And by the end of October the church was well on its way to being built. When Isobel rode down towards that part of the estate, she was shocked by all the activity going on there.

Chapter Thirty

It was Christmas again, and Edward now eight, loved his little sisters, and would often go along to the nursery to sit and play with them. The weather was awful and the work on the Church had to stop. Consequently, once again, they were all cooped up inside the house keeping warm, but all were extremely happy. This year their Christmas tree was the biggest they had ever had, and underneath the branches presents were stacked high. After a lovely day, the gifts were handed out, Mary was pleased with her bigger pram and doll dressed in a long dress and a coat, with a bonnet on her head. Edward with his white paper, books on paintings, and some new clothes was so happy. Baby Victoria had different shapes you could join, and they were in bright colours, and a rag doll.

The staff all received a gift, Alice was so happy with her new bonnet, Ben with is new Jumper, Florence loved her new slippers, so every-one was happy. Later that night alone with Dune, he gave her a bangle it was in gold, and had belonged to his mother, Isobel was in awe of it and, felt very privileged to have received it.

'It was my mother's I have treasured it for many years now, and I be please you like it so much. My sister would have been given it, but as you know she passed.'

'Yes, my darling.' And she pulled him close, then reached for the wrapped parcel next to her chair and handed it to him.

'Oh, my what have I got here.' He slowly tore at the paper, then whistled when the type of leather jacket, he always wore came into view. 'But darling this is wonderful, but how did you, have it made. Why it's simply great, I love it.'

'Dear, reliable Ben had it done for me. And yes, I was really pleased with it.' Content and happy he picked Isobel up and walked through to the bedroom.

The snow began to melt, and signs of life began to be seen everywhere. The men had started to work again, and the Church was almost built. Isobel often rode that way and, was extremely pleased with the way it was all coming together.

Ben told Isobel of a preacher he had heard of in the next village, so she rode over there with him to seek him out. The man was short, overweight, but had a pleasant face, and seemed really, nice. When told about the new Church, he said he would be only to pleased, to come and seek it out.

It was a large building put together with all the flint stone, and inside an alter had been made of wood, with a cloth cover. There was a wooden stand for the bibles to be placed on, and there were rows and rows of wooden seats for people to sit on. Isobel felt the Church had been built with a great deal of care. The Vicar as promised came with Ben in the horse and cart, he loved what he saw, and said he was looking forward to taking the service on Sunday. The holy day dawned, and the whole household turned out in their Sunday best, and happily made their way up the long, snaking, path that led to the new building. It was wonderful, and Isobel thanked God for all she now had. The service was perfect, and the man, truly, was a man of God.After the service, there were a few tables and chairs, for people to sit on, to drink lemonade, and eat biscuits. This was if they wanted to, wanted to, it seemed like everyone, desired to stay back for the refreshments.

Consequently Isobel, decided something more permanent, would have to be arranged for future Sundays. The vicar was enthralled with it all so much, he wanted to stay and become their permanent priest, which meant he too would need his own cottage eventually.

Isobel, sitting in the garden, smiled as Alice approached with the tray of teas, and biscuits.

'You should let one of the maids bring that out for us dear.'

'Oh, I really do not mind, I find it hard sometimes not working for you as I always did.' They laughed, drank the liquid, and enjoyed the fresh air.

'Alice, apparently, I must charge rent to the folks who move into the cottages.'

'Oh, really.'

'Yes, but I have told Ben, no, I will not do that. But he said, you must, because they are your houses, and people must pay a certain amount of money to live in them. He said it was the law of the land.'

'Well, I know this to be true. Florence told me that, she

and Ben used to pay rent to his Lordship years ago. But then, suddenly, the man who collected the money, just stopped calling on them for it. That's quite weird, do you not think.'

'Indeed, I do, very strange. I told Ben no, because I do not need it. But he insisted, I must because, I will be their landlord, and landlords are given rent money.'

'Well, if that is what's supposed to happen, you must Isobel, but you can charge perhaps just a small amount of cash.'

'Yes, that is what I shall do, then, I am doing the right thing.' They finished their tea, Alice stood to collect the tray, but she suddenly stopped, and put it back onto the table. 'Miss, I have... mm...' Alice, stuttered.

'Yes, Alice.'

'Mm...

'What are you trying to tell me?' Silence followed. 'Alice are you alright my dear. Are you well?'

'Oh yes, dear Isobel. It's just that, mmm...I...Oh. Ben has asked me to marry him, and I... I don't know what to tell him I...'

'Alice. Dear Alice, what wonderful news, wonderful. Yes of course you must marry him. Anyone can see how much you both love each other. Yes. Yes, my dear you both have my hearty blessings.'

'Oh Isobel. Thank you so much.'

Both stood and embraced. 'My dear, dear sister, I am so happy for you, so very -happy for you both.' Isobel felt the tears run down her face as she watched her lift the tray and walk back towards the open French doors.

Isobel was truly- happy for Alice, but she herself could not think of marriage yet, also she was not sure of what Dune's thoughts about a wedding would be.

There was great excitement about the forthcoming wedding and plenty to do. They all went into the big town, and material for the wedding dress, and bridesmaids was brought. Edward was to have a new suit, and more paper and paints were purchased towards his already growing collection. Isobel spent a great deal of money and, was pleased when she eventually arrived home with all her goods.

It was the end of May, and the day dawned, the weather was perfect, the sky was as blue as blue, the sun shone. The wedding breakfast was to be held in the big hall, with several more tables and chairs added for the extra guests. Mary and Edward were so excited, she was to be the flower girl, and she loved her pale cream dress, which matched her mamas. Edward in his light, blue double breasted, reefer jacket, his long trousers, with his dark blue buckled shoes, thought himself most handsome. There was much bustling and laughter as the young maids helped Alice to dress.

Isobel was a picture of beauty in her long off the shoulder dress, which was made differently from the bridal gown. She would walk down the aisle with her sister and take the flowers when needed.

Everything was ready, and one of the stable lads was to sit up on top of the carriage to take the wedding party to the church. Isobel walked into Alice's room and tears fell. 'Oh, dear, dear, one, you look so beautiful.' Her long, flaring dress, with a long vail that covered her face, had all been a gift from Isobel.

'Oh, dear sister, you are such a wonderful person, I cannot thank you enough.' And she smiled radiantly. Isobel smiled and took her hands. 'You dear Alice, have been by my side through thick and thin all my life. You are a strong wonderful person, and I love you very much, and you are of my blood, and I thank God, for you.'

'Yes, but it is me who is so lucky to have you as my sister, for which I to thank the Lord, also.' They hugged and laughed. Then, it was time for the bridal party to leave for the church.   Dune was Ben's best man, and has Isobel walked towards the men she thought how beautiful he looked in his chosen outfit. His brown leather trousers, his pure white shirt that bellowed about him, his brown knee length boots, her heart threatened to stop. How she loved this man.   The whole household, dressed in their best cloths filled the church, and there were quite a few gypsies, which Ben had become good friends with, sitting in the pews.   The preacher was so happy about the wedding, and as they slowly moved towards the alter, Ben's love for Alice was there for all to see.   The Church was full of happiness, and halfway through, baby Victoria cried for her mama, Nanny who held her, quietly, stood and walked to the entrance to take her outside. The service over, everyone outside in the fresh air, were laughing, dancing, and making merry. Soon it was time to return to the house where the grand party was to be held. The food was delicious, and the merry making went on till the small hours of the morning. There were many gypsies still there in the grounds, really enjoying themselves. Dune took Isobel's hand, and walked her towards a small group who were sitting on the ground, singing some of their old folk songs.

He spoke to them and silence prevailed. Dune took her arm, then he steered her towards the woman sitting in an extremely large wooden rocker chair, he lent down and kissed her head. Then he turned to Isobel, pulled closer to his body, he said. 'Darling this is my Nana Rosa.' Isobel looked at the beautiful face of the elderly lady, and, smiled. Her skin was so good, her thick hair was pulled from her face, and her black eyes twinkled. She was dressed in a long black dress, with a lovely colourful shawl about her shoulders. She was an extremely attractive lady, and Isobel was so please to greet her.

'I am so, happy to meet you at last madam.' Isobel stammered.

'No, no, it is I who be pleased to finally meet the lass who as stolen my Dune's heart, and my what a beauty you be Miss Isobel.' The lady smiled and reached for her hand. 'Yes. Yes, you are a good person, you have a big heart, and you are a loving and caring lady. This is all good for my boy.'

'Oh, yes. I have loved him since I was really small.' She whispered as Dune pulled her closer to his body. Suddenly another wooden chair appeared, and they sat with the group for quite a while. But Isobel was tired, it had been a long day, also Victoria might need to be fed. Goodbyes were said, and Rosa took her hand again. 'Bless you dear one and your life will only get better now that evil man is no longer with you. Rosa kissed it, then uttered. 'Till we meet again my dear.' Dune bent to kiss his grandma once again, then his hand around Isobel's waist they quietly walked from the group towards the house.

Chapter Thirty-One

Cottages were springing up all round the church area, some were even being built on the land near Florences. Life, and people were everywhere to be seen. But this was all going on far beyond the estate gates.

Alice and Ben were offered Florrie's cottage. It had been arranged to be stripped out, painted and new furniture would be placed inside. Florence now semi-retired was to move into the big house and have the suite of rooms that had been set aside for the Master. The man had never used them, but a new bed arrived, and several other pieces of furniture for her use, and the lady was overjoyed by her Mistress's kindness. Alice was sad, she didn't want to move from the house, she wanted to be near Isobel. Arm in arm, they had gone for a walk, it was the end of June, and the day was perfect. The girl smiled. 'Doesn't everything look lovely at this time of year.'

'It certainly does my dear. But tell me, you have been married to Ben for six weeks, what's it like being a wife to him?'

'Wonderful. Wonderful. He is a special man, my dear husband.'

'He certainly is, what he has done for us over almost five years has been so, so great. We would not be where we are today without all his help and doing.'

'Yes, dear sister you are right.' They stopped, Alice laid

the blanket she held onto the ground, and both sat down. 'Isobel.'

'Mm… oh, sorry. Yes dear.'

'I do not want to move into the cottage, I need to stay with you.' The girl smiled and took her hand.

'You do not want to live on your own in Florrie's cottage?'

'No. No I do not. Because I want to be with you, we have never been parted, and if I live up there, no, no, please dear Isobel let us stay where we are. I want to be near you always.'

'But, yes of course you can stay. I was just thinking of you and Ben, but if your chambers are where you want to live, that is absolutely fine with me.' They hugged and kissed each other's cheek.   It was decided that the priest would move into the cottage once it had been painted, and everyone was happy.

Dune, Isobel, and Ben rode out to the area where many mines were being worked. She could not believe how many there were, or the amount, of men needed to work them. Plus, the piece of land, they were all on was extremely large, and they were jotted everywhere.

'Gosh.' Isobel stated. 'Look at all the activity, I never thought the mines would be as busy as this.' '

'Yes. Also, Miss, this is one of many, you have areas like this all over the estate, and all are busy working mines.' Ben added.

'Really. Well, what am I to do with them all?'

'Your, going to let them work for you and there'll keep you in money for years. Ben told me this. Is that not right, my friend?'

'Indeed, it is, Dune.' Isobel smiled at the men, then stated, 'Okay, good, fine then that is what we will do. But now if we are finished Ben, I think I would like to go for a long ride. Tranquil has not been on a long run for ages.'

'Yes, Mistress, of course I can manage here.' He bent his head and rode off.' Dune looked at her then asked, 'who pays the men for you Isobel?'

'Ben does, he puts the money in sacks then rides off to pay everyone.'

'Do you pay them weekly or every two weeks?'

'Weekly. Why do you ask?'

'Well, do you think some of my kin folk could come along to work the mines. It will help them to make roots, because the majority wish to settle here, especially now you have let us move all our horses into that double field. The amount of space we have is perfect.' He smiled. 'And you allow me to stay with you every day and night, which is wonderful my love.' He lent forward and kissed her hard on the lips.

'Why, yes of course, they can, and we build more cottages for them, do you think they would like that Dune?'

'Yes, I am sure some might like to live in brick-built homes, although, it will be strange.' Dune leaned forward and kissed her, 'come my sweet, lets' go to our favourite spot.' She laughed, and shouted, 'race you.' Isobel eased

Tranquil forward, then both horses took off as if the bats from hell were after them. They arrived but the day was cold, and the wind was biting. It would be too cold to stay there, so they rode towards the nearest glass houses.

'Oh, no darling, being November, it will be much warmer back at home, it has become much colder since this morning. Come on let's go back.' She leaned over, and his kiss and caress melted her.

On, their return, they sat in the hall and drank tea, then they went to their rooms for their supper, then bed. Snow fell, day and night, there was no let-up in it, this trapped everyone inside the house, and work in all the mines ceased. It was one of the worst winters, Isobel had experienced since her arrival in Sussex. Consequently, Dune, and Isobel spent a great amount of time with the girls, and Edward.

'Dune,' Isobel laughed the baby is trying to climb up your leg.' He laughed and pulled her up into his arms. Victoria gurgled and clapped her hands, and Mary ran towards him, he reached for her, and she smiled as he fell back onto the chair and laughed. He sat one on each knee, moved his legs up and down. 'I be doing a jig.' He whispered. The girls giggled and clapped their hands, Mary kissed his cheek, and the baby copied her. 'Well thank you, dear ones.' He declared as his kissed them both back. Victoria and Mary had been with their Mama, and papa, for a couple of hours, and they were having great fun. Eventually Nanny came for them, it was bath and super time. Dune offered to carry Mary back to the nursery, and before he left, he pulled her tighter to his body, and kissed her head, then he carefully placed her feet onto the floor, smiled, then quietly walked from the room.

'Isobel, my people are so happy, and grateful, for all the glass houses they have been able to use during this terrible snow, and cold winter. You have been so kind and caring towards them, and I am forever grateful to you for this.'

'Darling, no it is my pleasure to help them out, not even poor creatures should be out in the bitterness outside. But tell me how is your Nana Rosa? Is she keeping well, and where is she staying?'

'Oh, yes she is good, she is inside one of the largest glass houses out there, she is well looked after, but thank you for asking, darling.'

'Dune, you know she could always come here to the big house, we have so many rooms, you only have to say my love.' He pulled her close to his body, and in front of the fire's warmth, he took her to their special place. Later, Dune did some paperwork and Isobel read her book. They retired and held in his arms Isobel slept almost instantly.

Days and weeks passed, then at the end of March the sun began to shine, and more and more people ventured outside. Work in the mines had started towards the end of February so normal life was resuming.

Sat by the open French doors in her study, Isobel smiled when Alice entered with a maid. They both moved towards her, Molly put the tray onto the table, curtsied, then quietly left.

'Do you know dear, we have been here five years next month, and hasn't an awful lot happened to us both.'

'Indeed, it has.' The girl smiled as she handed Isobel her coffee. 'You have three beautiful children, the love of Dune, and I have my Ben.' Alice sighed. 'We are so lucky Isobel, so lucky.'

'Yes, how true. We are blessed, so blessed. Edward is now ten years; Mary is three and baby Victoria is 16 months. You are wed to our dear Ben, and Dune is here all the time. Yes, with Mama gone, my sister in the church, to have you as my sister is a blessing. Your care of me through the years, has been something I have always treasured, dear Alice.'

'I have always loved to be with you, to serve you my dearest. I have been so lucky, your wonderful mama looked after me so well, and you have given me a perfect life here. Also, dear Isobel I am with child.' She left her chair and quickly reached her side. 'Alice, wonderful, wonderful. I am so happy for you and Ben.' And they hugged each other tightly. 'When do you think the baby will arrive?'

'I think possibly September.

A township about ten miles from the estate had begun to grow, because the village was getting larger. The ground around the Church had become, a small Hamlet, and nothing else was to be built on or near it. It was decided to put a new, high stoned, brick wall completely around the estate, then to move the enormous gates a little nearer to the stables, which would not affect the main house in any way.

Isobel was busy in her office when the young maid brought a letter in for her. 'Thank you.' The girl bobbed and left. This was not her grandmother's writing, she thought as she opened it. Tears fell, and she read the words. 'Sorry to inform you, but your grandmother, Mrs. Isobel Claremont has died.

The lady had another stroke and passed peacefully, in her sleep.' The letter was from grandma's solicitor, Mr. Benjamin Bronte. It also went on to inform that a young man called Isaac Jacobs, was coming to see her and explain all about her grandma's will, and the shipping company, which apparently, she, now owned.

Chapter Thirty-Two

That night in Dune's arm she cried for her beautiful grandma. Until she had been made to leave Durham and move here to Sussex, the dear lady had been a great part of her life. Mama was always talking of her and there were many letters back and forth to each other. There had been so many trips in the past. She had been fifteen when she went on her last visit to Cornwall to stay with her. But like her mama, she now prayed her dear, sweet grandma was also at peace.

It was Saturday, and the man was due to arrive about lunchtime. Isobel was halfway through her lunch when he appeared, so he was taken to the kitchen to have lunch and drinks, until the Mistress was ready.

'Lady Belington, how lovely to meet you. My name is Isaac Jacobs.' They shook hands. Isobel sat, he copied, and seated himself opposite her.

'As you know, I am an associate of Mr Benjamin, Bronte, your grandmother's solicitor. I do a great deal of traveling round the country to see his clients. And, I have a great deal of paperwork for you to sign, and a lot to tell you about your Grandmother's company and how it all works.'

'Yes, Mr Bronte, informed of my grandmother's passing, so thank you for coming all this way to see me.' There was so much to do, the man stayed for two nights. Consequently, when they had finalised all the paperwork, she was so relieved, because there was so much to take in. But she was also extremely saddened by the loss of her dear grandma. She was going to be extremely, rich, and had been flabbergasted by the amount the man said went into her grandmas account each month. She was to inherit all that the dear woman had owned, and with the income from the mines, she would become a wealthy lady.

They were all gathered buy the fire in the big hall, when Isobel walked in, Edward had his nose in a book, the girls were sat on the floor on a thick rug with some of their wooden toys.

Isobel looked at Dune, and Alice. 'Well, the man has at last gone, but I still cannot believe all he had to tell me.' She sighed and took the cup Alice offered her. She smiled at the babies and nibbled a fresh shortbread biscuit. 'What happens now. I shall have a vast amount of money each month, then there are the flint mines, which have brought a great amount of cash in already, there will be so much. What shall I do with it all?' Isobel declared. Dune smiled. 'What do you want to do with it all, my love?'

She looked at him. 'Dune there will be so much.' Both the girls stood and made their way towards their mama, Isobel picked up the baby, then she helped Mary up beside her.

Dune stood, his arms held out, he took Mary. 'You do not look comfortable, come and sit with your Da.' Her arms about his neck she kissed his cheek.

'Isobel. We just stay here, look how happy we all are.

You have your babies, and everyone around us are all kind and nice, my baby is on its way. What more could we ask for?'

'Yes. Dear, you are so right, but I think I'm still in shock with all that young man had to say.'

'Look.' Dune said. 'I have my horses, and they are doing really well. My uncle Salus has arrived to help me because we have so much work. You have all your builds, and I believe some of the men from around here, have found work quite a way away, so they will need to buy your stones. So yes, my darling, you just stay here and enjoy it all.'

'Yes. Yes, you are both right. So, if I let Mr Jacobs, help me run the company, I will just have more, and more money each month.'

'That's right darling.' Dune answered. 'With the man's help you will become, what's that word you like to use, oh yes, extraordinarily rich.' She laughed. 'Yes, yes, your right, but I shall be happy to do some work regarding the ships. So, if money is not going to be a worry for us, I think I might speak to Ben, about the second floor. It would be nice to have all the rooms there, cleaned, painted, and furnished. Do you not think Alice, dear?'

'Indeed. Indeed, Isobel it would be grand to see them spring back to life.' She declared.Nanny came to collect the girls, it was their teatime, bath, then bed. They both hugged and kissed, mama, Da, and Alice. Edward kissed and hugged them all, then he slowly followed them up the stairs.

'They are such lovely little girls, Isobel.'

'Yes, Alice, we are very- proud of them, is that not so Dune.'

'Ah, yes, they are most adorable, and so good.' He smiled and stood, he leaned down and kissed Isobel's lips, 'I'm away I will see thee later. Alice bye.' He bent and kissed her head. Then he disappeared down the back stairs.

'Would you like some fresh tea, dear.'

'Mm, yes that would be nice, but pull the cord the girl will come.'

She did and a young girl stood before them instantly. Isobel stared into the flame, she was thinking of grandma, Bella, she had loved her so much. The girl returned, the tea was poured, she bobbed and was gone.

Alice stood, 'Oh, Isobel, look at this lovely cake cook as made. Shall I cut us a slice each.'

'Please dear.'

'Alice, I will speak with Ben about the second floor. Because your special man will have them done and shining in no time.'

'Yes, I think he is kind of wonderful to.' And they both laughed. 'That cake was nice shall we have some more?'

'Mm please Alice, it was scrumptious. But tell me, how are you feeling now my dear?'

'Yes, a great deal better, thank you.' She smiled. 'The sickness is not as bad as it was, and I am not so tired, so yes quite good.'

'How many bleeds have you missed now Alice.'

'I think it is about five.'

'Oh, so your well on your way now, dear.'

Life went on in the big house, as the lovely, summer months arrived. Isobel spent a great deal of time with her three little ones. Edward was in the thrones of being taught to ride. A small colt had been brought back by Dune, from one of his horse deals, and the lad absolutely loved the small creature.

'Oh, Mama my horse is beautiful, he has such a shiny black coat, I think Dune is so kind for giving him to me.' He cried out as he walked towards her.

'In-deed, it was really good of him to buy you the animal.' She smiled. 'And I think your chosen name suits him very well.'

'Yes, well I love my black leather boots, and he seems to be the same colour so I thought Blackie would be nice for him.'

'Yes, it certainly is, my darling.' Isobel cuddled him. 'Right, young man, now you and I are going to get on our horses, and I am going to take you for a short ride. It took quite a while to reach the spot. But once there they dismounted, tied the animals to a tree, laid the blanket onto the floor, and Isobel, opened the cloth that held a small cake, and some biscuits. The cool stream was there if they needed to drink some fresh, clear water.

'Mother this country is so beautiful, I love it here, thank you. It is so peaceful.' With his thick pad and pencils, he sat and started to draw. Isobel smiled, 'I have looked at many of your drawings and paintings, and I think they are really good, Edward.'

'You do, thank you.' He stood, then hugged and kissed her. He was a beautiful lad, and Isobel could not forget the fact, that Ben had once told her some of the old staff believed him to have been fathered by her late husband, Lord William Belington. If this was so, then he was the legal heir, to all she laid claim to, because she had the two girls. Edward, should, automatically take up the reigns when old enough. But she had named him Claremont, to make him one of her kin. Well, thankfully she did not have to think about these issues now. But, also with Edward she honestly, believed he would possibly, become an artist. Consequently, he would not want the worry of the estate. She stood and brushed her skirt. 'Come, my lovely boy, we must away and get back, but I will tell you this. The next time we go into, Portchesterton, I shall make enquires about an art teacher for you. Would you like me to do that?'

'Like it. Oh, thank you, thank you. That would be wonderful.'

'Good, that's settled then, now let me help you up and we will ride back.'

'Yes, Mother, and thank you, I have really enjoyed today.' She pulled him close and kissed the top of his dark head, how Isobel loved this boy of hers.

It was May, and Dune who had been away for several days, rode into the courtyard. Isobel ran down the steps to greet him, he picked her up and carried her into the large hall. He drank beer, while she had her tea and biscuits, and they chatted for ages, then he took the stairs two at a time and made his way to the room where the bath was. An hour later he came back to the hall, he scooped Isobel up into his arms and they made their way to the bedroom.

Time just flew by, everyone in the summer months were always so busy. Alice was sitting beneath the shade of a tree, reading a book. Isobel smiled as she walked towards her. 'Oh, it was terrible in Portchesterton this morning, but the sea breeze was lovely.'

'Did you get all you needed?'

'Yes. But I missed you and, I am glad to be home.' A young maid walked towards them, the tray she held was placed onto the table. She poured their tea, then curtsied and left. Isobel stood and took the cloth off the plate, then she handed a plate to Alice, who cried, 'oh, dear Isobel our lovely lemon cake.'

'Yes, when I explained your condition, they happily wrapped it nicely. Anyway, how are you feeling?'

'Fat and extremely uncomfortable.' They both laughed, then ate the delicious cake.

'I was told of an art teacher who might come along to see what stage young Edward is at with his drawing and paints.'

'Isobel, that will be great, I think the lad is really good at both. Drawing and his painting.'

'Yes, I feel he has a talent for it to.'

Alice signed as she lay on the great soft mattress. She looked at Ben. 'Isobel is the most wonderful person I have ever known.'

'Yes, words fail me at her kindness towards you my sweet.' She smiled and took his hand. 'Ben, I have always been well looked after since the day I was born in the Manor house. The Mistress was a beautiful person, and Isobel and I have been together since we were two, and three years old. I am her half -sister, Fordham her father, was also my father. But forget the past, Miss Isobel is a beautiful, kind, caring lady, and I love her so much. He took her into his arms, as sleep took over their bodies.

.

Chapter Thirty-Three

The days were extremely hot, but a fire always roared up the large chimney, in the long hall, and Isobel sat by its warmth watched her children play on the rug. Little Victoria stood and walked towards her then climbed up onto lap.

'Mama, when will Dune be back home.'

'Oh, my precious one, you must call him da, or daddy. She hugged her tight and kissed her nose. 'I know not, but soon we hope.' Mary and Edward decided to join the baby on their mama's lap, and joyous laughter filled the room. The heat of July was too much for Alice, so, she would go outside in the evening for air, sometimes with Ben, and other times with Isobel. She was so uncomfortable; she did not know where to put herself. Everyone did all they could to help her, but she was having a bad time with the heat. Isobel had quite a bit more work to do regarding her grandma's companies than she thought and was kept quite busy at times. September arrived and the weather began to calm down, and on the morning, rain eventually fell, dear, Alice's labour begun. Ben rushed off to get the herbal lady. It seemed hours, but just before dawn reared its head a beautiful baby boy arrived for the happy parents. She and Ben were ecstatic, and Florrie was in seventh heaven. She was exhausted, and after she was cleaned up, and had cuddled the little one, she was given more of the heated herb, and went into a good sleep. She slept for most of the day, and nanny cared for the baby in the nursery.

Isobel, Florence, and Ben kept going to sit with him, but all the little one did was sleep. Alice woke quite early on the second day; she was refreshed and ready to care for her beautiful son. Isobel, with the baby snug in her arms walked into the room, and Alice cried as she watched her walk towards the bed. 'Dear, sister, it gives me so much pleasure to hand your most gorgeous son to you. Just like you did for me when my beautiful Mary was born.' The bundle was carefully placed into her arms, and Alice's face when she saw him was a picture, and they both cried together.

There was a knock, Ben and Florrie entered the room. 'Oh, Miss Isobel. Miss Isobel, is he not the most beautiful little one?' Florence declared.

'Yes, he surely is, absolutely gorgeous. I don't expect you have thought of a name for him yet have you, you happy parents.'

'Well, actually, yes we have.' Alice replied. 'We are going to call him James, after Ben's father.'

'Oh, such a lovely name. He looks like a James.' They all laughed, then Flo and Isobel quietly left the room.

Alice back on her feet was given the lovely grey Windsor pram to use, for the daily walks she took James on. The arrival of the baby brought such joy and happiness into the house, and life was good. Dune had been away for almost two weeks, when she was informed, he just entered the stables. A warm cloak about her body, she was out of the house and moved quickly towards where he was.

'Oh, my darling your back, how I have missed you.' She wailed. He pulled her close and his lips aroused her, 'Darling, darling, come, its freezing, let us get inside.'   Sat by the fire in the big hall, Isobel walked to the decanter and poured him a glass of whisky. Seated opposite him, she asked. 'did you get all the horses you wanted.'

'Aye, I did, there be a few beauties among them as well. I be pleased with them.'

'Good, my darling. I am so happy for you. Now come on we will eat in our rooms this evening.'   Later, sat together on the floor by the fire, Isobel curled up in Dunes arms, was content and happy. 'My Nana Rosa, is to leave for Ireland about next April time.'

'Is she, but why my love. I thought she had settled quite well here?'   She smiled.   'You always say she is good, when, I ask about her.'

'Yes, I know I do and, she does like it here, but she wishes to return, because it be near her time.'

Isobel lost her colour. 'Her time. What do you mean?'

'Her time to get ready. We gypsies, when, old usually know when we are near our time.' He saw her tears fall, and he pulled her closer to his body. 'No, no, my darling, this is not a sad time, it be a happy time. She goes back and gets all her things in order. There is always so much to do when you have been the head of a clan.'

Isobel, sighed, 'that is so brave of her.'

'No, she be a good age now, so she be ready.'

266

'But…Surely she must want you to go with her. She would not want to go on her own.'

'She will travel with her two brothers. They be a great deal younger than Nana. She will be in good hands. They will watch over her until everything she needs to do has been completed. So, my love, she will be well looked after.' He pulled her into his arms and lifted her from the ground. He walked to the bed and gently laid her down. 'My darling.' Dune murmured. 'If you knew just how much I loved you.' He gently took her clothes from her body, then both naked, he took up and beyond their special plateau.

The snow was thick on the ground, no one could move about outside, so the house was full, and every-one settled down to face the winter months inside. Isobel spent a great deal of the daytime in her study, there was quite a lot involved when you had many flint stone mines plus all the paper- work from her grandma's estate. Isobel sighed and put the pen down. Her back ached and she was tired, she stood and left the room. Out in the large hall, Dune and Ben sat with a mug of ale in their hands. She walked over to them and sat down. Ben stood, smiled, and excused himself.

'I have the most awful pain in my back.' She muttered.

'Have you my darling, come on let's go up and I'll massage it for you.' Isobel smiled, 'But I am also very tired.'

'Okay, just a massage then I will leave you to rest.' Back in her room Dune worked wonders on her back, and as she was so relaxed, she asked.

'Dune.'

'Mm. Yes my sweet.'

'Please tell me the story of when your Nana Rosa took you to the 'Holy Mountain.' Please.'

'Are you sure you want me to tell that story again?'

'Yes, yes you know how I love your stories from your childhood, plus your accent is so pure and smooth. I love to hear you speak.'

'Okay. If that's' what you want. Right, are you comfortable?'

'Yes, I am now, thank you.'

'Well, my darling I was about ten years old when we went there. We were ready to go, and Shamus, Rosa's white horse was packed with all we needed. My little Leah was to stay with Aunt, Mayer, Rosa's sister while we were gone. So, my Love are you ready.'

'Yes, I am Dune.'

It was June, and although it was early, it was very warm. Sat on Shamus's wooden seat Nana held the reins as she coaxed him through the camp entrance, out into the country- lanes. The sun felt warm, as the horse's hooves pounded the cobble stones, and the countryside looked beautiful. Trees, full of blossom, wildflowers scattered as far as the eye could see, filled the many fields we passed. Birds sang, light, fluffy clouds floating across the deep blue sky, made it a perfect summer day.

'I think we stop here boy, for a while.' Nana Rosa said,

as we pulled into a large space of the road. 'Yes, this be perfect for our lunch and me little nap.' Dune jumped onto the grass and reached for the wooden steps, he placed them against the side of the van which allowed his grandma to walk down to the ground. Dune busy with Shamus's food bag, tied it in a knot about his neck, then he poured water into a large metal container for the animal to drink from when ready. Nana Rosa made lunch, and Dune sat on the grass.

'Well eat the cold food for now me boy, then we can have hot when we settle somewhere for the night.'

'So be Nana,'

The cheese, cooked eggs, and delicious Soda bread, washed down with fresh milk, filled him for now. Lunch finished, he cleared everything up and stacked it all back in the large box, roped to the side of the van. Rosa settled in her rocker lit her pipe, then closed her eyes, while Dune wandered off to stretch his long legs.

That evening after many more hours of being pulled by Shamus, they made a camp in a very secluded spot, so a fire could be lit without a worry. A pot above the red flames was filled with prepared rabbit stew, which both enjoyed, and apple cider was drunk, but Dune was only allowed a little. The fire built high, Dune rolled his covers out and snuggled down to sleep by the heat. Rosa bent to kiss his head, then she walked up the steps and entered the van where her bed was. This was the daily routine until, eventually, the sign-post, to 'Croagh-Patrick,' Irelands. 'Holy Mountain,' was reached. Dune feared for Shamus as he tried to pull the Vardo up the very steep winding hill, he jumped down and stopped him. Rosa to dismounted, and with the van a great deal lighter, the animal was guided up to the very top. Once there, Dune, secured the horse with water and food, then he gathered wood for the fire. It was not yet dark, and he walked to the edge at the highest point, the scenes before him, he was in awe of. 'Nana Rosa, 'I'm stood here, it is the top of the world.'

She smiled and muttered. 'Aye lad, that you be. Stood on top of the great world.' As he digested the breathless views all around the North Mayo, Mountains, that overlooked the beautiful bay below with its many sunken drumlins, he added. 'And just look at the magnificent views to be sure.'

'Aye lad, it's something I've seen many a time afore, but I wanted you to come and see the beauty of it all for your - self.' He was overwhelmed, he ran across and flung himself across her lap, and kissed her cheek. Tears gathered, he was so like her beloved, daughter, Leah. He loved to show his love, and the way he cared for people, how she loved this wee grandson of hers.

To his sheer delight, Nana decided to camp there on the top of 'Croagh-Patrick.' For several nights, and Dune loved every minute of the stay. On the day of their departure back to the campsite, he vowed when full grown he would return to this very spot. He wanted, once more to cast his eyes over the most beautiful scenes he had ever witnessed.

Chapter Thirty-Four

It was the first day of July, the day had been awful, rain had fallen since dawn, and as they rode into the encampment, Tom was there to greet them. Dune's utter delight to see his Pa, he jumped to the ground and ran towards him. 'Da, Da.' Tom gathered him up into his arms and kissed the boy's head. 'Ah, look at you my boy, to be sure, look how much you've grown.' Rosa watched father and son unite.

'Oh, it be so good to see you my boy, so dam good.' Tom's eyes sought hers. 'You are well Rosa?'

'I, Tom, thanks be.' He hugged Dune tightly again, then asked. 'And the baby?'

'Little Leah, like her mama, she be a beautiful one.'

'Leah.'

'Yes, young Dune, he named her. She be over with my sister.' Tom looked to where Rosa pointed, but decided to go and see the child later. He reached for Dune again. 'Come on with yah son, your uncles be over in that barn, they want to meet you.' He looked up to this caring lady, who had helped him so much. 'Will that be fine with you Rosa?'

'I, it be. But, please, the lad is very tired, we have been on the roads these past seven days.'

'Ah, so be it.' He took the boy's hand.

'Rosa.' She looked down at him.

'Thank ye, thank ye so much.'

'You be very welcome Tom O'Malley. Your boy and wee one, be of my blood, so be sure it's blessed I be to have them.' Tears blurred her vision, as she watched Dune slip his tiny hand into his father's large one as they walked towards the battered barn.

'And that, was that my darling.' Dune uttered as he took her face and kissed her lips.

'Dune, I love to hear the stories you tell me of your childhood, because it was so different from mine.'

'I know my sweet, but now it's time to sleep. But I will tell you this, darling. One day hopefully I would love to take you there, it is somewhere I would love for you to see with me.'

'That would be wonderful, but we must take the children with us.'

'Yes, oh, yes indeed.' He kissed her nose, helped her up from the floor, then arm in arm, they walked through to the bedroom.

Isobel had been awake for ages, she pushed the covers from her body, and tried to sit up. Yes, there it was again, sickness filled her, her head ached slightly. She was completely full of queasiness, this had started a week ago, she felt like this till about lunch time, then she was a little better. But, overall, she did not feel good at all. She had not mentioned this to Alice or Dune, and of course with the snow neither could ride anyway. She had missed two bleeds, so she knew for sure, she was again with child. Joy filled her, because this time this precious little one would be from the man who truly had her heart. Dune never really made much fuss of the little ones, although he did seem to make a beeline for Mary. Yes, many a time she had found him with this little one on his knee, or if she cried or got upset, he would move forward to tend her. He made a great fuss of young Edward and thought, his beautiful Isobel wonderful for the way she had taken the wee lad in and called him her own.

He never ignored Victoria, and if he brought something back from his trips, he always gave it to the three of them. But it was Mary, Isobel noticed he seemed most drawn to.

December and the house was getting ready for Christmas again. Isobel was in Alice's rooms, she picked James up from the bed. 'Oh, my you are such a handsome boy, yes you are.' She crooned. The door opened and Alice came back in, she smiled and took her son, then sat opposite her sister, James happily took his milk from her breast.

'I cannot believe he is almost three months, Alice, he is a beautiful baby. How are you feeling, is everything good with you my dear?' Isobel enquired.

'Yes, I am feeling a lot stronger, but the baby has not slept for the past four night, so I am tired, other than that, yes things are good.'

'Alice, my dear, dear sister, tonight he must go into the nursery to sleep, so you may have a rest, and you must do this whenever you are tired, or just feel like a little rest.'

'Dear Isobel, I might just do that, just to get some sleep.'

'Absolutely, I will go along and speak with Nanny.'

Florence knocked and entered the office with Isobel's afternoon tea and cakes.

'Thank you, dear Florrie. But please do not rush off, sit and speak with me.' She heard the older woman's deep sigh as she eased herself into the chair opposite hers.

'Are you, okay dear lady, that was a big sigh.' Florrie smiled. 'Oh, sorry Miss Isobel. Yes, I am good, it's just my aches and pains as I become older.' She poured the tea, handed her a cup, then sat back to sip her own. They both sat in silence. Isobel placed her cup onto her desk, 'Oh that was a lovely, you do make a nice pot Florrie.' She smiled. 'Tell me dear are you well or just extremely tired.'

'Oh, yes, Mistress, I am well. But I do get very tired these days.' She laughed, 'It be me age.'

'Right, then I am going to retire you with full pay. Mrs Granger is only too happy to take over all your cooking duties, and chores. I want you to rest, you have worked so hard for us over many years now, so it is time for you to rest. You have your rooms; you just stay there and rest.'

'But, Mistress, I…I cannot except such kindness, I am a mere servant…I'.

'Florence, please, you are not a servant, you are family, and that is how it will be from now on. You are family, my dear.' She stood and walked towards her, she took her hand and helped her to her feet. 'Now, go to your rooms and rest.' Isobel kissed her cheek, then she pulled the cord. A maid arrived instantly.

'Molly, please take Miss Florence to her rooms. She is

to have whatever she needs.' Tears streaming down her face, the lady took her hand and kissed it. 'Miss Isobel, thank you, thank you so much.' Then the young girl led her from the room. The fire in the big hall was stacked high up the chimney and the heat from it was lovely. The girls had just been taken back to the nursery, and Isobel was miles away.

'Where are you, my love?'

'Mm… oh, sorry Dune. Yes, I was deep in thought. But your back that's good darling.' He bent and kissed her lips. 'I have just been to see the little ones, but nanny chased me out it was their bedtime.' He laughed.

'Oh, she keeps to a strict ritual with them, which is good for them both.'

'Yes, your right, but they are adorable.'

'Yes, they are both beautiful girls. But tell me, what was the weather like when you returned?' Is it still snowing?'

'No when I got back it had stopped. But now Christmas has gone, spring will soon be here.' He took her hand and knelt before her. 'Isobel would you like a small wine, I'm going to have one?'

'Mm…yes, yes please.' She watched him pour the liquid into two glasses, then he handed her one. Isobel had started to have the odd glass here and there. She drank a mouthful, 'mm, it is nice, yes I like this one.'

'Good, yes I quite like this one also, darling.'

'Dune, shall we take these up to our rooms, I need to speak to you about something that has been worrying me for quite a while lately. I know you will think me silly, but I have to tell you about it.'

'Yes, darling.' He stood and took the glass from her, then in silence they left and walked up the stairs. Seated by the roaring fire, they sipped their wine in silence. Dunes finished he stood. 'Would you like another glass?'

'No, I am good with this, thank you.' Also being with child again, she was not sure whether wine would be good to drink. Seated again, he looked at her. 'Right, what do you need to speak to me about?'

'Well, actually it's about the two girls. Mary is five and Victoria is three.'

'Yes, I know that darling.'

She nodded and smiled, then continued. 'Well, now at this age, they are changing and getting their identities, but what I cannot understand is how can Mary, and Victoria, look so much alike, and both image you.' He began to cough, he put the glass onto the table, and took a white cloth from his pocket to wipe his eyes, then he stared into the fire.

'Please I need you to explain what has happened here. Because Mary cannot be your child, you were not even here when I carried and gave birth to her. With Victoria I could not know who fathered her, but thankfully you did, she is so like you.' She stopped. 'Dune, surely you can see the likeness between you and Victoria. But there should be nothing between you and Mary, but there is, and this I do not understand. Because she is not of your blood, yet she images you strongly.' She saw the colour drain from his face, as he picked his glass back up, and drank the liquid in one gulp.

'Dune, this is worrying me, can you tell me why Mary is so like you, she even puts her head in her hands as you do when you are upset.'

Silence in the room, was broken by the fire's smoke as it crackled its way up the chimney. Dune placed the glass onto the table, then he stood, and lent down to brush her lips. 'Darling I have to go somewhere; I will not be long. I will be back quickly.'   Before she could answer, the door closed behind him.

He was relieved to find Ben in the kitchen, sat with a mug of tea.

'Oh, Ben, good you're here on your own.' He then went on to tell him about Isobel's worries, regarding the little ones.

'You mean, she sees Mary is like you. Blimey, Dune, was she your child?'

'No, no she was not. I want you to get, Alice and Florence and come up to our rooms, as soon as you can, and I will tell you all the story of my Mary.'

'But Dune, what do you think she will do, when she finds out what the three of us did, well the four of us did on that sad night?'

'To be truthful I think she would thank us, because of how happy she is with her beautiful little ones.'

'Do you really think so.'

'No, to be honest I'm not sure what she will say or how she will take it.

Chapter Thirty-Five

The thing is her baby, boy, had not survived. A young gypsy girl had passed, and there was a tiny baby left alone. So, we did what was best for the little one, we gave her to our Mistress Isobel. Because we did not want to see her with a broken heart.'

'That is so right, Dune, so very right.'

'Well, when I tell her, I just hope, she will forgive us all.' Alice walked into the room and smiled, then Dune sat her down and told what was about to happen.

'Oh Dune, I am not surprised, it is so true, both girls image you. Victoria is your daughter and Mary also favours you. I can truly, understand Isobel asking you about them because of this likeness. Is she your child, Dune?'

'No, no dear Alice, she was my little sister's baby. But now I must return upstairs and tell Isobel just what did happen, and I want you and Ben to come with me please. And, what about Florence?'

'No, no Dune she is not too good, she is really tired, and you know how kind Isobel has been with her, she needs to rest.'

He nodded, then the trio silently left the kitchen, and made their way up to Isobel's rooms. Ben tapped the door, opened it, and they entered, and all felt extremely, apprehensive. Alice walked over and kissed her sister's cheek, then sat down.

Dune stood with his back resting against the mantle, shelf and looked round the room.

'Isobel has asked me why Mary and Victoria look so alike, and why both image me. She cannot understand this because there is no way Mary could be my daughter.' He stopped, then, turned to stare at the flames, as they whipped high up into the chimney. He inhaled deeply, then turned back to face them.

'So now my darling, I will tell you the story of what happened on that extremely sad night, when we all had to deal with an horrendous, tragedy.' He stopped; he was finding it hard to speak. He took another deep breath, then continued. 'I had a little sister, her name was Leah, she was named after our Ma. She was a wonderful girl, an angel, and I loved her very much. She always lived in Ireland, but when she was fourteen, she got on a boat with two of our uncles and came to England. I knew she was here, but she was far away. Then eventually she travelled with some of our clan's people, to come here and be with me.' He stopped, there were tears in his eyes, and the silence in the room was strong. Then he cleared his throat and continued.

'But when she arrived, she was sixteen and heavily pregnant. She had been raped by the Master of the house's son, then had been thrown out into the street.' His head lowered into his hands, silence, again descended. He walked over to the chair and sat down. 'She forbade me to do anything to the boy, which made me really angry. But I did get a message to some of the clan quite near him, and justice was carried out.' Isobel, stood and walked towards where the decanter of scotch was, she poured two large ones, then handed a glass to Dune, and the other to Ben.

'Our people here loved her, and everyone was pleased to have her with us. She went into labour the day before you did Isobel, and the baby's birth was quite easy, considering her age. But the herbal lady could not stop the bleeding, which is what happened to my Ma, when she had Leah, so my baby sister bled to death, like our Ma did, and I was left with this tiny new baby.'

'Oh, Dune my darling, how awful for you, and your poor dear sister, so, so sad.' Isobel cried, as she left her chair, and sank to the floor by his feet.

Alice wiped her eyes, 'So sad.' She whispered. Dune finished his drink then continued. 'So, I was left with this tiny baby, my little sister was dead, then suddenly the herbal woman was stood in front of me. She told me she could give my wee niece a really good home with a beautiful, and wonderful lady, who had just sadly given birth to a still born son.'

He stopped, he reached for Isobel, and helped her up and back into the comfort of her chair. He knelt and looked straight into her eyes. 'My darling, you had a terrible birth, and when your baby was born, he was not breathing. Everyone here was in an awful state of shock, and heartache.' He stopped as he watched her face crumble and lose its colour.

'It was the herbal woman who told of my motherless

nice, and eventually the decision to get the baby for you was made, while you slept, heavily. I came here to the underground part of the house, and your dear son was given to me, and my niece was given to you. That was an awful sad night, and the only good thing to happen was, that you had been given Leah's baby to love and care for. I was overwhelmed with love for you. And that is why Mary is like me, she is of my blood, the same as my beautiful Victoria.'

Isobel was shocked to the core, coldness engulfed her, and her body began to shake, she clung to the arms of the chair, then tears fell, uncontrollable tears. Dune gathered her into his arms, and she sobbed and sobbed. Alice stood, tears streaming down her face, with Ben by her side, they quietly left. Dune lifted Isobel and took her through to the bedroom, he carefully laid her onto the bed, then he sat in a chair to watch over her. Eventually an exhausted sleep engulfed her, and Dune stayed by her side all night.   It was still dark when Isobel opened her eyes. She saw Dune fully clothed was beside her. She sat up slowly as the realisation of yesterday came back into her mind. She moved from the bed carefully and walked towards the fire. Sat in her chair, Dune words came flooding back to her. So, his dear little sister died giving birth, then my son is dead, and then there is a little one who needs a mother's care and love. This was a terrible situation everyone was in, but Mary is not mine, she is not my child. Dune woke, stretched, moved from the bed, then walked towards her and sat in the chair opposite her. 'Isobel how are you this day darling?'

'Shocked, numb, I cannot believe Mary is not my child.'

'When this was done, I took your dear son and put him in a lovely place so he could rest peacefully. I go and visit him weekly and take flowers for him.'

'Oh, Dune really, thank you for that.'

'When, the weather is better I will take you to where he is.'

'Oh, sadly, I cannot do that for some time, because I am with child again, so I must not ride. But just as soon as the wee one is born, I will come with you.'

'Oh darling, how wonderful, we are to have another baby.'

'Yes, yes we are.' She smiled. 'Dune is it early?'

'Yes, it's only seven o'clock. And it be black as night outside.'

'Can you please leave me on my own, I need time to digest your words from yesterday, please, I must think about all that has happened.'

'Yes, of course I will. I'll hopefully ride out and do some work with the horses.' He stood, then bent to kiss her lips. 'I just need to tell you this before I go. When I was told of your sadness, and that Leah's baby was going to be given to you, I was overwhelmed. To think you were to love and cherish part of my dear sister, I was the happiest man.' He smiled, and she could see his tears. 'I love the little one very much, because she is all that is left from my, Leah.'

'Oh, Dune, my darling, yours was a double tragedy. It

was hard for everyone, that night especially for you, and now it is really hard for me to know, that Mary is not of my blood.'

'Yes, I know this is a big shock for you my darling.' He smiled, then walked towards the door, and was gone.

Isobel was numb, she sat about for most of the day. She had a nice bath, changed her clothes then made her way to the nursery. She must find out, what her reaction will be, when Mary runs towards her to be picked up, and loved. Isobel opened the door of the nursery and thought how quiet it was. Nanny was sat in the wooden rocker near the fire, with a cup in her hand, and all the little ones were asleep. Isobel looked at the window it was dark, she had not realised the time. Nanny saw her and stood.

'Sh...sh.., nanny, no go back and relax. I just want to look at my babies.' Isobel walked towards Mary's little bed, then sat on the floor to watch her. She was so beautiful, and a most loveable little girl. She lent down and kissed her hair, the little one stirred and opened her eyes. 'Mama, mama,' she whispered sleepily, but then she threw her arms about her neck. Tears streaming down her face, Isobel collected her up into her arms, and walked back to where nanny was. 'I am taking Mary back to my bed for the night.'

'Yes, Mistress. Very well.' The woman smiled as she watched Mother and child leave. Back in her quarters, she laid the little one into her bed, then she laid beside her and held her tight in her arms. 'My darling precious one, do you know how much Mama loves you.' Mary kissed her lips, then, she snuggled in and went back to sleep. Dune crept into the bedroom, and the sight of Isobel sleeping with her arms tight about his little one, brought a lump to his throat. He pulled the wooden rocker closer to the bed, then sat to watch his two girls. Mary was wide awake and bouncy as she tried to brush Isobel's hair. 'Oh mama, please let me do it.'

'No darling, not just yet. Let me get up and sit over there on the stall, you will be able to brush it better there.'

'All right, mama.' Dune smiled as he watched the two of them chatting and laughing together. Then nanny knocked, it was time for Mary's breakfast and to get dressed. There was another knock and Molly came in with their tray of food.

'Dune I sat most of yesterday, and I did a great deal of thinking, and I am only going to say this to you once, 'I love Mary, and as far as I am concerned, she is my beautiful child. I never want to hear another word, about what happened on that terrible night. For, I truly know it must have been horrendous for you all. You will please tell Ben, it must never be spoken off again, and I will speak with Alice.'

'Yes, my darling. Oh Isobel, Isobel my love.'

'Now, come eat your breakfast.'

'Yes, my love, I am hungry.' Dune pulled out the chair for her, then he sat opposite. Once he had eaten, he went off to work with his horses. Isobel after her bath and clean clothes, went to see Alice.

Chapter Thirty-Six

Isobel knocked then opened the door. James was on the floor moving about and gurgling, it was still quite early, and Alice was eating her hot rolls with eggs.'

'Oh, Isobel, I am so sorry. I am not even dressed yet.'

'No worry my dear, you carry on.'

'Would you like a cup of tea?' The girl asked.

'Yes, yes please. I am sorry to be so early, but I have been up since the crack of dawn with Mary. But she is back in the nursery now.' She saw Alice's handshake, and the colour leave her face has she handed her the tea. Isobel knew, the guilt of that night would have waved heavy on this dear girl for a long, long time.

'Alice, have you finished your breakfast?'

'Yes, yes I have.'

'Good, I am going to take the baby to the nursery, you get dressed and sort yourself out, then come down to my study, I need to speak with you.'

'Yes, thank you dear Isobel.' She picked James up from the floor and handed him to her.

'Oh, you are such a beautiful boy, yes you are cheeky.' The baby gave her the biggest smile. Isobel kissed Alice's cheek, 'I will see you later, when you're ready, there is no rush.' And with that she cuddled the baby and walked to the door.   It seemed no time, before there was a knock on the study door, and Alice entered.

'Come let's sit down by the fire, we will be more comfortable there.' She pulled the cord, and Molly quickly appeared. 'Can we please have some coffee.' The girl smiled, curtsied, then she was gone.

'Did James settle alright when you left him with nanny.'

'Yes, he went in and was happy to see the girls.' Isobel looked at Alice. 'I have to talk to you about what happened on that terrible night.' She took her hand. 'Please Alice, let me speak first.' She smiled. 'I know it must be the last thing you want to hear of, but Dune did clarify much for us all yesterday. And I know it must have been a terribly hard, decision, for you all to make.'

Tears fell, her body shook as she sobbed, and sobbed. Isobel moved to sit next to her, and she took her in her arms. 'Hush… there, there.' She was trying to console her, for she herself was all cried out.   Molly arrived with the coffee, the tray was quickly placed on the table, then the girl hurried out. Eventually, Alice was calmer, and Isobel walked over to pour their drinks. They drank in silence.   Then she whispered. 'Isobel, if you only knew, how what we did that night haunts me, and still does. Sometimes, I wake from a sleep crying, uncontrollably, and that night comes vividly back to me. The guilt I felt, and still do. But you were the one we were all concerned about. Had you woken two days after this all happened, and been told the truth, I think it would have broken you. I really do.' She rubbed the hand that held hers. 'We agreed to change the babies with the herbal lady, because we did not want you to suffer any more. Had you woken to find no baby, my dear, sister, I think it would have broken, your heart.'

'Oh, Alice. Dear Alice. I know this to be true, you would never do a single thing to hurt me. It was a terrible, terrible, tragedy, for you all to deal with. I know you all did what you thought would be best for me. So, I will tell you this as I have told Dune, Mary is my beautiful daughter, and this must never be spoken of again.'

'Isobel, I…I'm just so relieved, that you now know the truth.' She put her head in her hands and cried again.

'No, no dear Alice, come on no more tears, please, we never speak of it again. It is finished.' She smiled, 'But I do have something nice to tell you. I am with child once more, and I'm so happy about it.'

'Oh, oh, Isobel that is wonderful news.' She stood and they hugged each other tight.

'Come on Alice, let's go up to the nursery and see our beautiful little ones.' Arm in arm they left the room and made their way up the stairs.

Dune returned late that night, and like always he ate his supper in the kitchen. Then he made his way up the stairs and went straight to the room with the bath. Refreshed, and clean, he knocked Alice's door. 'Hi Dune come in.' Ben said as he turned to let him enter.

'No, mate I won't. I was looking for Isobel, but I can see she's not here.'

'No. I think she might still be in her study, she said she had a great deal of paperwork to do, when I left her earlier.'

Alice informed.

'Right, many thanks. See you all later.' The door closed, and he descended the stairs and walked round to find her. Isobel in her chair near the fire, was fast asleep. Dune looked around, then he scooped her up into his arms, and slowly left the room. He carefully placed her on the bed, she moved then curled into a ball, and sighed. He covered her, removed his cloths, lay down beside her, and slept instantly. It was early the next morning, Isobel stirred then sat up, Dune was still beside her, and sun streamed into the room. 'It is a beautiful morning, and oh, Dune I am still clothed, that's the second night.' She whispered as she moved closer to his sleeping body, to kiss his ear, and eyes, she was pulled across him and his mouth took hers. Her cloths removed they sealed their final agreement on their darling Mary.

Dune was in no hurry to dress, and laying in his arms, Isobel said. 'I am with child again. I am going to have your baby are you pleased about this, only yesterday you seemed unsure.'

'Yes, my darling of course I am, but I worry about you and your reputation.'

'What do you mean, Dune. My reputation what does it matter about that.'

'I'm a gypsy, my darling, you are a beautiful, educated lady. Mistress of this great estate, you bare a title, you are Lady, Isobel Belington. What will people say and think.'

'People, what people. With Mama, father, and my Nana

all gone to their rest, and that terrible man Belington, thankfully no longer here, who is there for us to think about. I love you and you love me.' She smiled and took his strong hand. 'You do love me don't you Dune?'

'What a silly question, you know I do.'

'So, Dune, my darling we have no one to worry about, and we are being blessed once more with a child to be born around June.'

'I be happy, my darling, I be, so happy.' He kissed her lips, then took her once more,

Spring arrived and so much activity outside began, the massive lawns and gardens needed to be done, the horses were allowed out in a fenced off field, while the stables were cleaned and repainted. The lovely summer days, everyone spent most of their time outside, there would be picnics, walks and trips into Portchesterton.   Isobel was extremely large and very- uncomfortable. She wondered if she might have got her dates wrong, it was the beginning of June, and there was no sign of the little ones' arrival. Isobel sat in her study was going through a great amount of paper- work, she could not believe the amount of money she had already received. It was quite unbelievable.

She was tired, she pulled the rope, and the maid, knocked, and entered.

'Molly, could you please bring me a pot of tea.'

'Yes, Mistress. Right away.' She bobbed and left. Isobel stood, and made her way to the open French doors, the air creeping into the room was a bit cooler. The girl reappeared, she placed the tray onto the table, poured the liquid into a cup, curtsied, and quietly left. Dune was away for a few days to buy some more colts, his horse business was doing extremely good, and there was plenty of money coming in from him also.

'Isobel. Miss, Isobel.'

'Mm…Oh, Alice, sorry, I must have fallen asleep.'

'Yes, you did. It's quite late, here let me help you up.' Once she was up on her feet, she pulled the girl into her and kissed her hair. 'My dear sister. How I love you.'

'And I you my dear, dear Isobel. Come, I will help you up to your chambers, and with her support, they walked out and up the stairs.

'This baby is on the go day and night, gives me no rest Alice, it fair wears me out. I shall be glad when it is here with us.' She smiled. 'Consequently, I get tired.' They reached her rooms and the girl helped her to her chair, but Isobel said. 'No, no, sorry Alice but I prefer the settee, it seems more comfortable for me now.'

'Yes, that's like my James, he still moved when he was being born.'

'Where is he now.'

'He is in the nursery. I've had no sleep again for the last four nights, and Nanny said she does not mind having him at all.'

'Good, will you stay in here with me for a while.'

'Absolutely, Isobel for as long as you want me to.' She knelt and took her sister's hand and kissed it. They smiled.

'Would you like a nice pot of tea dear?'

'Mm, yes that would be nice.' The girl pulled the cord and sat by the heat they waited.

Isobel was so big and extremely uncomfortable, she spent most of her time now in her room. She would sit on the balcony to get some air, but now she just wanted the birth to arrive. It was the end of June and it was dark when a sharp pain woke her. The room was dimly lit, as she left the bed to pull the cord. Young Molly knocked, rushed in, and declared. 'Mistress, you be good?'

'No, a pain woke me, and there's another coming now. Oh, yes, I think the baby is ready to come. Please, get Alice for me.' The girl bobbed and was gone. Alice, hurried into the room. 'Oh Isobel, is it your time dear?'

'I believe it is.' And other pain caused her to cling to the bedclothes. The girl still behind Alice, listened to her instruction, then she fled from the room and descended the stairs. Molly brought more lanterns, clean towels, and plenty of hot water arrived. Florence then opened the door and walked over to the bed to hold her Mistress's hand. Isobel smiled, 'How are you dear Florrie? I have not seen you for a few days, are you well.'

'Yes, dear lady, thanks to you and your kindness I am indeed well. But how are you, Alice said the baby is coming.'

'It is, my dear, but if you just hold my hand, it will help me.' Florence was only to, happy to help in anyway, she could. Ben had gone for the herbal lady, and now in the early hours the baby was on its way. The room was well lit, and a fire roared in the grate, and Florence was still sat nearby, she wanted to stay.

Chapter Thirty-Seven

The contractions were strong, and Isobel cried out. Sweat poured from her as the herbal lady felt her tummy. 'Now, I want a big push when I says push. Ready. Push, yes that be it lady and again, push, no stop, stop, and the baby suddenly, appeared in her hands. 'Keep still, yes that's it, good.' The old lady smiled as she finished, then she handed the baby wrapped in a towel to Alice.

'It be a boy, Isobel,' The girl declared. But it was the look on her face that made her stop and keep hold of the little one. 'What is it dear?' She cried.

'Oh, I have more pains, and there coming and going, oh and oh, oh, I want to bear down again.' Isobel cried. 'Oh, I want to push.' The old woman came back to the bed, and after she had felt Isobel's tummy, she declared,

'I think there be another baby there. Yes, yes there is. Now, Mistress, I know you be tired, but I needs a big push, when I says, a big push. Ready, push, and again stop, stop, now one more big push now, another baby appeared in her hands, and it screamed its little head off. Isobel was exhausted, but she smiled and cried with everyone in the room.   Twin boys, her delight was for all to see. Alice sat by her, had hold of one and Isobel propped up had the other next to her on the bed.

'No wonder I was so uncomfortable most of the time Alice, dear.'

'Yes, but my dear sister what a wonderful gift you have here, two beautiful sons. God has blessed you. (and they both knew what she meant.) 'Yes but, now you must sleep, I will take them to the nursery, and fetch them back when you are well rested.' Alice left with the one she held, on her return she lent down to kiss Isobel's head. 'Sleep well dear.' She whispered as she collected the other wee one up into her arms and left the room.

Dune returned the next day, and his happiness was overwhelming, when told of his twin sons, birth, he was the happiest man alive.

The boys, now a few weeks old had been named, Eugene and Thomas, after Dune's father and grandfather. They were such good babies, and they certainly brightened up the house and all in it.   The night of their births Ben had made a second crib, and Isobel sat by her fire, had the two babies close to her. She was ecstatic, like Dune, she felt very blessed. The two girls and Edward were also thrilled to have two baby brothers. Everyone was happy.

Dune's nana Rosa had not left for Ireland yet. She was going at the end of July. She told Dune she wanted to see the two new babies.

Isobel had been thrilled, and he'd brought her to the house one afternoon for tea, and it had been a wonderful few hour, spent with her. All she ever talked of was Dune and Leah. The children, and the twins had been brought down to see her, but when they had been returned to the nursery, Mary had stayed behind. Nana had cried, and told Isobel, you will be truly blessed for what you have allowed to happen with this beautiful child. She came back to the house several times after that, and all the little ones would come down to the special, room Isobel had had made ready for visitors. And for this dear lady to be in Isobel's home, made her feel blessed and happy. She was sad when Dune told her this was to be her last time because she was ready to leave for Ireland. But, when they said their final goodbye, nana Rosa had taken Isobel into her arms and kissed her cheek. 'Bless you always. You are a beautiful lady.' Then she was gone.

The house was now quiet, and although the day had been hot, the room was now cold, sat near the fire Isobel read her book. She yawned it was time for bed. Dune would not be back tonight, he said there was to much for him to do. But in the early hours of the morning, he crept into bed and pulled her into his arms. She stirred, his lips on her, his body pressed against her, but both so exhausted just held each other and slept. The next morning Isobel went along to the nursery to watch the little ones playing, she went there as much as she could, and now sat near the fire, she watched her twin son's sleep. Edward normally at a class with his tutor, was downstairs, in his study rooms with his paper and paints. His tutor now, much older, had been back home for some time with an illness. And just that morning a letter had arrived from him. It had stated he was sad to say that due to his health he would not be back to teach the boy. But he had a grandson, Mr. Henry Turner who had taught school for some years now, who would love to become Edward's tutor. There was an address to write back to him.

Isobel wrote and told him to ask the young man to come to see her at the end of August, which he did. He was an extremely nice man, and she had employed him straight away.

Edward, after a week of teaching loved his new tutor. Isobel also put extra money into old Mr. Turner's last wages.

Dune was in her study, doing some much-needed paperwork, when she walked in with the baby in her arms.

'Oh, my darling and who have you got there, Thomas or Eugene?'

'Come look, see if you know which one, I have.' He smiled, left the desk, and walked to where she was near the fire. Isobel removed the blanket, and his black eyes stared up at her. 'Well, Dune which son is he.' He took him from her, then sat on the chair, he lent and kissed the little one's nose.

'This be our beautiful son Eugene.' He declared. She sighed, 'how did you know that.'

'Because, by his tiny left ear he has a wee mark, look.' Isobel moved towards him and sure enough, there was the smallest of marks near the ear. 'I think that might be the only way, that will allow us to tell the boys apart. I shall look for it in the future.' She laughed. 'Are you coming up our supper will soon be there?'

'Yep, I'll finish the rest in the morning.' He piled some papers together, took the baby from Isobel, and together they made their way back up to their chambers. The twins were good lads, and they slept most of the time, but now, both were awake and crying for their feeds. Isobel always went along to the nursery, and while Alice nursed Eugene, she fed Thomas, this became a regular routine, and the girls used to love to watch mama feed the babies.

Isobel was quite exhausted at the end of the days now and was only too glad to climb into bed each night. She had just settled when Dune returned from his days work, he too worked long hours to make up for all the time he couldn't get out because of the weather. She was not asleep, and through the dimmed light she watched him remove his clothes as he walked towards her. He lifted the covers and slid in beside her. She melted against him, his lips came down, but, exhausted or not he made such tender love to her, that she slept like a baby.

Time passed quickly, and the twins kept their mama, and Alice busy, as did the little ones. November came in quietly and there was no snow to be seen. The girls and James were wrapped up very warm, the babies well covered in the pram, as Alice and Nanny took them all for a long walk. It was cold but if you kept moving you were alright. The girls loved to go out in the air, and when they all eventually returned indoors, their little cheeks glowed.

Isobel sat in her study, wondered what Mr Isaac Jacobs could possibly want of her. The letter from him had arrived two weeks ago, and he was due to visit her today. She had all her paper -work out that referred to her grandma's' companies. So, what could be the problem. Mr Benjamin Bronte, Grandma Bella's solitaire had died so what could it all be about. Well, he would be there soon enough. She needed to be patient. The man arrived with an assortment of luggage, which confused her even more. The man's belongings were stored in the room allocated for him, then when he had sorted himself out, he was shown into her study.

'Hello, Mr Jacobs, how nice to see you again, although I am surprised being November, we normally have snow by now.'

'Yes. I am extremely lucky the month is quite good, which is great for me.' They shook hands and he sat on the chair that faced her. 'Although, I do not want to be in this area for too long just in case the snow starts.'

'I am a little confused about your visit, I thought everything was all good.'

'Yes. Yes, My Lady it is. The thing is, when Mr Bronte passed, he had no relations at all, no one, consequently he kindly left his law firm to me. For which I am truly - grateful.'

'Oh, that was nice of him, was it not.'

He went to speak, but she stopped him. 'Look you must have been on that road for many days, would you like to rest, then have your lunch before we begin. We can discuss all we need to later in the afternoon.'

'That would be nice, your Ladyship, but I afraid I cannot, we must discuss our business now, because I have a coach coming for me at two o'clock. I must leave early because, I wish to reach the next family's estate before dark. I will be staying there for several nights. Mr. Bronte did a great deal of business for the gentleman there.'

'Oh, yes I see, but you must eat.' She pulled the cord, and a young girl appeared. 'Please, ask cook, to make some sandwiches, and pots of tea for Mr Jacobs. Molly.' She curtsied, then left.

Isobel still in awe of all he had told her walked into the big hall, she smiled at Alice as she walked towards her. 'I cannot believe you are here, in the quiet all on your own.'

'Yes. After our walk nanny took them all up for their lunch, and a sleep. I have not seen anyone or heard a peep.'

'Wonderful.' Isobel pulled the cord. The girl arrived quickly. 'Tea and biscuits please Molly.' She smiled and walked away.

'Well, Mr Jacobs has already left, I thought he would stay the night, and travel on tomorrow.'

'Really, he has come a great distance.'

'Yes, I told you Mr Bronte died, but what I did not know was, he had left everything he had to Mr Jacobs. So, the young man has gone and sold the old premises and has brought new ones in London. Consequently, during his journey here, he has stopped at quite a few clients to inform them of his big move.' The girl arrived with the tea, she poured two cups, bobbed, and left. They sat in silence for a while, Alice stood and walked over to the table. 'More tea Isobel?'

'Mm…sorry dear, I was miles away. Mm… yes, please.' Alice seated again. 'Was it all good with the man then?' She queried.

'Yes, oh yes. Everything is fine and it will all stay the same, except he told me that there is a man who wants to buy grandma's company, he wants her ships.'

'Really, is that what he said.'

'Yes, and he has offered a substantial, amount of money for it all.'

'How do you feel about that then, Isobel?'

'To be truthful, I am not sure. I told him I need time to think about it. He said I had till the end of next week. So that is when I have to give him my answer.'

'But you like what you have to do regarding your grandma's company don't you?'

'Very much, but I will speak with Dune, before I decide.' The tea and biscuits all gone Isobel stood. 'I am going up to see the children, coming dear?'

'Yes, indeed.' The girl stood, and arm in arm they made their way up the stairs to the nursery.

Chapter Thirty-Eight

Later that night sat by the heat of the fire, Isobel went back to her conversation with Mr Jacobs. This man who wanted to buy her ships, why, she had grown to love the work she did regarding the company. She also liked the money it brought in each month. It had also given her something to do other than, just looking after family and the estate. She wondered what nana, Bella, would have done had she received such an offer. Would she sell and make life a great deal easier, or carry on with what she had? Isobel was in her twenty-fifth year, still quite young. She would speak with Dune, but she was sure she would not sell, because her grandma always kept it all close to her heart.   It was late that night, when Dune returned, he opened her door and from the threshold said.

'Hello, my love. I won't come in I be off for my bath, see you when I've had it, unless you wish to join me.' She laughed, 'Away with you Dune, O'Malley and get cleaned up.' He smiled and closed the door. Much later sat together she told him of Mr Isaac's offer for the ship company.

'How do you feel about it? It was your Grandmas business?'

'Well, I am still young. I not sure what I want to do. I only do a small amount of paperwork now, but look, at all the money that comes in monthly from it all.'

'Yes, but this man has offered you a great, amount to

take it off your hands, and make it his.'

'I know, I think it's because I'm still young. I like to be busy.'

'Well, only you can make the decision my love.'

The next morning there was a watery sun, and Isobel decided to take Tranquil for a ride. Her maid had run to the stables to tell of her wishes. She smiled at young Bert as he helped her mount. 'Thank you for your quickness lad.' She uttered as she steered the animal out into the courtyard. The boy stood to attention and bowed his head.

Isobel rode as if the devil himself was after her, she had ridden for quite a few miles, when she suddenly brought the horse to a slow stop. She rubbed Tranquille's head and stared about her. Where was she, she had never been this way before. She did not recognise any of the land markings, where she was? How could this have happened she could not remember going a different way. She had ridden from the front of the house, but it had not led her to where she wanted to go. This scene was so different from those she was used to. There was a mountain, and it was extremely high, there were flat fields, then she saw hills, like the hills she could see from the back of the house. She coaxed Tranquil to move on a little further, suddenly a group of trees came into view, and as she moved closer the thickness of them seemed to go on and on. Could it be a forest?

She decided to return to the house, she would ask Dune if he would gather some men to ride out and search this part of the estate. Just to see if there was anything here for them to use.

Possibly, there could be more mines out this way. The whole area felt extremely weird, and it was all new to her. She returned at a slower pace, and she felt the coldness creep into her body. Then suddenly small snowflakes began to fall, and she knew winter had arrived.

Isobel made her way to the nursery, but it was empty. Nanny must have taken them all down to the big hall, she did this sometimes in the winter for a change of scenery. She walked in and the girls ran straight towards her, she tried to pick both up but declared.

'Oh, my darlings how heavy you have become.' Little James was busy on the carpet with several wooden cars, and the boys were rolling about on the rug. They all sat and had a lovely afternoon, tea, cakes, and milk was enjoyed before their return to the nursery.

Life was good. Isobel had a beautiful family, there was plenty of money, and the community was growing daily. Consequently, all she wanted now, was to marry the man she loved with all her heart. But it also puzzled her, when the subject of marriage was approached, he always used the excuse about her status, and the fact he was a mere gypsy. Dune had been gone for almost one week to buy more horses and would be back any day. Isobel sat with Alice by the fire in the big hall, smiled as she watched the twins trying to roll about on the large carpet with some toys.

'They are all one's work these days.'

'Yes, indeed they are dear sister, but it's good that young

Molly goes in to help nanny now at different times. So, I am thinking of getting another nanny, there is an awful lot for our nanny to do now.'

'Yes, your right there is.'

'When we next go into Portchesterton I shall enquire about the extra help.'

Then, the sudden appearance of Molly to collect their tea tray, Isobel asked. 'Molly you have been helping nanny in the nursery haven't you dear?'

The girl bent her head and replied. 'Ay, my lady. I have.'

'Tell me do you like to help with the babies, or would you still like to help me, which do you think you would prefer?' She kept her head bent, but never spoke.

'Please Molly, please tell me which one of these duties you prefer to do the best?' She looked up. 'Oh, to be with all the little ones with nanny.'

'So be it, Molly as soon as I can get a couple of new maids, you will work with nanny in the nursery, you will become her helper.' The girl's eyes shone, and the biggest smile appeared. 'Mistress oh, Mistress, thank you. Thank you so much.'

'No, no.' Alice said. 'Let Molly go there now, its winter and I would love to take care of you dear, Isobel.'

'You are sure Alice, until we can get new help.'

'Absolutely. Absolutely, my dear sister.'

It was decided and young Molly, who would have a dress like nanny's was delighted.

December, and Edward now fourteen, had a lovely party

and everyone received gifts. Time went by quite quickly in the winter and before Isobel knew it March arrived with the sun often in the sky. She had decided to keep Grandma's companies, consequently the amount of money that arrived in each month was exceedingly high, even after she had paid everyone their wages. It was a pleasant morning, so Dune was taking Isobel to see her son's grave. They left the estate, she followed him closely. Although neither was to speak of that terrible night again. Last evening, Isobel spoke to Dune about what she felt in her heart, because of today's trip. They were speaking of their children, and how blessed they both were. Isobel said.' Mary is a beautiful little girl. Was your Leah, lovely? I ask you this because, I know you think about her a great deal.' Dune just stared into the fire as she continued. 'Your love for your sister is still so strong, I feel that if anyone other than I had taken her baby, it would have broken you.' He put his finger on her lips, then said. 'Through your love and care of Mary, I have seen her grow. Watched you nurture her, she is a beautiful child, like our daughter Victoria, and our beautiful sons. I miss my baby sister every day, but to have Mary, is like watching her grow again. You have always had my heart, dear Isobel, I could not love you more.' He took her hand and they walked through to the bedroom, and again she was in heaven.

This part of the land was again strange to Isobel, and they had ridden a fair way out. Suddenly, Dune eased up, then stopped. He dismounted and helped her down. They moved towards the stream that ran past a vast amount of tress. It was a beautiful spot, Dune took her hand and led her to a small clear area, there she saw the cross, the stones beneath it, and the flowers laid upon them. Isobel sank to her knees, and tear fell freely.

'I come here each week and speak to your son, my love, and I keep his grave nice for you.'

'Dune.' She touched the stones and could see it was well looked after. She sat for a long time and Dune left her to herself. Her tears, just fell and fell, she prayed, prayed for the Lord to love, and keep her son with him always. Time passed, and dusks encroachment was slowly descending. Dune walked towards her slowly, he handed her his metal cup filled with crystal clear water, she was thirsty, she smiled, drank it then handed it back to him.

'Darling.' He muttered, 'it will be dark soon, we should return to the house.'

'Mm…Yes, you are right. He helped her to her feet. She smiled and pulled his face towards her; she kissed his perfect lips. 'Thank you, my darling Dune, for your care towards my dear sons place of rest.'

'My darling it be my pleasure to come here and visit the wee one. Now we must go.'

He helped her mount, Isobel turned for one more look, then she eased Tranquil to trot on. Together in silence they rode back to the estate. They were back at the stables and has they walked towards the house, Isobel stopped, 'Dune, I almost forgot, did you go to that strange piece of land I told you of?'

'Yes, we did. There was about ten of us, and we all found it quite interesting. Isobel, you have so much land out that way, that you could even sell some of it off. If you're never going to use it, be rid of it. I say.' He smiled. 'Also, you have a vast amount of salt mines, and we found many more flint-stone mines as well.' He smiled and pulled her close to his body. 'You my love are rich woman.' She smiled. 'I will speak with Ben; he will sort it all for me. He is a wonderful man. Which is what I keep telling Alice.' They both laughed as they entered the front porch and made for the big hall.

Isobel was out at the stables because Alice was being taught to ride. The girl was nervous, but she loved the horse Isobel had given her. She had been learning for some time and had started to become confident, and like her sister, she too loved all animals.

The session finished, she went off for her bath and a change of clothes, then the two of them went along to the nursery. It was lunch time when they entered and Isobel smiled as she watched the twins trying to each mashed food, so life was much easier for her now, where her two lovely boys were concerned. They stayed for a couple of hours, then the little ones went down for a sleep. The girls returned to Isobel's rooms and tea was ordered. Alice poured and handed a cup to Isobel. 'Thank you dear.' She smiled. 'Do you know what I have decided to do when Dune returns?'

'No silly of course I do not.'

'I am going to marry him; we will have another big wedding like you and Ben had.'

Alice never spoke and her expression changed.

'What is wrong dear, why the sad face?'

'Well, I too love your man, and you know this to be true. But Isobel, as much as we both care for him, he is a gypsy, and you my dear one have an extremely high status.'

'Yes. Yes. I know, but we are here in our own little world, life is so good, we have so much. Who here would not want the marriage to take place, we are all mixed in together, and your Ben has I have often said, is such a wonderful man? But for him I honestly believe we would never had moved so forward.'

'Yes, you are right. Who is there to stop you?'

Later alone in her quarters, Isobel reflected on her earlier conversation with Alice.

Yes, there was the Church with the priest. Two new shops with accommodation had been built. Cottages were jotted all around the town that was growing, and people just seem to make their way towards where they all were. Once between the sheets, she decided, she was going to marry the man she loved, and that was that. Just as soon as he returned, the wedding preparations would begin. She smiled, snuggled down, and went straight to sleep.

Chapter Thirty-Nine

It was a beautiful morning and after her visit to the nursery she decided to go for a ride. Alice was not yet ready to do the long rides yet, so she set off on her own. The sun shone, and she rode quite steadily. Eventually back at the stables, she dismounted and made her way to the house.

It was late when Dune opened the door and crept towards her. He carefully collected her up in his arms. She nuzzled in and stirred as he placed her into the bed. He waited a moment then quietly left and made his way to the bath area. His toiletries finished he climbed in beside her, he yawned, he was tired, his eyes closed, then he was asleep. The next morning, he was up and gone before Isobel moved. She could not remember how she ended up in her bed, then she saw some of Dune's clothes on the floor and knew he had returned late last night.

She hoped he would be back later so they could talk. Dune returned home late afternoon and went in search of Ben who was in the kitchen with a mug of tea.

'Ah, there you be my friend.' He sat next to him, and the cook poured some tea into a mug for him. He smiled. 'Thank you, Agnes.' She smiled back then went back to her vegetables.

'Ben how be thee, well I hope.'

'Yep, and you Dune.' They went on to discuss wire, wood, and a multitude of things, then Both stood, and left the kitchen. Dune made his way upstairs and walked into Isobel's room, but she was not there. Nor was she in the big hall. Where could she be, oh yes in her study. He made his way there, and sure enough she was seated in her chair with the French doors wide open, with her book in her hands. So, pleased to see her after such a long absence he moved quickly to her side. 'My darling why do you hide in here?' Taken back, she smiled and whispered. 'I am not hiding, sometimes I think a change is good for one. Plus, you have again been gone for so long. You promised me once that you would never leave me again, and you have.'

'No, no, my darling. I told you I would never travel to Ireland ever again, and I have not.' He beamed broadly, she stood and fell into his open arms. He lifted her high and almost ran from the room, up the stairs, into her bedchamber, placed her on the bed. He took her again to their favourite place, and both were fulfilled.

Isobel and Dune had breakfast together, then once they were dressed Isobel asked him to stay with her because she wanted to speak with him. Eventually sat with their coffee and biscuits, Isobel knelt before him, then whispered. 'Dune will you marry me. Please.' Colour left his face, and he looked away. 'Isobel, we have talked of this very often, I have told you no because of the status you carry, and I am just a gypsy boy.'

'Man.'

'What.'

'Man, you are just a gypsy man now, not a boy anymore.'

'Ah, yes, that be right.' He smiled. 'Darling, aren't we happy as we are?'

'No, no I want you to marry me Dune, I love you so much, and apparently you keep telling me you love me, so what is there to stop us. I have told you so many times status mean nothing to me at all.' She rung her hands and stood. He looked at her, then he knelt before her. 'Isobel... Isobel...I never wanted to tell you this, but I fear now that I must. He took a deep breath. 'Now what I am about to tell you, you must listen to it all before you answer me anything. Do you promise me you will, keep quiet?' Baffled by his words, she nodded, then murmured. 'I promise Dune.' He smiled and lifted her hand for his kiss. 'Right then.'

'When I was fourteen years, I was married to a member of another clan. It was really an act to bind two groups of people as one. We never consummated the marriage; she went her way and I mine, which was straight back to you.' He looked at the tears as they rolled down her face. 'My darling, I was asked to carry out this deed, which is often done in our clans, but if I had paired up with another girl of our clan, we would never had married, but she would have accepted me.' He stood and sat back on the chair.

Isobel looked into his eyes. 'Can I speak now?'

'Yes. Yes, my darling.'

'So, the truth is, you cannot marry me, because your already wed.'

'Well, yes. Yes, that is it.'

'Dune, why have you always acted like a free man. We

have three children together, and I have always wanted marriage with you.'

'But Isobel, this is a tradition with our clans, had I fallen for another girl in my clan she would have accepted me, no trouble.'

'Well, I am sorry Dune, but I do not see that way at all. As far as I am concerned you are a married man.'

He stood and walked towards her. 'But darling, please can we not carry on as we are, we are both so happy.'

'No. No definitely not. I want marriage, or nothing.'

'So be it.' He shouted and walked from the room.

Isobel stared at the closed door. In all the time and years, they had been together, they had never had a cross word. But it was a big thing to find out the man you love is already married. Why could he not see that. She knew Dune would be back, and they would talk about it all sensibly. But she just could not see a solution to her future, if he kept his marriage which was not even consummated as an excuse. True, yes, they were happy as things were, but she wanted him for her husband, and if this did not happen, well, would she ask him to leave. But his clan and any other gypsies that wanted to stay there could do so, to hopefully make a new life there in Sussex.

Isobel decided not to mention to Alice about what had happened between her and Dune, because after their disagreement he had loaded up and left, and he had been gone now for several months. She began to wonder if he would ever come back to her. Because she would forgive him, and carry on as they were, the man had her heart, and she hated it when he was not there with her.

Although it was January, there was hardly any snow on the ground, so Isobel decided to go for a ride. Tranquil desperately needed to be exercised. Once she was saddled up and ready, they set off towards where she thought her beautiful son had been laid to rest. True she had only visited the grave once, but she was sure she knew which way to go. The sky was dark and was getting darker with every move they made. There was to many trees, and the countryside did not look familiar, yet again. She stopped and stared around her; she had been sure her baby's tiny grave had been in this direction. Rain began to fall heavily, and she could hardly see, where on earth was, she? Drenched from the rain, she wiped the water from her face. Yes, she knew where she was, and that was lost.

She managed to stand Tranquil beneath a great amount, of trees, but there was no shelter from them. She decided to ride back, but the rain was awful, then suddenly, several glass houses came into view, she was so relieved as she made her way towards them, and with the help of a rather thick tree trunk she managed to dismount from her horse. Her hand on Tranquille's face, she reassured him as they both entered inside, and the door was closed firmly behind them.   Relived to be out of the bitter weather, she decided to light a fire. There were quite a few old logs scattered about inside, which she quickly gathered up.

When she was a small child, she would visit the stables

with her precious Mama, and old Joe had taught her much about life, animals, and things you can do to survive. He had told her to always attach a bag to your horse when you take long rides far away from the house. This she always did, so now she was extremely grateful for his words of wisdom. She collected the soaked bag off Tranquil and sighed as she reached inside it. In her hand was the piece of flint stone. Then she reached in and pulled out the bag which contained six small biscuits. Then there was the fair size blanket, and the water container, which she always took with her. She was extremely thirsty, but she only took a couple of mouthfuls. The fire was going in no time, and the warmth felt good. She stripped her cloths from her body placed the rug about her and opened the biscuits. She took two and would have another two later. The heat from the flames was great, but sat there all alone she felt extremely vulnerable, and prayed, that no one else would ride that way, while she was there. Her stomach rumbled, she was very thirsty, but instead she laid in front of the flames and fell fast asleep. She kept waking and each time added more wood to keep the fire going. Fear ran through her, is this where she would die?'

Eventually she opened her eyes and decided to sit up. The weather outside was still bad, she could hear the wind as it howled around, and the rain was so heavy it hit the roof with a vengeance. With no idea where she was, Isobel reached for the last biscuit, then quickly replaced her clothes. They were very damp, but they would have to do.

Isobel guessed it was quite early, as she noticed dawn's slow eruption outside. What should she do, stay put or leave and try to find some way back to the house? She must have fallen asleep again because, the heat from the fire was nice. She woke with a start and felt a little nervous. She stood and moved towards the door, 'oh, no.' She blurted. 'Snow.' And it was coming down quite heavy. She could not stay here, she must leave. The fire was almost out, so with the door wide open, her feet placed onto the tree stump again, she managed to throw her body up into the saddle. Tranquil, felt her weight and eased himself through the open doorway. The wind was bitter, but she urged him to ride on. They moved quite well, but she had no idea of where they were headed. The sky was almost black, and fear ran through her frozen bones. Isobel truly, believed she was going to freeze to death. Lightheaded, she felt very odd, but as the black oblivion took her body, and she fell to the ground, she never saw the group of riders who had spent all night searching, quickly ride towards her.

Chapter Forty

'Mistress. My lady. Isobel.'   Her eyes opened and the light hurt her head. 'What… what. Where am I.'

'Mistress. Dear Mistress, you have been lost to us all, and we have been so worried.   Ben and some men searched all night for you. What happened, where did you go.' Alice took her hands and kissed them.

'Oh. Dear, dear sister, I am so sorry, but when I left here to go for my usual ride, I went in search of my baby's grave. I wanted to visit it.'

'Yes, but Isobel, you never ride far in the winter months, because the weather is so cruel.'

'I know my dear, and I am so sorry, that I did something so stupid, like trying to find his tiny grave on my own.'

'Well, your safe now, and that is all that matters. Here let me help you out of bed, you must be starving. I have food and a nice hot pot of tea for you to drink.'

'Ah, bless you dear, dear Alice.'

'But how did you manage? It was a bitterly, bitterly night.'

And Isobel went on to tell what she did while lost out in the cold.

The fire roared up the chimney and sat close to it, Isobel enjoyed, the steamed fish with a little potato, and she was very thirsty. Alice would not leave her side and later that night the two girls had supper together. Then she helped her get ready for her nice clean, warm bed. The next morning, Isobel and Alice went along to the nursery and spent most of the day there with her precious little ones. That night they had their supper together again, and Isobel felt so loved. She had eventually told Alice about the Dune situation. But she, herself was resigned, he was not coming back to her. It took several weeks for Isobel to forget the ordeal, but she still shivered when she thought of what the outcome could have been. The high flames as they sped upwards to the chimney, mesmerised her and she was deep in thought. Her eyes were heavy, the book fell to the floor and sleep took her.

The door opened and Dune stepped inside. Lord, Isobel was so beautiful, he quietly moved towards her then sat in the chair opposite her. Her eyes suddenly opened, and she whispered; 'Dune, Dune is that you?'

The heat from the fire crackled, and it was the only sound that filled the room, as both stared at each other.

'When did you get back?' She suddenly asked. 'And have you seen the children?'

'Late last night. And yes, yes, I have, and they are all so beautiful, and we are so lucky to have such beautiful little ones.' She nodded and smiled. 'You have been away for almost five months, it has been a long, long time.' He turned to stare into the flames, then he stood and moved closer to her, he went down on one knee. 'Lady Isobel Belington, would you please marry me.' He reached for her hand and placed a beautiful pale blue stoned ring on her finger. Isobel was speechless, as she stared into his handsome face. Dune continued. 'My darling I love you so much, and I do want to marry you with all my heart and soul.'

'But. I..I.'   He stood and drew her up into his arms, his lips descended, and she forgave him everything.

'Isobel, I have a great deal to tell you my darling, an awful lot to explain to you.' He took her hand and kissed it.

'Oh, my darling, darling, after all these years, are we finally going to be able to marry?' He pulled her down in front of the fire and once she was comfortable in his arms, he began to explain his situation.

'Apparently, in my world I am of Royal blood, and to marry me is a privilege for any young gypsy girl. But because I do not wish to marry a girl from our clans, but wish to marry a beautiful, white girl who is titled, I am able to do this purely because of the status she now has.'

'What… what …did you say?'

'I said, because, you are an outsider, but you have a title, I can marry you.'

'Do you mean, that if I had not married that disgusting man Belington, you would not be allowed to wed me?'

'That is exactly what I am saying.'

'This is fascinating, really fascinating, are you telling me your status is higher than mine.'

'Exactly. Yes. Yes, in my world it is.'

'But what about the young girl you married all those years ago?'

'Yes. Well, when I arrived in London, I was sent over to Ireland, because all the paperwork was there. I was told it should never have happened, again through my status. Consequently, it was wiped away, like it never happened, which now makes me a completely free man.' She smiled as he pulled her close, his lips descended and again she was in heaven.

'My love, oh, my love.' He whispered. 'We can marry now whenever you want.'

She smiled and snuggled tight into him, and for some time silence filled the room. Eventually she moved, and he helped her up onto her feet.

'Thank you, Dune.' She sat in her chair, and he followed suit and sat opposite her. 'What's this I hear you got yourself lost, and the weather was bitterly cold?'

'Yes. Because we have not had much snow, I took Tranquil for a ride, I tried to find my baby's grave, but ended up lost. It was a bitterly cold day, it even snowed. I was out all night.'

'Yes, I know. Well thankfully your safe now, and never do that again. I will take you as soon as the weather gets better.'

'Thank…you... Dune, I shall look forward to that.' She smiled.   Isobel was still digesting all he had stated. 'So, are you saying we can arrange our marriage, and are you happy to wed in our Church Dune?'

'Yep, I am. We can do it right now if you so wish it my darling.'   Delighted, she stood, 'do not move,' she shouted as she lifted her dress and was out the door. She returned several minutes later with Alice, and Ben in tow and everyone was extremely happy, and they all drank a toast to the happy couple. Early the next morning, Isobel with Dune by her side entered the nursery, and the little ones were all thrilled to see their, Mama and Papa together again.

It was the day of the wedding, and May was such a lovely month to get married. There was great excitement everywhere, and the sun shone. Isobel's long white off the shoulder wedding dress had been made beautifully. Alice, Mary, and Victoria wore cream long dresses, and each had a lovely bunch of fresh picked flowers to hold. The twins now two years, and little James were dressed in pale blue velvet suits, long white tights, blue shoes, and tiny blue hats on their heads. Edward's suit was a darker blue with long trousers, dark blue shoes, and he had a hat which he held in his long hands. He was to give Isobel away, for which he was terribly excited about. Dune's outfit was leather, dark brown in colour, trousers, knee length boots his frilly shirt as white as white, and his brown waist coat magnificently made, he looked adorable. Ben was his best man, and he looked very handsome in his new clothes as well.

It was noon, as the carriage drew up on the gravel, nanny and Molly were already there waiting with the little ones. Edward helped Alice out, then he turned to his Mama, he smiled, took her hand, then helped her alight. The service was about to start, the priest was happy to stand and wait for the bride as she slowly walked down the aisle to take her place before him. She and Dune smiled, he took her free hand, Alice was given her flowers. It was a nice service and when the gold ban, which one of his clan's men had made was placed on Isobcl's finger, the whole congregation cheered and clapped. The holy man declared them man and wife, Dune pulled her close and kissed her lips. All the paperwork completed, they turned and happily made their way towards the open doors.

Outside everyone cheered and clapped, dancing began as Isobel and her husband climbed back into the carriage, for their short journey back. Food filled all the tables inside the large hall, there was also food filled tables out on the grass, and drinks flowed freely. Folk were everywhere as they danced, eat, and drank good health to the Mistress and Master of the Manor, which carried on late into the night.

Isobel sat in the nursery, with Mary on her lap, smiled when Dune walked in. 'Here you are darling, I have been looking for you.' His hand caressed the child's hair from her face.

'Nanny came for me, she has been sick, and cried for me. I think she has eaten too much sweet food.' She whispered. He smiled, 'Do you want me to take her from you, she's fast asleep now.'

'Please Dune.' He carefully took her into his arms and walked towards her bed.' Isobel stood and joined him. 'Do you wonder about your sister when you see how this little one grows. Because like all our children, Mary is incredibly beautiful.'

'Always. Yes, always, as you say she is extremely beautiful. My sister was like our mother, whose beauty also took the breath from you. But you my darling have a big heart you are a wonderful, caring person. I dread to think what might have happened to her if she had not been given to you.' She smiled as tears gathered. She took his arm. 'Come.' She whispered. 'Nanny is asleep, we do not want to disturb her.' She took his hand. 'I am quite tired too; shall we go to our rooms?' They quietly left and back in their chambers Dune poured two glasses of wine, which both sipped by the fire.

Dune smiled and pulled her close. 'How I love you my darling.'

'And I you, my lovely, husband.' Isobel placed her glass on the table and reached for his hand. 'I often sit and think of all we have achieved since the three of us moved here to Sussex. We have our wonderful children, we have accumulated, a loving family. And those terrible times with that man Belington, I have erased completely from my mind.' She smiled.

'I honestly believe Dune, had we stayed in Durham, we would not be as blessed as we are today. I feel so blessed.'

'As do I Mrs O'Malley.' He smiled and lifted her up into his arms, then walked through to the bedroom.

Life was good and roughly one hour's ride from the house a town was forming, and Isobel was going to call it, 'Claremont.' It was to be named after her Grandma, Isobel Claremont, because her money had paid for everything, from the very start of this adventure. Houses, like those built in Portchesterton were being built and people were buying and moving into them. Consequently, People had started to visit the house and Isobel has lady of the manor was thrilled. Dune mixed well if a dinner party had been arranged and everything was good. Life for Isobel, now twenty-nine, was rather hectic at times, but she loved every minute of it. The girls, the twins, with dear James were all in school with Mr Henry Turner, Edward's tutor. The boy was now seventeen, and away at boarding school, and art was his main subject. He was gifted; he was an artist. Alice, and Ben had a beautiful daughter, they named her Bella, which Isobel adored. But sadly, dear Florence had passed.

Isobel, had over the last five years had the house almost restored as new, the only floor not yet finished was the fourth one, and she had named the house, 'Claremont Manor.' So now her Grandmother was all over the area they lived in because she had every right to be there. When she and Alice, arrived there eleven years ago, that awful man Belington had left the house broken and severely neglected. But now it stood tall, distinguished, and was a home to so many. Yes, 'Claremont, Manor' would stand for many years to come in her mama' and grandmother's honour.

Lightning Source UK Ltd.
Milton Keynes UK
UKHW011319200522
403286UK00002B/112

9 781800 310926